A Wedding
BLUNDER
IN THE BLACK HILLS

A Wedding
BLUNDER
IN THE BLACK HILLS

KIM
O'BRIEN

BARBOUR
PUBLISHING

Cover design: Faceout Studio, www.faceoutstudio.com

Published by Barbour Publishing, Inc., P.O. Box 719, Uhrichsville, Ohio
44683, www.barbourbooks.com

*Our mission is to publish and distribute inspirational products offering
exceptional value and biblical encouragement to the masses.*

 Member of the
Evangelical Christian
Publishers Association

Printed in the United States of America

Nothing is so common as the wish to be remarkable.
WILLIAM SHAKESPEARE

Chapter 1

H e's your *dentist*, Mom. I'm *not* going on a blind date with your dentist."

Millie Hogan stabbed her knife into the tub of mustard then swiped it across a piece of pumpernickel. She'd only broken up with Karl Kauffman a couple of weeks ago, and already her mother was trying to set her up.

Peering over the top of the glass deli counter, Howard Glugan, the chief of police and one of the café's regulars, strained to watch. "Take it easy, Millie," he said. "I'd hate to charge you for assault and battery to a slice of bread."

Millie managed to laugh. She arranged slices of ham and swiss cheese on the bread, stuck a colorful toothpick through the center, and added a handful of chips. "Pie, Chief?"

"What kind?"

"Blueberry, pecan, or rhubarb."

"I could manage a piece of rhubarb."

Millie cut him an ample slice and rang him up on the register.

"Of course you're going out with Dr. Denvers," her mother stated. "It's all arranged."

"Then unarrange it. Shouldn't you be working the grill?" Millie turned to the town's librarian. "The usual, Mrs. Ellison?"

"Yes, please. I hate to say it, dear, but Eva's right. Dr. Denvers is a real catch."

Her mother laughed as Millie ladled out a bowl of chicken noodle. She knew Mrs. Ellison liked a buttered roll and a cup of herb tea with her soup. She'd practically grown up here in Dosie Dough's, and the same people had been ordering the same thing for years. She knew most of the people seated at the booths and tables. Unfortunately, this meant that everyone was so familiar with one another that they ended up discussing everything in front of everybody, like now.

"Why are you so stubborn?" her mother said. "Just because you broke up with that policeman doesn't mean you give up on all men."

"And bless his soul is that boy cranky," Aunt Lillian remarked from her wheelchair. She was sitting with the other aunts at her usual spot at the table in front of the bay window where they could see the town square and comment if they saw something interesting. "He's practically shaking the parking meters in hopes of giving some poor soul a ticket," Lillian continued. "Can't you talk to Karl, Chief?"

The chief wiped his mouth with a napkin. "I don't discuss police business."

Millie scooped out a generous portion of tuna salad. She really didn't want to talk about Karl Kauffman anyway. He kept leaving parking tickets on her car with notes that said, *Call me.*

"I hear we've got more snow coming." Millie glanced over at Aunt Keeker for help. Of all the three women who made up Eva's best friends and Millie's "aunts," Keeker could always be counted on for a lively discussion about the weather. She particularly enjoyed being the bearer of bad news when it came to storms, and today she was wearing her sheepskin bomber hat, a sure sign that Deer Park was due for a major snowfall.

"As a matter of fact—" Keeker started.

"Dating is like riding a horse," her mother interrupted. "If you fall off, you should get right back on again."

Millie lifted the lid off the steaming pot of tomato soup. She was pretty sure the nearest her mother had ever been to a horse was watching a rerun of *Bonanza* on television.

"Mom, I'm done with blind dates. I'm not going out with the electrician, the UPS guy, or anyone else." She ladled the soup into the bowl and in her best and most dramatic stage voice, declared, "I'm off men. Forever."

"Let's not get melodramatic," her mother said dryly. "You know you like going out on dates."

"That was before," Millie said. "I've decided to concentrate on my acting career now."

"Dr. Denvers is perfect for you," her mother insisted. "Smart, good looking, and nice. He has that doctor thing going, too. You'd have excellent medical benefits."

Millie gave her a look. "We have medical coverage, Mom."

"But he's a *dentist*," Aunt Mimi called out from the aunts' table. She was a tiny woman with a cloud of permed apricot-colored hair that matched the coat of the toy poodle that snored in her lap. "Do you know how hard it is to get good dental benefits?"

"If she's going to date him," Jeff Gulden, a thin, wiry-haired mechanic with huge ears and a chronically sad face, said, "could she at least wait until next week? I have a root canal scheduled for Friday, and it'll probably go better if the doc doesn't have a broken heart."

"Remember it took Erv Michels two weeks before he stopped throwing the UPS packages into the bushes after Millie dumped him?" Aunt Mimi agreed. "Not that I blame you, Millie honey, for passing on that boy. I saw him kick his dog when he thought no one was watching." She stroked her poodle lovingly.

"All of you," Millie said, waving a serving spoon, "need to stop talking about my social life. If you want to help me, think of things for me to write about in my application for *Chef's Challenge*. The deadline's coming up." She pointed to the back kitchen. "Mom, don't you think you ought to go flip those burgers?"

"Lottie's got the grill." Her mother's brow creased. "I don't know why you keep trying to get yourself on those mindless reality shows. What if some crazy person saw you on TV and started to stalk you?"

Millie blinked innocently. "Well, I guess if he was single, you'd probably try and set me up on a date with him."

Her mother pursed her lips firmly together. "I'm just trying to help you, honey. I don't want you ending up like me, with no one to keep me warm at night."

"I'll keep you warm," somebody called out. Millie thought it was Will Gavinski, who worked on the sunflower farm ten miles north of town.

Millie didn't think that thirty-one was exactly ancient, however, she let her mother's comment pass. "What can I get for you today, Mr. Lawrence?" Millie asked the next customer in line.

"He'll have liverwurst," Millie's mother announced before the manager of the town's movie theater could reply, "and I'll get it. You need to go home and get ready for your date."

Millie swiped a generous amount of mayo on the bread. Hadn't her mother heard a word she'd said? So what if David Denvers was a good dentist. It didn't mean he'd be a good date. In high school, he'd been a year ahead of her. She remembered a nerdy kid on the short side with big glasses and ears that bent out slightly at the sides.

"If you like him so much, Mom," she joked, "why don't you go skiing with him?"

Her mother set her hands on her ample hips and locked eyes with Millie. "If you won't, I will. I'm not standing the boy up."

The restaurant became so quiet that Millie could hear the hum of the refrigerator in the back room. Was her mother serious? This from a woman who got in her car to drive twenty yards to the mailbox?

At age sixty-four, overweight, and a diabetic, the last thing her mother needed to be doing was putting on a pair of skis. As if reading Millie's thoughts, her mother said, "I'm sure my old skis could still get the job done."

Her mother had to be bluffing. Millie folded her arms and ordered herself not to give in.

"Don't wait up for me," her mom continued. "Unlike some people"—she paused to give Millie a significant look—"I have not forgotten how to have fun."

"Mom, you can't go skiing. You could hurt yourself."

"Before you were born, I used to be quite the ski bunny, and I still have the trophies to prove it."

She might have been a ski bunny once, but Millie tactfully restrained from pointing out that most bunnies didn't top the scale at over two hundred pounds. "Mom. . ."

"Your father has been gone for twenty years. It's high time I put myself back on the market. You gotta live, Millie."

I would, Millie thought, *but you won't let me.* Immediately she felt a stab of guilt. This was her mother, who loved her more than anyone else in the world. If her mother sometimes tried to run her life, it was only because she wanted Millie to be happy.

"You're acting crazy, Mom. Skiing is risky."

Her mom rolled her eyes. "I'm not a novice. And if I do get

hurt, at least I'll be with a doctor."

"Dentist," Millie corrected.

"They both go to medical school," Millie's mother announced. "Don't worry about me."

Clumping across the wooden floor in her trademark UGG boots, her mom added, "I'll tell him you were having female problems, Millie, but you want to reschedule."

Why? Millie scrunched her eyes shut. *Why me?* She didn't know whether to laugh or cry. Her mom loved her dearly yet couldn't see she was killing her. Watching her mom's broad frame navigate around the crowded room, Millie knew she should stop her, and yet part of her wanted to let her go. If she kept caving in to her mother's demands, she'd never get her mother to leave her alone.

Why couldn't she have a mother who didn't guilt her daughter into blind dates or wield her health as a weapon?

Her mother had reached the coatrack. Hardheaded, stubborn, and proud of every drop of German blood—that was her mother. Millie clenched her jaw. Her mother wasn't going to win. Not this time. "You'd better check your blood sugar before you go."

"No time," her mother replied. Her hand was on the doorknob. "See you later, honey."

The door was open now. A cold draft snaked its way across the floor, and she could see the light bouncing off the gleaming heaps of snow half burying the parking meters on the sidewalk.

"Hold it," Millie ordered. "If I do this for you, you have to promise me—no exceptions—that this is the last time you set me up on a blind date."

Her mother turned. "Of course, dear."

"No meddling of any kind in my social life."

"Scout's honor," her mother replied and held up two fingers

for Millie to see.

"No more talk about me getting older or settling down or having kids."

"I promise."

Millie studied her mother's face a moment longer. She probably couldn't trust her, yet she didn't want her going off and trying to ski just to make a point. "Okay," Millie said, "I'll do it. I'll go skiing with Dr. Denvers."

Her mother's face relaxed into a broad smile. "David will be waiting by the ice sculpture of the dolphin—and sweetie, don't forget to floss before you go."

Chapter 2

It'd been years since Millie had skied. In the ladies' room at the ski lodge, she squeezed into her one-piece ski outfit. The zipper was a bit tighter than she remembered, and the sleeves seemed to have shrunk. Then again, she'd been sixteen when she'd bought this outfit.

Sixteen. She'd had such big dreams then—of going to Hollywood and being discovered or living in Manhattan and starring in a Broadway show. She and Oprah would nod to each other casually at cocktail parties, and Millie would appear periodically on shows like *Larry King Live* and *Good Morning America*.

Millie tugged her zipper. She'd never seen herself as a permanent fixture at Dosie Dough's, and at the rate she was going, the best she could hope for was a spot on *Dr. Phil* for a special on dysfunctional relationships. All too easily she could picture her aunts, mother, and former dates squeezed onto one couch while Millie sat across from them trying to explain that she didn't have commitment issues—just a desire to find out if there was more to life than what Deer Park had to offer.

Surveying herself in the mirror, Millie couldn't decide if she looked more like a fat Judy Jetson or the Michelin Man. In either case, the way the material strained at the zipper suggested that the first time she hit a mogul she was going to burst out of this ski suit like a parboiled tomato.

She tucked her mass of dark, curly hair into a bright yellow Turtle Fur hat and settled her goggles on top. Who cared what she looked like?

Blinking, Millie stepped outside into the blinding light of snow reflected off the mountain. She scanned the group of skiers who clustered in groups around the ski racks or slid past on their way to the lift line.

She didn't see a short man with glasses who had ears that kind of stuck out at the sides waiting next to the ice dolphin. Then again, it'd been years since she'd seen him. After high school, he'd gone to dental school in California and gotten married. According to chatter at the café, he'd returned to Deer Park six months ago to take over his father's dental practice.

Pushing up her tight sleeves, she checked her watch. It was a little after four o'clock. Maybe he wasn't coming. She felt something hopeful stir inside, and then a deep voice said, "Millie? Millie Hogan?"

A medium-sized man wearing black ski pants and carrying a pair of Rossignols over his shoulder walked up to her. "David Denvers." He extended his free hand for Millie to shake.

"I know," Millie said. "I mean, I remember you from high school."

"Me, too," David said cheerfully. "Only you looked a lot taller then."

Back then she'd been a giant compared to him. Not anymore. He wasn't a very tall man, but he still had several inches over her. His face was lean now, and he carried the skis easily. The glasses were gone, too. She couldn't tell if his ears still stuck out though. His wool ski cap hid them.

"Nice to see you again," Millie murmured, reduced to falling back on good manners and hoping that he wouldn't bring up the time when she was in ninth grade and he had asked her out in the middle of the cafeteria line. She'd said no, and the cafeteria lady had looked as if she wanted to throw the spaghetti and meat sauce at her.

"Hope you haven't been waiting long," David continued, glancing over his shoulder. "I was getting us lift tickets." He handed her a sticker and a thin metal hanger.

"Thanks," Millie said, threading the thin wire through her coat zipper. "Let me pay you back."

"It's my treat," David said.

"I insist." The more she let a guy pay for her, the bigger the guy's expectations at the end of the date. Millie never intended to feel obligated to anyone.

David shrugged. "We can settle this after we finish skiing. We don't want to lose the light."

Millie bent to put on her skis. She hadn't used them in years and was more than a little relieved when the bindings snapped neatly shut. "David," she said and straightened. "I should warn you, I haven't skied in quite a while. Would you mind starting out on a blue trail?"

David didn't answer. She looked over her shoulder and saw a slender blond standing nearby. The woman was wearing tight black ski pants that outlined her long, thin legs and a black ski jacket that ended at her trim hips. The woman's big blue eyes were fixed on David.

"David," Millie prompted sharply enough to get his attention.

"What?" His voice sounded strained, and the way he now looked at Millie reminded her of someone who was trying to put a good face on something unpleasant, like spending the afternoon with an IRS auditor.

Great. She could win a Michelin Man look-alike contest, and her date wished that he were with someone else. Her toes pinched in the boots that, like the snowsuit, had mysteriously shrunk in the closet. When she got home, she and her mother were going to have a very long conversation.

When David saw that Cynthia had followed him to the ski area, he almost groaned. During the past few weeks, he'd tried talking to her, ignoring her, and once hiding from her in the office supply room. Cynthia, however, had proved to be both unshakable and relentless.

He supposed that he could get a restraining order, but he suspected that Chief Glugan would laugh at him if he tried. Cynthia wasn't threatening or dangerous. She was just a lonely young woman, recently divorced, who like him had returned to Deer Park after being away for years. Besides, his parents and Cynthia's parents were good friends. He suspected the reason she was so good at finding him was that his mother was helping.

Digging his ski poles into the snow, David pushed forward, heading for the lift line. He had a vague plan about getting to the top of the mountain ahead of her then disappearing with Millie down one of the lesser-known trails.

The lift line moved agonizingly slow. He had to fight himself not to glance over his shoulder again to make sure she wasn't standing right behind him. He wished with all his heart that two weeks ago Cynthia had walked into a different dental office. He probably shouldn't have complimented her so much on her dental hygiene or accepted that offer of coffee and donuts. She'd mistaken friendship on his part for something more.

It didn't help either that his mother was firmly on Cynthia's side. *"You can't mourn Lisa forever,"* his mother had said when all of this started. *"Bart needs a mother, and you need a wife."*

"She's stalking me, Mother. That's not a good start to a relationship."

"Of course she isn't stalking you. Her family and ours have been friends for years. Besides, David, it's been five years. How much longer are you going to wait?"

Giving in to the urge, David glanced back over his shoulder. Cynthia beamed at him. David groaned involuntarily.

"Are you okay?" Millie asked.

"Oh, yeah."

"You sounded in pain."

"I'm fine."

"It's this date, isn't it? I'm going to kill my mother," Millie announced. "How'd she blackmail you into this?"

David looked more closely at Millie, whose face was all but hidden under a fluffy yellow hat and goggles. It had not occurred to him that he was not the only one who had been talked into this date. "She didn't blackmail me."

"Then what?"

"Nothing. I haven't been skiing in a long time. And she said you hadn't either."

Millie studied his face. "Look, we don't have to do this. We can end this date right now. No hard feelings."

David glanced back at Cynthia. If he backed out of the date now, it'd only encourage Cynthia to pursue him harder. Of course, he couldn't explain this to Millie. "We're here," he said. "It's a beautiful afternoon. We should enjoy it."

A moment later, the chairlift lightly bumped the back of his legs, and he settled back as the cable pulled the chair into the air.

"If it wasn't blackmail, then it was a bribe," Millie mused. She was wearing a one-piece down outfit with a lot of insulation. Their shoulders touched, although he was aware that she was sitting with as much space between them as possible. "What'd she promise you? Apple caramel pie? Black Forest cake? Strudel?"

David cast a nervous glance over his shoulder. There were only two lift chairs between Cynthia and himself. "She didn't bribe me. I wanted to come." The false note in his voice hung in the air as obvious as the small puffs of his breath. "Hey, how about this weather? Feels like snow, doesn't it?"

Talking about the weather. How lame was that? He wiggled his fingers inside his thick gloves to warm them and tried not to think how long it'd been since he'd been on a date.

"Snow?" Millie picked at the thread of conversation. "We're already ten inches above average for the year."

He looked at her to see if she was being serious or poking fun at his awkward attempt at conversation. "At least the trails will be in good condition."

The chair bounced slightly as it rolled over the top of a support tower. They glided past ponderosa pines, their branches glistening with two inches of fresh snow. Far below them, skiers traversed the slope gracefully. David envied their freedom.

The wind picked up as they neared the top of the mountain. Seeing the safety netting below, David raised the safety bar and inched to the edge of the chair. The lift leveled, and David pushed off. Millie skied off beside him, mirroring his movements as they slid away from the lift area.

David wanted to waste no time putting distance between

himself and Cynthia. If they hurried, they might be able to choose a trail without Cynthia seeing them. "Let's try Sidewinder," he suggested. "It's on the far side of the mountain, but it's usually not very crowded."

"What color trail is it?"

David kept moving. "It's a blue trail. An intermediate."

"Okay," Millie agreed.

It was windy and much colder at the top of the mountain. Most of the surface was flat, and they had to use their arms and move their skis in an awkward ice-skating motion. Both of them were panting by the time they reached the top of Sidewinder.

Normally David would have paused to admire the view. Today he just wanted to get out of range of Cynthia. "You first," he said.

Millie pushed off. He felt something inside him relax as she put a nice edge into the first turn. The snow sparkled in the late afternoon sun, and the air that filled his lungs tasted pure and chilly. His face burned pleasantly from the cold, and the world opened up to him in a way that he had almost forgotten.

Casting one more look over his shoulder, he used both his arms to swing off the lip and launch himself down the slope. The powder felt as good as it looked. He took the fall line at the edge of the trail where fewer skiers had skied and the snow was deeper.

He picked up speed quickly but controlled it with quick, short turns that sent the snow spraying behind him. Just in front of him, he watched Millie making her way down the trail. She traversed the mountain easily although cautiously, avoiding the few moguls that had formed out of the turns of other skiers.

Millie paused where the trail flattened. Digging his edges into the snow, David checked his skis to a hard stop next to her. In the distance, the ski lodge looked tiny, a dollhouse version of the sprawling wood-and-glass building.

"This is great," Millie said, slightly breathless. "I'd forgotten how much I like to ski."

"Me, too," David said.

She lifted her goggles onto the top of her fluffy yellow hat. "Hope I'm not holding you back."

"No. Not at all. You're a terrific skier."

"Thanks. You're pretty good, too."

For a moment their gazes met. Millie's eyes were the same, a clear shade of gray as they'd been in high school. She had a nice smile, too. He liked the slight crookedness of her incisors. It was an honest smile, the imperfections telling him it was the smile God had given her.

Looking at her heart-shaped face and stonewashed eyes, it was impossible to think so many years had passed. She looked exactly the way he remembered from high school. She'd been the girl of his dreams, and he'd prayed that she'd go out with him. It hadn't worked out that way, but he had no regrets or complaints. He'd had seven amazing years with Lisa. God had blessed them with a son, and he thought it was more than one man could ask for or want.

It surprised him though to look at her and feel the slightest stirring of interest. He remembered she'd been a girl with big dreams—voted most likely to be a movie star. Instead, she'd stayed in Deer Park.

"I'm really glad you could come today, Millie," he said, but couldn't help glancing up the hill to make sure they hadn't been followed.

"Me, too," she said, sounding unconvinced.

"We should probably get going."

She peered down the trail then back at him. "It's getting steep.

Maybe you'd better not watch me—this might not be pretty."

He laughed. He'd forgotten that she had a great sense of humor. It amazed him to realize that if it hadn't been for Cynthia, he'd be genuinely enjoying himself. "I'll be right behind you," he promised.

She tugged her goggles into place, took a deep breath, then pushed off.

He watched her bend and rise out of the turn and felt that little spark of interest again. Not that he was going to do anything about it. He already had one too many women to deal with. A quick glance confirmed Cynthia was schussing down the slope with determination toward him.

He considered waiting and telling her to back off, but the trail was steep, and he'd promised Millie that he would stay close to her. Pushing off the lip, he let his skis run down the hill and wondered what it was going to take to get rid of Cynthia Shively.

Chapter 3

Hi, Mom," Millie called as she dumped her boots and ski suit in the laundry room. "I'm home."

Following the sound of the television, Millie hurried into the family room where her mother sat in the leather recliner watching the Food Network.

Her mother punched the MUTE button and stared up at Millie. "You had a great time, didn't you? I told you he was perfect."

"Well, not exactly." Millie eyed the bag of caramels in her mother's lap. "How many of those have you had?"

Her mother giggled. "I don't know, and I don't care. Tell me about David. Did he kiss you?"

Millie reached for the bag of candy, but her mother lifted it out of her grasp.

"Paws off, Millie. I'm serious. You get your own." Her fingers tightened as Millie managed to get a hand on it. "Look," her mom said in an obvious attempt to distract her, "*Dinner: Impossible* is coming on. Robert Irvine is practically exploding out of his T-shirt."

Millie snatched the candy from her mother's grasp and studied the brightness of her mother's eyes. She didn't trust the excitement she saw in them. "Have you checked your blood sugar?"

"Maybe later." She glanced at her mother, but as usual Eva

avoided her gaze. "Millie, relax. Every once in a while it's okay for me to eat a little candy. Besides"—she wagged a finger at Millie—"I'm eating those caramels for your own good."

Millie crossed into the kitchen. Pushing aside the familiar clutter on the counter, she searched for her mother's blood sugar monitor. She found it beneath a Pottery Barn catalog and her mother's red wool hat. Taking a clean lancet and a test strip, she returned to the family room.

"It's not okay for you to eat this stuff," she informed her mother. "And you know it. If your blood sugar gets too high, you could go into shock or pass out."

"Stop being a wet blanket." Her mom rose from her chair and stepped behind it. She looked prepared to make a run for it if Millie came one step closer. "Besides, I'm not finished yet." She pointed to her teeth. "My filling is still in place, but don't worry, honey, I'm going to loosen it if it takes all night."

Millie blinked. Who on earth would *want* to go back to the dentist? Then it hit her. A matchmaking mother would welcome an excuse to go back to the dentist if she was interested in setting her daughter up on another date. "Mom," she said sharply. "He has a girlfriend. She was following us all afternoon on the ski slope."

Her mother waved her hand indifferently. "If the girlfriend was serious, David would never have agreed to go on a date with you. He's not that kind of man. So, Millie, the appointment is at nine. You'll take me of course."

"Mom, you're scaring me."

"If it's a girl, you can name her after me. And if it's a boy, you can call him Everett. Rhett for short. Isn't that cute?"

"There isn't going to be a first child," Millie interrupted, advancing a step. "And I'm not taking you to the dentist tomorrow.

Now come here and let me test your blood."

"Vampire." Eva made a cross with two fingers. "Stay back."

Millie struggled to keep her temper. *It's the diabetes talking,* she reminded herself. Her mother's moods often were directly related to the levels of her blood sugar. If it was high, her mother's spirits soared. She went about the house singing, almost giddy. Low blood sugar, on the other hand, made her defiant and irritable.

"Come on," Millie coaxed. "If you let me test your blood, I'll tell you a little more about my date."

Her mother's face brightened instantly. "You're going to break the Hogan curse; I just know it. You're going to be the first Hogan woman in three generations to get the happily-ever-after."

Millie took another step toward her mother and wondered how she was going to put a positive spin on a date that had consisted of David covertly peering around for glimpses of another woman while she pretended not to notice.

"He's grown," she said. "I don't tower over him like a giant anymore. Now give me your hand if you want to hear anything else."

"Oh all right." Her mother extended her right hand. "Did you notice his eyes? They're the color of the Caribbean Sea."

Millie placed the pencil-shaped instrument on the pad of her mother's index finger and pushed a button. The device released the needle in a loud *click.* A small dot of blood formed on her mom's finger, and Millie dipped it onto the test strip.

Her mother was capable of using the device herself, and it never failed to puzzle Millie how her mom could take such a casual approach to a potentially life-threatening disease.

She stuck the test strip into the monitor and waited. A few seconds later, the number flashed on the screen. "380," Millie announced. Worry made her voice sharp. "Did you take any medication today at all?"

"I'm not senile. Of course I did."

Millie studied her mother's face. Eva's brown eyes sparkled, and a becoming blush the color of pink geraniums bloomed in her cheeks. She didn't look like a woman on the verge of a diabetic coma, but that was the problem. With diabetes, you couldn't tell what was happening on the inside.

"I'm going to call your doctor," Millie announced, wondering if she should simply take her mother to the emergency room. "You keep watching *Dinner: Impossible*."

"I want to hear about your date," her mother insisted. "Wait until you're in the dental chair and he leans over you. I haven't had such a hot flash since I went through menopause."

Millie knew Dr. Wong's number by heart. She left a message with the answering service and hung up. Although she pretty much knew the drill by now—*"Keep a close eye on your mother and check her blood sugar in an hour or so"*—she still needed to hear the orders come from a physician. She didn't want the one time she should have called to be the one time she didn't.

Sinking into one of the ladder-backed kitchen chairs, she tucked a piece of hair behind her ear, but it wasn't long enough to stay, and it fell forward, tickling her cheek. She pushed it again anyway. A cup of coffee, half empty from the morning, sat on the table. Millie sipped the cold beverage and waited for the doctor to call.

She stared at the yellow walls. For as long as she could remember, she and her mom had been saying they'd change the color, but whenever they got to the paint store, they ended up coming home with the same shade of egg-yolk yellow. The fading print of a rooster hung over the Formica table, and the speckled linoleum floor was thirty years old.

A gallery of photographs on magnets covered three sides of the refrigerator. Her gaze lingered on the sight of herself elbow deep in bread dough and her mother standing beside her laughing.

Millie couldn't remember what had been so funny, but it didn't matter. The photo captured the essence of her mother, who thought the only good life was one with joy and laughter. Of course her mother didn't have to worry—she had Millie to worry for her.

"Millie? What's taking so long?"

Millie hesitated. She needed a few seconds before she faced Eva again. She reminded herself she and her mom were the M&M's—Mom and Millie. She, Millie, was the plain kind; Eva, the flamboyant, nutty one.

She picked up the bag of caramels and bit into one unhappily. *She's my mother, and she loves me. She's just trying to do what she thinks is best.*

Millie popped another caramel into her mouth and then another. She chewed unhappily and wished the doctor would hurry up and call. Suddenly her teeth clamped down on something hard as a rock. She moved it around her mouth, but with growing certainty realized this couldn't be a caramel. Her tongue found an unfamiliar gap in the back of her mouth.

She didn't need to see the silver evidence to know that she'd just dislodged a filling, and from the size of the hole, maybe even part of her tooth.

Chapter 4

Aris waited for him as he stepped into the kitchen. Seated at the wooden table, his housekeeper was wearing an ankle-length down jacket. Her long silver braid extended from a fur hat with a raccoon tail. She gave him a sour face and tapped the face of her watch.

"Sorry," David said, remembering belatedly that his housekeeper met with the Garden Club at the library on Tuesday nights.

"Oh well, it's no problem," Aris replied in a tone that said the exact opposite. "Tuna casserole's in the oven, salad in the refrigerator." She swung an industrial-sized purse over her shoulder. "Your mother called. She wants to know if you can take her to the Saint Francis cemetery this weekend."

To photograph ancestral graves. His mother's latest obsession. David nodded. "How's Bart?"

Aris shrugged and picked up a key ring that jingled with at least a dozen keys. "He's upstairs on the computer. Says he's working on homework, but. . ."—her eyes narrowed—"when I brought him milk and cookies, he almost dove into the computer screen trying to cover up what was on it." She put her hand on the doorknob. "We should check his IMs."

David shook his head. A month after Aris had moved with

them from California, she had joined the Deer Park Garden Club. It hadn't taken her long to become moderator of the club's online "loop," a position that allowed her to review all the notes posted on the web page. With the new responsibility she had acquired some new computer skills and an insatiable urge to become a cyber detective.

"Instant messages," Aris said very deliberately, as if he hadn't understood the acronym. "I can show you how to pull up his history. We can trace where he's been. Make sure he hasn't been visiting the wrong websites." She paused dramatically. "The web is full of nudie pictures."

David shook his head and tried not to think about how Aris knew about these places. Still, she made a good point, and he made a mental note to ask Bart what sites he'd been visiting online. "No thanks, Aris."

The elderly housekeeper shrugged. "Okay then. I'd better get going, or I'll be late for my meeting."

With a blast of frigid air and the firm click of the door, Aris left him alone in the kitchen. David hung his parka on a hook. He gave Tank, their English bulldog, a pat on the head then crossed into the living room.

Pulling aside a hand's width of the cranberry-colored drapes, he pressed himself tightly against the wall and peered out the window. *This is ridiculous,* he told himself. *I'm acting like a fugitive in my own house.* Still, he couldn't resist gazing up and down the street.

There—in her cherry red Miata—was Cynthia Shively. She had a pair of binoculars trained on the house. He let the curtains fall and stifled a groan. Turning, he saw his son, Bart, standing behind him.

"Hi, Dad," Bart said cheerfully. "She's late tonight."

David stiffened. He didn't like the idea of Bart being any part of this whole unpleasant business with Cynthia. "She stopped at KFC on the way home from the ski hill." He'd felt a brief moment of hope when he realized she wasn't going to follow him the entire way home. But then he'd seen her pull into the drive-through and knew she wasn't giving up—she was simply gathering ammunition in the form of one of Bart's favorite fast-food options.

"KFC?" Bart's eyes lit up. He was eleven years old, not quite five feet, and had the appetite of a starving Russian soldier. "I love KFC."

David was pretty sure his mother had made sure Cynthia knew this and that it was very likely she'd be knocking at the door in a few minutes to offer them some. He ruffled Bart's short black hair. "We've got tuna casserole in the oven." He tried to make this sound like a good option and watched his son's face fall.

"Every night it's either tuna casserole, chicken noodle soup, or macaroni and cheese."

"Not every night." Although privately David agreed that they had eaten enough of these foods to last a lifetime, he also knew that without Aris their lives would be completely chaotic, not to mention more than a little bit empty. She might have started off as their housekeeper, but somewhere along the line, Aris had become family. When he'd talked about moving back to South Dakota, she hadn't blinked. She'd just nodded and said she was tired of Los Angeles and that she hoped he planned on buying a house big enough for them all.

He glanced down into the always serious face of his son, a face slowly edging its way toward manhood, but still round and soft. He made a split-second decision. "Come on, buddy, we'll go to Pizza Palace tonight for dinner."

"No!" Bart said so loudly that David blinked in surprise. "I mean," he added more quietly, "we should stay home. It's a school night, and I have a lot of homework to do."

Something pinged David's parental radar. "Aris said you finished your homework."

Bart folded his arms, and an expression of guilt washed across his boyish features. "Well, I just remembered that I have more, uh, math homework."

"It's only six o'clock," David pointed out. "We'll be home by seven if we leave now."

"I'm really kind of tired tonight."

David's suspicions raised another notch. Usually Bart jumped at the opportunity to go to Pizza Palace. Not only did he wolf down enormous slices of pepperoni pizza, but also the two of them enjoyed playing the arcade games afterward. "What's the matter?"

Bart's gaze slid past his face. "I just want to stay home tonight, that's all. Maybe I'm getting sick or something."

David placed his hand on Bart's forehead. No temperature. He sighed. All he wanted to do was turn on CNN and collapse on the couch with the newspaper. The last thing he wanted was another problem. And yet one look into his son's eyes and David found himself prepared to do whatever it took to erase the look of unhappiness from Bart's face. "Okay, buddy," he said. "We'll stay home."

Not even a hint of a smile formed on Bart's round face. "Thanks, Dad."

David hesitated, unsure of the words that needed to be said to draw his son out. If he pushed, the boy would clam up. And yet if he didn't, how would he find out what was bothering Bart and help him?

The phone rang.

David guessed it was his mom calling about the Saint Francis cemetery. Well, he wouldn't answer. The phone rang twice more, and then the answering machine picked up. David's voice, sounding low and deep and not quite the way it sounded to himself, asked the caller to leave a message.

"Hey, Barty," a voice called in a high, squeaky voice that was obviously a boy trying to sound like a girl. "This is Lauren. I *love* you. I want to get *married* to you. I want to have your babies!" There was a sound of air kisses, a chorus of not-so-nice male laughter, and then the caller hung up.

David looked at his son's tomato-red face. "Bart?"

Wordlessly, the boy turned and charged up the stairs. His door slammed shut in reply. A moment later music blasted through the house.

Tank shuffled into the room and glanced up at David. Heartfelt sympathy seemed to flow from the bulldog's liquid brown eyes. The thump of the bass drew David's gaze to the ceiling. He pictured Bart facedown on his bed, blasting his music as if he could drown out his own thoughts. David knew a lot about unwelcome thoughts. They slid through your mind like ghosts, and the more you tried to bat them away, the more they multiplied.

What he didn't know was how to reach his son who was growing up faster every day, becoming more distant, more plugged into his computer, his friends, and his MP3 player than he was to David. At the same time, like now, he knew the tough exterior was nothing more than a thin shell that Bart hid behind. Inside, he was still a little kid—smart as all get out—but not particularly tough.

David glanced down at the bulldog, who wagged her stubby tail hopefully. "What do I do, Tank?"

The round bulldog flipped onto her back and stuck four short paws into the air. "Play dead?" David asked. "That's the best you can do?"

The dog wiggled happily on the floor, almost but not quite in time with the beat of the music. David rubbed the back of his neck and glanced up once more in the direction of his son's room.

He put his foot on the first step of the staircase. Bart probably wouldn't talk to him. Quite possibly he'd make things worse by pushing the boy. David was a man, but not so old that he'd forgotten how much he'd wanted his father's approval, not sympathy. Maybe the best thing to do was ignore the whole telephone thing.

From the upstairs, the music continued to pound. David looked up the stairs and sighed. He knew he would have to talk to Bart about girls—something he had not expected to do for a long time. He'd give Bart a few days to get past the embarrassing phone call, and then he'd talk to him.

Chapter 5

The sound of easy-listening music filled Millie's ears as she stepped inside the second-floor office. Glancing around the small, windowless room, she walked past the burgundy-colored leather couches to the receptionist, an older woman with ash-blond hair, a narrow face, and a friendly smile looked up at her. "Can I help you?"

"I'm Millie Hogan. My mother, Eva, is scheduled to see Dr. Denvers at nine, but I'd like to take her appointment if that's okay."

"Millie Hogan?" The polite smile remained on the receptionist's face, but something flickered in her eyes. Setting her reading glasses on her nose, she studied the appointment book with the concentration of someone who'd been told they had two minutes to study before a pop quiz. "I'm sorry," she said. "We can't just substitute patients like this."

"Why not?"

The woman's gaze stayed in the appointment book. "Because"— she paused—"your name is not in the book."

"Can't you add it?"

"There's another name there already."

"But my mother isn't coming," Millie repeated.

"I could probably fit you in a week from next Thursday," the receptionist said.

"I don't think I can wait that long," Millie said. "Look, I'm sure if we ask David, he'll be glad to let me use my mom's appointment."

"Dr. Denvers," the woman corrected sternly, "cannot be bothered with scheduling conflicts."

Millie ran her hand through her hair. Why was the receptionist being so difficult?

The hall door opened, and a woman stepped inside. Millie immediately recognized the woman from the ski hill. She looked even more stunning in slim-fitting winter white pants and a camel-colored wool turtleneck. Her gold necklace and earrings were flawless.

The blond stepped across the room on thin heels that gleamed as if they'd never set foot in a snowy, salt-strewn South Dakota street.

"Veronica," the blond exclaimed. "I made muffins." She handed the receptionist a basket covered with a checkered cloth. "Banana chocolate chip. And they're still warm."

"Oh, they're David's favorite," the receptionist exclaimed. "I'll go get him right away."

She must have pressed a secret bell or something because almost immediately the door to the patient area opened and David appeared in the doorway. He was wearing a white, thermal shirt beneath a pair of light-blue scrubs. His face brightened when he saw her. "Millie?" he asked. "This is a nice surprise."

Before she could reply, the blond said, "Have a muffin, David."

"They're your favorite—banana chocolate chip," the receptionist confirmed. "Wasn't that thoughtful of Cynthia to bring them?"

A tiny muscle jerked in the corner of David's mouth. His gaze swung to the tall blond who beamed back at him. "Try one," Cynthia said. "They have a secret ingredient that I think you'll like."

"Uh, no thank you," David said, backing up a step. "But maybe later."

"Now's a good time," the receptionist said. "Your nine o'clock patient just canceled."

"Actually," Millie said, "I'd love to take my mother's appointment. I lost a filling and was hoping that you'd be able to take a look at it."

Relief washed over David's face. "Come on back, and let's have a look."

"David, you can't do that. I don't have her insurance information."

Millie took her insurance card out of her wallet, handed it to the receptionist, and followed David into the examination room.

"Thanks, David." Millie set her purse on the windowsill. "Your receptionist sure is protective."

"That's my mother."

Millie's head swung around. "Seriously?"

David smiled apologetically. "When I took over my dad's practice, I sort of inherited her, too. She's actually very good at the job."

"Oh. Say no more." Thousands of hours of running the café with her mother flashed through her head. Sometimes her mother nearly drove her crazy, and other times her mom's sense of humor had her laughing so hard she could hardly stay upright. She settled into the reclining dental chair and tried to relax as David snapped on a pair of latex gloves.

"So what happened?" David asked, adjusting the arm of a high-tech light. He pressed a button, and the seat reclined. The world tilted, and she found herself staring up at the tiled ceiling blocks. He aimed a strong light on her face, and she was suddenly conscious of every imperfection of her face.

"I was eating caramels," Millie confessed. "Suddenly I felt this little hard rock in my mouth and a space where my filling used to be."

"Caramels?" David repeated, frowning. He rolled his stool closer to her. "I was just telling your mother yesterday that eating caramels was almost guaranteed to pull out a filling."

"I know," Millie said. "I confiscated the candy from her."

"That's odd. She thanked me yesterday for telling her." He frowned thoughtfully. "Well, let's take a look." He picked up one of the slim, stainless steel tools lying on an adjustable tray and gently probed the hole in Millie's mouth. "Does that hurt?"

"Sort of," Millie said. With David's hands in her mouth, it came out, "Thort off."

"That's a pretty big hole back there," David mused, bending so close she smelled the faint odor of soap. "I'm going to clean it up a bit and then patch it."

"Great," Millie said. She just wanted the whole thing over. She flinched though at the sight of a scary-looking needle in David's hands.

"Just some Novocain," he said cheerfully. He dabbed her gums with something that tasted like banana then injected her. Millie focused on his eyes and decided her mother was right. They were the exact shade of the Caribbean. Not that either her mother or herself had ever actually seen the Caribbean. Nope. For them it was Lake Bluckman, which they'd dubbed Lake Blue Lips, because even in the summer the water temperature rarely rose to sixty degrees.

"We'll just give you a few minutes to let that numb up." David gave her a confident smile. He had nice teeth, even and white.

"I had fun skiing yesterday," he said casually, perching on the stool and watching her with that look doctors use when they're making a clinical assessment while trying to appear as if they aren't.

Millie nodded. "Me, too." She was trying not to touch the cavity with her tongue, and her gum felt increasingly foreign and tingly. "I was really sore this morning. I'm not used to so much exercise."

"We got in a lot of runs," David agreed. "How's that gum feeling?"

"What gum?"

David laughed. "Open, please."

"Uh, David," Millie said, eyeing the scary-looking tool in his hand. "I want to apologize for yesterday. My mother never would have made you go on a blind date if she knew you already had a girlfriend. I'm really sorry if we caused you problems."

"Girlfriend?" David repeated.

"Cynthia—the muffin woman. I saw her yesterday at the ski hill watching us."

"She's not my girlfriend," David said, his face tightening slightly.

Millie's eyebrows drew together. She'd seen the way the woman looked at David. "She isn't?"

"No," David said firmly and advanced with the drill.

"Oh." Millie involuntarily shrank back. "She was following us all day. She couldn't take her eyes off you. And here she is today in your office."

"I know," David said calmly.

"So, she's what? A bill collector?"

He laughed. "No."

She was prying but couldn't seem to help herself. Dental offices always made her a little nervous, and the sight of the adjustable arm of the drill struck dread in her heart. It was getting harder to feel part of her mouth, and she concentrated on getting the words out clearly. "A stalker then?"

David's cheeks turned pink. "Don't you remember Cynthia Shively?"

The name was familiar, but Millie couldn't quite place it.

"Dr. Shively? The optometrist?" David prompted.

"She's his daughter? You're kidding me." But it clicked. The Shivelys had several children, and all of them had attended private boarding schools, mostly in Europe. "That's Cynthia Shively? I thought she was in France married to some bigwig plastic surgeon."

"She's divorced," David explained. "Came back to town a couple of weeks ago. We had coffee because she seemed kind of down, and ever since then I haven't been able to get her to stop following me."

Millie was fascinated. "She's stalking you?"

"Aggressively pursuing," David explained. "Our mothers are friends. They sort of made some kind of marriage pact while we were in elementary school."

Millie would have laughed, but David looked so unhappy over the whole situation that she felt a bit sorry for him. "How long has she been stalking—I mean, aggressively pursuing you?"

"A couple of weeks," David admitted. "I hoped if she saw me with you, she'd realize that I'm not interested in her. It didn't work."

So he'd only gone out with her to try and shake Cynthia. Millie should have felt insulted. Instead, she was relieved. David hadn't wanted to be on that blind date with her yesterday any more than she had. No wonder the date had felt so awkward.

"It's not that you're not an attractive woman, Millie, but I'm not looking for a relationship right now."

"Neither am I," Millie agreed. "But my mother, well, she'd probably throw herself in front of a bus if the driver was male, single, and she thought it'd get me a date."

"Don't say that in front of Cynthia," David said dryly. "It might give her ideas."

She met David's gaze and felt the understanding pass between them. "My mother was only eating caramels because she wanted to dislodge her filling. She planned to have me come with her so she could get us together again. She already has names for our children."

"You know. . . ," David began then shook his head. "Bad idea. Very bad idea. Probably wouldn't work."

Millie sat up as straight as the sloped chair would allow. "What? What probably wouldn't work?"

David reached for a surgical mask. "I was just thinking. . .that maybe. . .no." He shook his head. "It's a bad idea. Let's get back to your tooth. That's something I can fix."

"You can't do that," Millie protested. "You can't tell me that you have an idea and then not say what it is."

He'd put on the surgical mask, which was cheating, since it hid his expression while he could see her entire face very well. He tried to move the arm of the drill into position, but she pushed it away. "Tell me."

He hesitated a second longer then said, "Okay. I was thinking that if we pretended to keep dating, then maybe Cynthia would stop stalking me. Plus, your mother would stop setting you up on blind dates." He paused. "We'd both get a little breathing room."

Millie blinked. Pretend to date David? Wouldn't that just fuel her mother's dreams of grandchildren? Then again, if she didn't go out again with David, she suspected Cliff Johnson, the pharmacist from CVS, was next on the list.

"You know, that's a fantastic idea," she said. "It might be hard to pull off though. I mean, to be believable, we'd have to do a good job of pretending that we were really into each other."

"But only when we were around other people," David pointed out. "And only for a short time."

"And then, when we break up, we could tell everyone that we have a broken heart and need time to recover. I would probably have to take a vacation," Millie mused. "You know, get out of town for a little while." She brightened at the prospect.

"And by then Cynthia would have found someone else."

"We could call it off sooner if either of us wanted," Millie qualified quickly. "With no hard feelings. You know. If it wasn't working."

"No hard feelings," David echoed. "So what do you think?"

"I don't know. What do you think?"

"It might be worth trying."

"As long as we both understand that it's only pretend." Millie looked at him carefully. "When we go on dates, we bring a book or something. No personal questions."

He seemed to consider the plan a bit longer then extended his hand. "I'm fine with that," he said.

The latex hand felt a little weird. To be honest, the whole plan felt a little weird, but Millie figured this was the only way to get her mother off her back.

Chapter 6

Both Cynthia and Mrs. Denvers were wearing polite smiles when Millie returned to the reception area. Given what David had just told her, Millie could almost see their brains whirling, trying to calculate just how big a threat she was to them.

"Did everything go well, dear?" Mrs. Denvers asked.

Cynthia covered the muffins and looked prepared to defend them physically if Millie so much as stepped in their direction.

"Yeth," Millie said, the Novocain making the right side of her mouth feel roughly the size of a bowling ball. Remembering her role, she added, "David ith a wonderful dentith."

As if on cue, said dentist popped out behind her. "It was so wonderful to see you again, Millie," he said into the back of her head and with way too much emphasis on the word *wonderful* to be completely believable.

Millie shifted so they could actually look at each other. "You, too," she said, smiling—well, at least she hoped she was smiling. For all she knew, she could be drooling like a Newfoundland. "And I'm really looking forwarth to tomorrow evening."

"Yes, tomorrow evening," David repeated so loudly that someone standing by the building's elevators could have heard. "I'll pick you up at seven, right?"

Millie winced. David might be a good dentist, but so far he was proving to be a lousy actor. "Right," she agreed, trying to signal with her eyes for him to tone it down a bit.

He didn't seem to get the message, because the next thing she knew, he was patting her shoulder much too enthusiastically. To make it worse, his gaze stayed pinned over her shoulder, probably watching his mother's and Cynthia's reactions.

This won't do, not at all, Millie thought. *Better help the man out.* She raised herself on the tips of her toes and gently kissed his cheek. The side of her mouth that had feeling registered the warmth and smoothness of his skin. She let her lips linger for a moment then added, "Thanks for fixing my toof, David."

"Anything else you need fixing, you just call me," David said, still sounding like a really bad actor reading a script.

"I will." Millie gave him a final, sultry look. "Thee you tomorrow night." She strutted past Cynthia and David's mother. "Have a nith day," she said grandly, putting a little hip action into the final few steps to the door.

As she stepped into the hallway, she heard Mrs. Denvers say, "David, don't you know who that girl is?"

She paused, held her breath, then heard David say, "Not entirely, Mother, but I intend to." The words sounded believable—as if he really meant them. As Millie stepped toward the elevators, she thought that maybe this plan might just work after all.

It started to sleet on her way back to the café. The gigantic éclair on top of the café's roof glistened in its case of ice. The wind had picked up, too. When she stepped out of her car, icy wind grabbed the door and slung darts of frozen rain against her cheeks. She hunched over and hurried into the café.

At least half a dozen customers looked up, called a cheerful,

"Hey, Millie," and waved as she moved inside the warm restaurant. A log crackled in the corner fireplace, and the smell of freshly baked bread sweetened the air. Millie hung up her coat, and as Tim McGraw sang softly in the background, she braced herself for the onslaught of questions.

"You get your tooth fixed?" Jeff Gulden asked. His perpetually sad face looked even more worried than usual. He'd finished his plate of scrambled eggs and hash browns. Millie automatically scooped it up and checked the level of his coffee cup.

"Yes, thanks," Millie replied. Half her lip felt numb, but her tongue no longer felt huge in her mouth.

She picked up a few more empty plates on her way back to the kitchen. Dumping them in a tub near the sink, she grabbed two orders from under the warming lights and ran back to the front of the restaurant before her mother could start asking a million questions. Millie didn't want Eva getting suspicious if she gave up the information too easily.

She set the plates down in front of the older couple at table five then picked up the coffeepot from the hot plate and began walking around the room refilling cups.

"How's it going, Mrs. Benson?" Millie asked. "Cold enough for you today?"

Like most of the regulars, Mrs. Benson was retired and spent weekday mornings at Dosie Dough's sipping coffee and reading the morning paper. She looked up at Millie and smiled. "It says in the paper that it's going to get even colder." She held her cup up for a refill. "Obviously global warming has not come to South Dakota."

Millie laughed and moved to the next table. A husband and wife were seated with their two young kids. Tourists, she thought and topped off their cups, all the while engaging in small-town talk.

"Millie," Aunt Mimi's voice boomed across the room. "We cannot wait a second longer. Come over here and tell us how your visit with Dr. Denvers went."

The coffeepot jiggled in Millie's hands. It wasn't as if she could pretend that she hadn't heard what Aunt Mimi had said. Although Mimi was so tiny her head could barely be seen when she drove a car, she more than made up for it with her voice. Naturally loud, it boomed across any distance. When she'd worked as a crossing guard, her voice had kept both traffic and children well in line.

"Talk loudly," Aunt Lillian called from her wheelchair at the bay window. "I want to hear everything." As usual, her white hair was tucked into a neat chignon. Today she was wearing her favorite pair of faux diamond chandelier earrings—the same ones she'd worn the night she'd been named Miss South Dakota in 1965.

"Not much to tell," Millie said but smiled as if there were a lot to tell. "Where's Aunt Keeker?"

"Right here, honey," Keeker said, walking out of the kitchen area with Millie's mother. "I was just talking to your mother for a moment." She fingered the brim of her Chicago Cubs baseball hat. "How'd your appointment with Dr. Denvers go?"

"It went fine," she said.

Keeker exchanged a look of satisfaction with Eva. "And that's the power of a good hat."

Millie gave what she hoped was a believable sigh and shook her head. "Aunt Keeker," she said, "getting my tooth fixed had nothing to do with your hat."

"We're not talking about your tooth." Keeker's large brown eyes blinked innocently.

Keeker firmly believed in wearing lucky hats. When a friend got sick, Keeker would trot out the herbal hat; when someone had sleep problems, she wore her dream-catcher hat; and whenever Millie started to date someone, she wore her lucky baseball cap. The cap, she claimed, had helped the Cubs break a fifteen-game losing streak back in the seventies.

"Tell us about the doc," Eva pressed.

Busying herself with the coffeepot, Millie shrugged in response to her mother's question. "I don't know what to say."

"Say you're going to see him again."

The room became dead quiet. Millie could feel all gazes turned toward her, waiting for her response. Even Thomas and Melvin Dittmore, the twin brothers who sat in front of the fireplace playing a game of chess that involved about three moves a week, had stopped studying the board and were looking at her instead.

"Well." Jeff cleared his throat. "I don't mean to pry, Miss Millie, but my root canal is scheduled for Friday, and if you think it'd be better for me to give the doc a couple of days to himself, I'd sure appreciate your saying so."

Could she really pull this off? She wasn't sure, but the sight of Cliff Johnson, the CVS pharmacist, casually eating a cinnamon roll at table three helped make up her mind. Picking up a hot pot of coffee, she walked over to Jeff and filled his cup. "Keep your appointment, Mr. Gulden, and don't worry about a thing."

"That means she's got another date," Aunt Mimi boomed out, startling her little poodle so badly it jumped up on the table and started mindlessly barking. "Hallelujah!"

Millie chuckled. "Is there nothing better to discuss than my social life? How about that malfunctioning traffic light on Bender Road?"

"She's got a date," her mother confirmed, beaming.

"If you ask me, she doesn't look too happy about it," Jeff

ventured, the wrinkles in his weathered face deepening. "Maybe I should reschedule."

Millie touched the right side of her mouth to make sure the expression she'd formed was indeed a smile. "I am happy," she said. "It's just the Novocain. I feel like I have a fat lip."

Aunt Keeker placed her hand, blue-veined and gnarled with arthritis, on Millie's arm. "I have a feeling," she said, "that he could be the one. I'll wear my red beret on your next date. I wore it when Roland kissed me for the first time. It fell off when I swooned, and he caught me."

"You don't need to do that," Millie said, but she smiled and squeezed Keeker's hand back. No matter how many times Keeker told this story, her eyes still filled. Millie wondered if she'd ever feel that way about anyone.

"What Millie needs," Aunt Mimi said, her small, wrinkled face breaking into a smile, "is a new dress. Something that shows off her figure." She stroked her dog. As long as Millie could remember, there had been a small apricot poodle in Mimi's lap, and all of them had been named Earl Gray. This one was probably Earl Gray the sixth or seventh, and it was the nastiest one so far. It had snapped at everyone in the café. "Wouldn't Millie look pretty in something the same orange color as your coat, sweet baby dog?"

Millie's tongue rolled over the place where David had fixed the cavity. Aunt Mimi had a good idea. She'd make that trip to Swaggers and buy herself something pretty to wear on her next pretend date with David. She wouldn't buy a marked-down dress either. A full-priced dress said she was serious.

Picking up a rag from behind the deli counter, she began wiping down an empty table. She wanted to rewrite her essay about why she'd make a good candidate on *Chef's Challenge*—a new reality show on the Food Network. Of all the dozens of casting calls she'd responded to, this one was the most suited to her. The show was a combination of *Survivor*, *Amazing Race*, and *Top Chef*, and Millie felt sure she had all the right skills necessary.

Somebody honked, and Millie automatically glanced out the front window. It was a big black Expedition, impatient with the car in front of it, which was waiting for a parking spot. Probably a tourist coming to town for the skiing. She looked past the gray, slushy street and sharp-tipped grains of sleet. The mountains were lost in the haze, but she really wasn't looking for them.

Someday her cell would ring, and it would be a casting director calling for her. She imagined herself in a chair in front of a mirror almost as big as the café's front window. Her hairdresser and makeup artist would be fussing over her, preparing for taping the next episode of *Chef's Challenge*. If she tried hard enough, she could almost hear the whispers of their voices. Closing her eyes, Millie smiled and dreamed of being somebody.

Chapter 7

Hah!" Bart exclaimed as his Porsche 4000 sideswiped David's Audi. David's remote control vibrated in his hands. His car spun around and ended up, once again, on the TV screen facing backward.

It was worth it to see the look of excitement on Bart's face. "Come on, Dad. Catch up to me. I'll wait for you."

"So you can crash into me again," David observed, valiantly manipulating the controls so that his racer once more faced the correct direction.

Video games weren't his thing. He much preferred playing chess or backgammon, or even a long game like Monopoly. But Bart's generation played video games—increasingly sophisticated ones, too. David had to admit that his son, who pretty much tripped over his own feet in any kind of sport, could play any kind of video game like a professional.

From her place at their feet, Tank snored peacefully, ignoring Bart's shout of satisfaction as David's car once more plunged into the side rail.

"So," David said casually. "How was school today?"

"Fine."

Bart's racer accelerated, achieving a speed of 120 miles per hour, and left David's car in the dust.

"Those kids give you any trouble?"

Bart's gaze stayed glued to the television screen. He appeared not to have heard.

"Anything you want to talk about?" David accelerated his Audi with the determination of a father on a mission. Showing more skill than he had the entire game, he chased down Bart's car then deliberately slammed into it.

Both cars hit the side rail. Bart whooped in joyful surprise. "Good one, Dad!"

"You know," David said. "When I was your age or maybe a little older, I liked this girl. She was gorgeous—tall, wild brown hair, and a smile like an angel. I used to follow her around like a lost puppy."

He glanced at his son, who studied his remote control as if he'd never seen one in his life.

"There was this thing at school called Teen Night. Nothing big, just music and dancing in the gym. Finally, I got my courage up and asked her to go with me." David paused. "We were standing in the cafeteria line." He tried to see some sign that Bart was listening.

"And?" Bart asked, still fiddling with the remote but doing nothing to actually move his car.

"She looked down at me—I was about three inches shorter than her—and said no."

"I'm sorry, Dad."

"The point is that I asked her, and it didn't work out. That's the way it is sometimes."

Bart snorted. "It's not that simple anymore, Dad."

"No, it probably isn't," David agreed, thinking, *Talk to me, Bart.* "Nobody called me up on the telephone and harassed me. In fact, the cafeteria lady felt so sorry for me that I got extras at lunch for about a week."

Bart lifted the television remote. "At our cafeteria," he stated flatly, "you don't want extras."

His son turned up the volume of the television, and with a screech of tires and the roar of an engine, he once more focused his attention on the screen.

David surprised them both by reaching over and removing the remote from his son's hands. "I can't help you if you don't talk to me."

"Talk about what?"

"You know. That phone call."

"It's no big deal, Dad," Bart said without looking at him. "I have two Laurens in my address book on my phone, and I texted the wrong one. She forwarded the message to a bunch of people."

Ouch. David tried not to wince. Although he would have paid money to know what his son's message to the girl had been, he forced himself to assume Bart's casual tone and expression.

"Well," David said. "I'm sure this all will blow over."

Bart shot him a look that said it would when you-know-where froze over. Instantly David knew he'd said the wrong thing.

"Maybe you shouldn't let it blow over," David heard himself suggest. "Instead of taking your licks, you should use what's happened to your advantage."

"Huh?"

"Yeah," David said, searching his brain for a plan. "This girl you like. Why not text her again? Maybe she'll be flattered that you like her so much that you keep trying. Getting her to go out with you would make everyone stop teasing you."

Dead silence. Bart didn't look at him. "You could ask her to go to the movies," David suggested, knowing that he was doing all the talking but seeming unable to stop himself. "There must be something PG you could go to—or ask her to go ice-skating with you."

The image of his own unsuccessful skiing date with Millie flashed before his eyes. He stomped it down as quickly as he could. That was different. Neither of them had gone on the date for the right reason.

Bart punched the POWER button on the game console, and David had the sickening feeling that his son also was shutting down any further discussion about girls or dating. He could have kicked himself for failing. There was so much he wanted to say to Bart about this new stage of his life, but he didn't know how. Even now he wanted to hug his son but knew Bart would only shrink away.

"PG is for little kids," Bart stated without emotion. "And even if our movie theater was showing one, my friends wouldn't want to go. Mostly they like PG-13 or R movies."

Eleven-year-olds watching R-rated movies? What in the world are their parents thinking? David bit back the lecture forming and said, "Why don't we check the newspaper and see what's playing and then go from there?"

"If I see something good," Bart began, "could we have popcorn and sodas and candy?"

"You bet." David pushed down the dentist inside him that told him Bart shouldn't eat popcorn with braces on his teeth. He thought, too, of Lisa and how their first date had been to see *Titanic*. Would it help Bart to hear how awkward that date had been? How he'd dropped his soda and soaked the feet of the people in the row in front of them? Or would it merely serve to remind Bart of the mother he had lost?

"Dad?" Bart was studying his face, his eyes owlish behind the thick lenses of his glasses. "How do you get a girl to like you?"

David swallowed. He wasn't ready for this. Not ready at all. Yet he had no choice. The question had been tossed to him, and he could either fumble the ball or answer it as best he could.

"Well," he began, dismissing his first answer—the "just be yourself" answer that had probably been said about a hundred million times. "There's lots of ways. You compliment her. You give her gifts. You find out about her likes and dislikes." He paused. "You go slowly, Bart. You talk to God about it."

A long pause, and then Bart said, "Oh, okay," and punched back on the game console, filling the silence between them with the noise of a band that seemed to be shouting rather than singing.

David thought, *That's it? That's all he's going to say?*

Apparently it was. David followed Bart's cue and picked up his remote control. On familiar ground, he allowed himself to relax. All too soon he had a feeling that Bart would think playing video games with him wasn't cool.

He shot Bart a sideways look as his car drew even with the Porsche. He wondered if all parents had as much trouble letting go as he did or if it was because he was a single parent that watching Bart become more independent made him want to jerk him back into childhood. He felt as if he hadn't had enough time to fully appreciate it.

Above the ear-jarring music with lyrics that sounded like someone with a sore throat was screaming, "Raba-daba-jam, JAM!" over and over, there was a screech of tires and Bart's car fell back. A second later the finish line flashed in front of David's car. As he crossed it, his heart beat a bit harder, not because he'd won, but because he knew it was Bart's way of saying that maybe he wasn't ready to let go either.

Chapter 8

The doorbell rang at 6:55 p.m. Millie smoothed the folds of her new black silk dress—exquisitely cut but much too lightweight for the January night—and reached for the matching satin handbag.

Her mom, as if fearing that David might change his mind if kept waiting for longer than two seconds, flung open the door. "David!" she cried. "So wonderful to see you!"

Although it wasn't a date, not a real one anyway, Millie gave him credit. His dark gray pinstripe suit fit his lean torso perfectly, his shoes were polished, and in his hands were two red roses.

"For you," he said and extended one of the flowers to Millie. "You look very nice."

Millie's nose wrinkled. *Very nice?* That's what her mother said whenever Millie cut her hair too short. It was not something you said to a woman who'd just spent a hundred and fifty dollars on a dress she had bought specifically for him. She arched one eyebrow. "Thank you," she said. "You look very nice, too."

He gave her a flower and a small kiss on the cheek. The cool fragrance of his aftershave wafted over her. It smelled classy and expensive. And the long-stemmed rose was fresh and neatly bundled with baby's breath. She decided to forgive his lukewarm compliment about her appearance.

"Mrs. Hogan," David said, stepping back. "This rose is for you."

Her mother took the rose, and her face flushed with pleasure. "This is so sweet of you." Her mom turned the flower to admire it from another angle. "Thank you."

"You're welcome." He smiled, and in the space of a few seconds an awkward silence fell among them. This surprised Millie, because her mom was never at a loss for words. She was turning the rose in her hands, and there was a soft look on her face as if she was remembering another time and another rose.

"So, Eva," David began, breaking the silence. "How's that filling working out for you?"

Her mother beamed. "Perfectly." She turned to Millie and winked, making it clear it wasn't just her filling that she was talking about.

Millie touched David's arm. She didn't want him to get side-tracked with talking about dentistry. "Maybe we ought to get going."

"Oh, we have plenty of time," David said. "Our reservation isn't until eight o'clock."

Okay. The flowers had been romantic, but settling in for an extended visit with her mother wasn't. Millie had the awful thought that with any encouragement, he'd be happy to plop down on their couch and talk to her mom. That definitely didn't sound like a romantic first date.

Fortunately, Eva shook her head. "No, no, you kids get going." Her mother waved her arms as if she were shooing chickens. "*Dinner: Impossible* is about to start. That Robert Irvine is a fantastic cook. You ever watch the Food Network, David?"

"No," David replied. "I'm not much of a cook, I'm afraid."

"Everyone can cook," Millie's mother assured him. "It's just a matter of practice. I have some very easy recipes, and I'm sure Millie wouldn't mind showing you how to make them."

Millie almost laughed. Touting her culinary skills was just another way her mother was trying to make Millie seem like wife material. She handed her mother the rose. "Could you put this in some water for me? David and I really should get going."

"It was good to see you, Eva," David said. "Have a nice night."

"Enjoy yourselves," her mother said, fingering a rose petal. "But drive safely."

Millie grabbed her coat out of the closet. Slinging it over her arm, she yanked open the front door without even putting it on. The blast of cold air immediately stung her cheeks, and the slice of wind went straight through the hair she'd spent an hour straightening. She didn't look back as she hurried to David's SUV.

"Well, all in all, I think that went pretty well," Millie said, settling into the cold leather seat in David's black Lexus.

The car jolted slightly as David shifted into REVERSE. "You think so?"

"Absolutely. The flowers were a great touch." Millie checked the back of one of her earrings to make sure it was tight.

"Thank you."

She leaned back and watched the scenery flash before her eyes—houses frosted with a few inches of snow and streetlights throwing buckets of light onto the slick black street. They rode in comfortable silence through Millie's neighborhood then turned right onto the back road that led to town. "You know, I like what we're doing—this not dating," she said. "Normally I'd be trying to come up with stimulating conversation or wondering if you liked my dress or if I had lipstick on my teeth. This is much more relaxing."

David smiled. "I know what you mean. There's no pressure, no awkward silences while you wonder what the other person thinks of you. No expectations."

"Nope," Millie confirmed. "We're just two people helping each other out."

"Um-hum," David murmured and glanced in the rearview mirror.

She followed his gaze. "Is Cynthia following us?"

"I thought I saw her car a little ways back," David admitted. "But I guess I was wrong. I made sure she was within hearing range when I told my mother our plans." He flashed a sideways grin. "I told my mother that I thought you might be the one."

The one? Millie sat up straighter. She hadn't expected him to make such a bold statement so early in their relationship. "You think she believed you?"

"Well," David said, "she got very quiet and asked me if I was taking any new medications."

They both laughed. "You have to go more slowly, David, or you're going to give your poor mother a heart attack."

"I tried subtle," David said. "It didn't work."

Millie smoothed her dress. "I guess you're right. Sometimes it's best to be direct, especially when it comes to relationships. You have to make a clean break. Dragging it out just makes things worse."

She'd learned this firsthand. Men tended to ignore the signs that things weren't working out. Things like avoiding eye contact, not talking very much, and/or claiming to be too busy to go out rarely did the trick. People tended to see what they wanted to see and ignore the rest. "When I need to break up with someone, I tell them it's been nice, and then I shake their hand and say, 'It's over.' "

David slowed as the lights of the town came into sight. "And they just go away?"

"Most go passive-aggressive. Erv—the UPS guy—threw my packages in the bushes for two weeks before he got over it, and Karl Kauffman—he's a policeman—left me a couple of bogus parking tickets. But basically they knew going into it that I wasn't looking for a serious relationship." She noticed a Jonas Brothers CD sitting on top of a recording from the Chicago Symphony Orchestra.

"People should accept that a person doesn't have to be in a relationship to be happy," David said.

"Exactly," Millie agreed. "Marriage isn't for everyone. Some of us want other things."

David shot her a sideways glance. "Like what?"

Millie glanced out the window. Lights were still on in the CVS, but the windows to the adjacent UPS store and dry cleaner's were long dark. Ahead, the parking lot was half empty at the movie theater that had been playing the same two films for a month. "Options," she said, "which is something this town doesn't give you."

He took her to Ben's, which was the expensive restaurant in town. Mostly people went there to celebrate important family milestones, and it was pretty much booked all through the warmer months for wedding receptions. Millie was suddenly glad she'd worn the new black silk as she followed David through the foyer, where an enormous stone swan statue spat a flow of water. The crimson and gold carpet sank luxuriously beneath her feet.

"Hope this place is okay," David said as they waited to be seated. "I just thought, you know, that if we wanted people to think we were dating, I should bring you somewhere nice."

The last time Millie had been here was a few years ago when the aunts had brought her mother here to celebrate her sixtieth birthday.

There'd been a terrible scene when Aunt Mimi had tried to sneak her dog into the restaurant in a large purse and they'd been discovered. Aunt Lillian had jumped to Mimi's defense, but her story about Earl Gray being a service dog didn't keep them from getting escorted to the door. Millie remembered all of them grumbling as they walked back to the car, and then Keeker had triumphantly pulled out the loaf of french bread she'd stolen off the table when Lillian and Mimi had been arguing with the manager.

"It's perfect," Millie replied as a woman in black with oversized silver jewelry led them to their table.

Couples bent over tables talking. A tall guy in a brown suit laughed and clinked glasses with a cute redheaded woman who ducked her head as if she'd just received a very lavish compliment. Across from them a bald man with a silver mustache and his white-haired wife were sharing a large piece of chocolate cake. On the dance floor several couples were moving slowly to the piano player's rendition of Elton John's "Your Song."

Millie picked up her menu and studied the selections. She tried not to worry when she saw the prices.

"See anything you like?" David asked.

"It all looks great." Millie lowered the menu. "Hope you know we're splitting the check."

"I appreciate the offer, but I can't let you do that."

She studied the serious line of his mouth. "David," she said. "Don't you know going dutch is the number one rule in the official book of un-dating?"

"You must be studying an old version," David replied and broke a piece of bread off the end of the loaf. "According to the International Council of Un-dating, or ICU, the number one rule is to make people believe we are actually dating, which means the guy picks up the check."

"The ICU?" Millie laughed.

"Which covers both national and international rules."

"I see. . ."

"U," David finished.

"No. I mean, I see what you're saying, but I'm paying you back when we get in the car."

"Millie," David said. "Thanks for offering, but I've got it. What would you like to drink?"

"Water. If I agree to let you pay this time, will you let me get the check next time?"

"No," David said. "When we're on a date, I pick up the check."

"That's not fair," Millie pointed out. "Why should you always have to pay?"

"To do otherwise would be an insult to you."

He said it matter-of-factly, but Millie's skin tingled pleasantly. She liked being treated as if she mattered to him, even if they were only pretending. She lifted the menu to hide her pleasure and resolved to order the second cheapest thing on the menu.

The pianist struck up a melancholy tune. "Maybe we should suggest a Jonas Brothers' song," Millie suggested.

David's eyebrows pushed together. "The Jonas Brothers?"

"I saw the CD cover in your car. I figured you were a fan."

He laughed. "Oh. My son likes them."

Millie blinked. A son? He had a son? Why had she not heard this before? She vaguely remembered the conversation that had swirled around Dosie Dough's when David had taken over his father's practice, but mostly people had been speculating on whether he'd be as good a dentist as his dad or if they should look for someone older and more experienced.

She realized that she was gripping her water glass way too hard and consciously relaxed her fingers. She was going to kill her mother for failing to mention David's son. She never dated men with children. Never. Her mother knew that.

"He's eleven going on sixteen," David said, and there was an undeniable note of pride in his voice. "Want to see a picture?"

Millie set the water glass on the table with a definite thump. "I don't date men with kids."

He frowned. "Why not?"

"Because kids complicate things."

"Such as?"

"Breaking up. I don't want to have to tell some boy or girl that I won't be seeing them because I've broken up with their father." She shook her head. "I'm sorry, David, but we're going to need to rethink our plan."

"I understand your reservations," David said. He realigned his silverware then looked up at her again. "But I don't think we'll be together long enough for Bart to get attached."

Millie cocked a brow. She wasn't used to men being so clearly uninterested in her. Although it wasn't flattering, it was intriguing. "I agree. If we date, it would have to be short-term."

"Just long enough to be believable," David began.

"And short enough that there's no hard feelings at the end."

David nodded. "Of course, if you don't like being around kids, then you're right—this plan wouldn't work."

"No, it's not that at all. I love kids. I just wouldn't want to hurt anyone." It was her turn to realign the silverware. "What would you tell him about us?"

"I'd tell him that you're a very nice woman and that I'm going to be spending some time with you."

"You don't think he'd see right through us?"

"He's very smart," David agreed. "But we won't be around him that much—and when we are, we'll just be ourselves. You know, friends." He picked up a spoon and turned it over in his fingers with the same dexterity Millie remembered from the way he'd handled the dental tools. "I haven't dated much since my wife's death. This might be a good thing for him."

Millie dropped her gaze to the pretty little pearl ring on the fourth finger of her left hand. Maybe she was being a little too rigid. David had made some good points, and she would be careful to make sure that she kept a safe distance from Bart—for his own good of course. She could look at this as a test of her acting skill—a perfect opportunity to work unscripted, just as she would on a reality television show. She found herself nodding. "Okay, I'll do it."

David smiled in relief. "Good," he said.

They turned back to their menus. A waitress silently materialized at their table before Millie had decided what to order. She ran her finger down the price list. She was pretty sure David would call her on it if she ordered the cheapest thing. "The artichoke and chicken ravioli looks good."

"I'll have the New York strip steak."

As soon as their waitress left, David said, "In the interest of making our plan a success, we should probably get to know each other a little better. I should know what your favorite color is and things like that."

"That's a good idea," Millie agreed. "It's periwinkle. What's yours?"

"Gray. What's your favorite movie?"

Millie frowned. Gravestones and rain clouds were gray. So were trash cans and elephants. "Gray is depressing," she said. "We need to find you a better color to like."

"Hold on," David said, his eyes narrowing and his body stiffening slightly. "I can't believe it." He lowered his voice. "It's her. Cynthia. She's here—and heading right for us."

"Don't worry." Reaching across the table, Millie placed her hand over David's, startling him so badly that he nearly knocked over his water glass. "Remember, we're on a date. Look at me like you mean it."

David leaned forward and locked gazes with her. After several moments, Millie realized that he wasn't blinking. "Not like we're having a staring contest," she whispered, "but like we're really into each other."

Just to show him what she meant, she leaned forward and gazed deeply into his eyes. They really were lovely. Full of color and depth. She'd never seen that particular shade of blue before either. She felt something in her stomach flutter. Her gaze lowered past his sculpted nose to the molded fullness of his lips. She considered kissing him— not because she was attracted to him or anything—but simply in the spirit of being a good team player.

She might have done it, too, if David would stop looking at her as if he were an optometrist sizing her for contact lenses. She kicked him under the table.

"Hello, David," a husky female voice said, and Millie looked up to see Cynthia Shively standing over them wearing a lemon chiffon dress with multilayers that parted in all the right places.

"You remember Millie Hogan," David said gesturing.

"Yes, of course," Cynthia said smiling as if David had just awarded her the Miss America title. "I hope your tooth infection is clearing up."

"It was a filling," Millie corrected. "A very small filling."

"Of course it was." Cynthia laughed as if Millie had said something highly amusing. Even in the soft light, her perfectly aligned teeth gleamed pearly white, clearly demonstrating that she was a no-cavities kind of girl.

"What are you doing here?" David asked.

"Eating dinner," Cynthia replied innocently. "Your mother stopped to talk to the maître d' about a table. I'm sure she'll be along shortly."

Sure enough, Mrs. Denvers, wearing a floor-length blue dress that looked as if it had been plucked straight from a rack of mother-of-the-bride gowns, was making her way steadily toward them.

"Good news," Mrs. Denvers said after murmuring a polite hello to Millie. "Our table is almost ready."

"Why don't you have a drink with us while you wait?" Millie suggested, ignoring the frantic look David was signaling with his eyes.

"We'd love to," Mrs. Denvers said. She motioned to one of the waiters, and almost magically two additional chairs appeared. "We don't mean to intrude on your date"—she paused to give David an inscrutable look—"but we needed to celebrate."

"Celebrate what?" David asked.

"Cynthia's return to Deer Park," Mrs. Denvers said. "We should have a toast to a long, happy life here." She looked around for a waiter. "What are you drinking, Millie?"

"Ice water."

"Oh, that's right. I forgot. With the medication you're taking for that awful gum infection, you shouldn't have anything alcoholic. Hope you don't lose that tooth."

Millie smiled sweetly. "Thank you for your concern, Mrs. Denvers, but David replaced my filling, and I'm just fine now." She shot David an adoring gaze. "Aren't I, pooh bear?"

He blinked twice. "You certainly are—*muffin*." Turning to his mother, he added, "Want me to check and see if your table is ready now, Mother?"

"No," Mrs. Denvers said. "It's all taken care of."

A few minutes later, Mrs. Denvers's table did open. Millie wasn't surprised when it turned out to be one right next to theirs. She didn't fight it when Cynthia suggested they push the two tables together.

"Do you see what I'm up against now?" David asked. They had escaped to the small dance floor and were slowly moving as the pianist played the love theme from *Titanic*.

"It'll be okay," Millie assured him, moving her feet slowly in time to the music. "Once they see how happy we are together, they'll give up."

David's eyes crinkled attractively. "I hope so, *muffin*."

"That reminds me," Millie said, enjoying the firm band of his arm around her. "You have to come up with a different endearment for me. Calling me muffin makes me feel fat."

"You aren't fat," David stated firmly. "But would you prefer *honey*?"

"It's still food-based, but better." She breathed in a little more of his faint but expensive-smelling soap.

"You're awfully choosy," David complained, tightening his arm around her and smiling down at her when she glanced up in surprise. "How about something Italian, like *cara mia*?"

She laughed. It was amazing, really, how easy it was to pretend to be thoroughly enjoying herself. She should have come up with this idea of un-dating years ago. There was no pressure wondering where this date was going or worrying about someone else's feelings. She looked up at him flirtatiously from under her lashes. "Since when do you speak Italian?"

"There's lots of things you don't know about me," David said.

His face loomed closer. "You ready for a dip?"

The next thing she knew, she was bent back over David's knee, her hair all but touching the floor, and David was standing over her, holding her effortlessly. Someone applauded, and from this upside-down position, it almost looked as if Mrs. Denvers was smiling at her.

When she returned to the table, Millie excused herself to the ladies' room to check her hair and makeup. Inside, she plunked down in a purple upholstered chair with gold fringe and regarded her image in the mirror. Her hair was getting curly even though she'd spent an hour straightening it, and the freckles across her nose and cheeks looked more pronounced than ever. She dabbed a little powder on them.

The door opened, and Mrs. Denvers walked into the room. She zeroed in on Millie and seated herself on an upholstered chair next to her. They regarded the other's image in the mirror. Mrs. Denvers took out her lipstick. "I'm so grateful that you're sharing your evening with David with Cynthia and I."

"No problem," Millie replied.

Mrs. Denvers began outlining her lips. "Cynthia's mother and I have been friends for years," Mrs. Denvers said, still regarding Millie in the mirror. "When Katherine was trying to decide what boarding school Cynthia would attend, she consulted me. We studied every school in the country before we sent Cynthia to France. Katherine was determined that her daughter was not only going to get a first-rate education, but also learn how to be a lady. We were both so proud when Cynthia married that plastic surgeon—of course the marriage didn't take—but when Cynthia came back to Deer Park just like David, we saw all along that God had been working behind the scenes. It was much too big of a coincidence for everything to happen the way it did."

Millie's stomach tightened. Something in the other woman's eyes told her that Mrs. Denver had something else to say. Something unpleasant about Millie. She wanted to bolt from the room, but at the same time felt firmly rooted to the seat.

"Look," Mrs. Denvers said pleasantly, blotting her mouth with a tissue and still addressing Millie in the mirror. "I know you see an attractive, educated man like David and think you're holding a winning lottery ticket." She smiled sympathetically, but then her lips tightened. "David has to be protected from his own niceness." She snapped the top back on the tube of lipstick. "I don't want him hurt again."

Millie's chin came up a notch. "I may not speak French," she said, "but at least I'm not a stalker."

Mrs. Denvers put her lipstick back in her purse and snapped it shut. "Give my regards to your mother. Tell her we miss seeing her in church."

Millie stiffened. Neither she nor her mother had set foot in church in two decades. "I won't have people staring at the back of our heads," Eva had said. "Either pitying us or judging us or just plain wondering if we're going to burst into flames."

Judging, just like Mrs. Denvers was doing right now, and the woman couldn't have made it any plainer that Millie wasn't good enough for David. She might not have said it, but the word *tramp* was easy to read in her eyes.

Standing, she stretched herself to her full five foot eight—five foot eleven, actually, in her shoes. She wanted to say that going to church didn't make Mrs. Denvers better than Millie, but she refused to let David's mother know that the comment had hurt her. Instinctively, she knew a better way to get back.

Leaning forward, Millie pouted her lips as she studied herself in the mirror. She gave herself a final smoldering look that said she was every mother's nightmare. And then putting everything she had into the sway of her hips, she strutted out of the room without a backward glance.

Chapter 9

Tank greeted David at the back door with an enthusiastic, if not somewhat asthmatic sounding, series of welcoming snorts. Her rear end swung back and forth so energetically that the plump bulldog nearly lost her balance.

Straightening, David dropped his keys on the counter and slung his coat over the back of a kitchen chair. "Hey, Aris, I'm home."

No response. Crossing into the living room, he found the housekeeper sleeping on the leather couch. He started to pull a thick knitted afghan over her, but her hazel eyes snapped open.

"I wasn't sleeping," she stated. "I was just resting my eyes."

David smiled. "Go back to sleep."

Aris sat up and surreptitiously wiped a small amount of drool from the corner of her mouth. "I'm fine. How'd it go? Your date with Millie?"

"Great," David replied, stiffening slightly. Before he'd left, Aris had made sure he knew about Millie's reputation for dumping a man after a few dates. His mom had basically given him the same lecture a couple of days ago, and it had really bugged him.

"You're going out with her again." Aris shook her head sadly.

"She's a very nice woman." She was funny, smart, kind. He remembered all these things from high school. She'd been beautiful back then, too, with those big gray eyes and generous smile.

"I don't think this is a good idea," Aris protested. "She'll only hurt you."

"Not likely," David said, thinking of his foolproof plan. Although he felt the same attraction for Millie as when he'd been fifteen, he had no intention of getting personally involved. He wasn't a nerdy little kid with a huge crush anymore. He was a grown man—a father—and could clearly see that he and Millie weren't right for each other. If he ever got serious about someone, it would be with someone more grounded. Someone more like his wife.

"I'm just warning you," Aris said. "You've got a faraway look in your eye."

"I most definitely do not," David declared, blinking. "The only things in my eyes are my contacts."

"If you say so," Aris said, clearly not agreeing.

David decided to change the subject. "How's Bart?"

Aris sat up a bit straighter. "Ah yes. We need to talk. You know how I was telling you about all those sites on the Internet? The ones with the nudie people?"

David's stomach tightened. He hoped he wasn't about to hear that his son had been visiting one of those sites. "Yeah?"

"I wanted to make sure that Bart wasn't logging on to any of those places or visiting those chat rooms—those are the places where the child predators lurk," Aris explained. "You might think you're talking to another eleven-year-old boy, but you're really communicating with—"

"Aris, I'm familiar with the dangers of online chat rooms. Bart and I have talked about them. Are you telling me that he disobeyed me?"

"Not exactly," Aris said. "I sort of distracted him with peanut butter cookies, and while he was eating them, I sneaked up to his room and took a peek at his computer."

David felt his features freeze. Aris had been part of their family before Bart had even been born. She'd been their housekeeper then their nanny. While he and Lisa had been building their dental practice, Aris had spent hours playing LEGOs and watching Disney movies with Bart. He'd never forget coming home one evening to watch Aris and three-year-old Bart dancing as Sebastian the crab sang "Under the Sea." But violating Bart's privacy? "You distracted him with cookies and then peeked at his computer?"

"You'll be happy to know that when I checked his history, he hadn't been to any sites with nudies."

David ran his hands through his hair. He didn't like that Aris had invaded his son's privacy. At the same time, he knew that she'd been trying to check up on his son—something that maybe he might not be doing enough.

"That's good," he said but didn't let his guard down completely.

"I decided that as long as I was there, I ought to check his e-mail. You know, make sure that he didn't have any inappropriate communications. You should see the e-mails I get advertising all sorts of enhancements for parts of your body that. . . Well, let's just say there are some pretty sick people out there."

"I know you mean well, but you shouldn't invade Bart's privacy like that. He's a good kid."

"I guess you probably don't want to hear what I found then."

Despite himself, David's interest piqued. "Is it something that I need to know as a father?"

Aris shrugged. "Probably, but seeing that you don't want to invade his privacy, I guess you don't want to know."

David forced himself to relax his jaw. He'd seen enough patients with teeth worn down from grinding to know how much damage that could do. "Obviously you think I should know what you discovered, so just tell me."

"Okay," Aris agreed. "But first, did you know that there's a program, a kind of spyware, you can use to pull up everything that's on somebody's computer, even if they delete it?"

Although David wasn't a computer expert, he knew about parental controls. He nodded.

"You wouldn't believe the things that people share over the network." She shook her head. "Enough to turn my hair gray. Oh right, my hair is already gray." She laughed.

I don't want to hear it, David thought, sensing that with any kind of encouragement Aris would happily spill the beans on her fellow garden club members. He closed his eyes and sighed. *My housekeeper, the cyber spy.* "What did the e-mail on Bart's computer say?"

"It was an IM," Aris corrected, obviously enjoying drawing out the story as long as possible. "And the tricky thing about recalling those IMs is that they're not in the deleted folder where most e-mails go. You have to recall them by—"

"Aris, just tell me!"

"The message read, 'Next time you'll lose more than your hat if you don't leave Lauren alone!' The alias was 'GorillaGuy.' "

David rubbed the skin on his face hard. He felt something primitive and fierce rise up in him. No way would he stand back and let a bully go after his son. He'd call the parent tonight. Go over there if he had to. The phone calls he could dismiss as a prank, but stealing Bart's hat? That was an act designed to humiliate, and he wouldn't have it. The only trouble, he realized slowly, was that he didn't have a name.

"I was thinking that if we log onto Bart's computer, we could draw out GorillaGuy. You know, pretend to be Bart."

David shook his head. "No."

"We could tell GorillaGuy," Aris added, completely ignoring him, "that we'll chop-suey him if he doesn't return Bart's hat."

"No," David replied firmly. "We can't chop-suey anyone."

"Of course we can," Aris assured him. "There are instructions for everything on the Internet. It's simply a matter of using the right search engine. I like Bing."

"It's not that," David said. "It's the wrong thing to do."

"What? You're just going to sit there and let Bart get bullied by this. . .this King Kong person?"

David nearly smiled at the look of outrage on the elderly housekeeper's face. She looked prepared to go one-on-one with GorillaGuy if necessary. As much as he felt the same way inside, he knew it wouldn't help Bart, not in the long run. "I'll handle this."

"How?"

"First, I'll talk to Bart and get him to tell me the name of the bully. Then I'll talk to the principal and the guidance counselor."

Aris laughed. "In what world do you live?"

David just looked at her.

"In a perfect world, your plan would work perfectly. In reality, David, you're not going to get anything accomplished unless you're sneaky. Our best strategy is to covertly draw out this bully and then. . ." She hesitated. "I don't know. Maybe we threaten to chop-suey him if he doesn't stop."

"That's not how I do things," David said. "I'm going to talk with Bart in the morning." He thought a moment. "If you could sleep late tomorrow, I'll make a good breakfast and talk to him one-on-one before school starts."

Aris rolled her eyes. "You cook breakfast?" She snorted. "That's funny."

"Even I can manage eggs and bacon."

She shook her head. "I think you're going to need me there—but if that's the way you want it. . ." The look in her eyes suggested a disaster of epic proportions was imminent.

He nodded. "I think it should come from me."

"Okay, but you're going to have to tell me everything he says."

"We'll see how it goes," David said. As he walked upstairs, he rubbed his face wearily. The pleasant glow from his un-date with Millie was fading, and it pained him to think of some kid picking on Bart. He dreaded the conversation with Bart in the morning. How was he going to explain just how he attained this information?

What David really wanted, he realized, was for Bart to come to him for help. He hadn't—and there had been plenty of time when Bart had been sitting on David's bed as he got ready for his date with Millie to ask.

That Bart had shut him out of a major conflict in his life was another issue—and something else he was going to have to address. Sighing, David walked down the silent hallway. All in all, a root canal was so much easier than parenting, and in the long run it was much less painful for everyone.

Chapter 10

The next morning all the aunts were huddled outside the café when Millie and her mother arrived just before five o'clock. She quickly unlocked the door. "What are you all doing here so early? Is everyone okay?" Millie scanned their red, weathered faces. It couldn't have been more than ten degrees, and she had no idea how long they'd been standing there. "Aunt Lillian," she said. "Can you feel your toes and fingers?"

"All eight of them," Lillian quipped from her wheelchair. "We're here early, Millie, because we want to hear the details about your date with David last night."

Her mother flipped on the lights as they moved inside the café. Aunt Lillian flicked the lever on her electric wheelchair and rolled into the room. Aunt Mimi, clutching her dog, clip-clopped in the three-inch high heels that just brought her over the five-foot mark, heading straight for the kitchen. "Hold on while I get my tea," she called. "Nobody say anything interesting until I get back."

Millie hurried to the stone fireplace and began stuffing newspaper between the layers of logs and kindling. The last time Aunt Lillian had gotten so chilled, she'd developed a bad case of bronchitis. Who would have guessed the one morning she was running late would be the one morning they would decide to show up at 5:00 a.m.?

"What time did he pick you up?" Aunt Keeker asked. Her flyaway gray hair stuck out from beneath a black bowler hat out of which an enormous purple ostrich feather flew.

"He came early," her mother informed everyone smugly. "Brought us both roses. I'm telling you, when he walked in the room, it was like the temperature went up five degrees. He isn't cheap either. He took her to Ben's."

There was an appreciative chorus of *oh*s and an exchange of impressed looks.

"The boy is smitten," Aunt Keeker pronounced. "As you can see, honey, I'm wearing my ostrich plume fedora—typically the male bird flaps his wings and shows his feathers when he's trying to attract a mate, but I have found that it works just as well when the female wears it."

Aunt Mimi's voice boomed from the kitchen. "You all are saying interesting things without me."

"He brought Millie flowers, and Eva had a hot flash," Lillian yelled. Her voice softened. "I want to hear if you had a good time. Did you, sweetie?"

Millie stepped back as the kindling caught fire. She closed the wire gate. "Aunt Lillian, it's warmer over here." Of all her mother's friends and Millie's aunts, Lillian was the most fragile. She'd been a Realtor, and had, in fact, sold Eva the small house on Cherry Lane more than thirty years ago. The two women had quickly discovered they had two things in common—a shared love of freshly baked pastries and parents who lived with them. They started meeting for coffee and muffins and had been friends ever since. While a degenerative neurological condition had progressively weakened Lillian's arms and legs and ended her Realtor's career several years ago, her mind was as sharp as ever. With no kids of her own, Lillian, of all the aunts, was like a second mother to Millie and could read her almost as well as Eva.

Millie ducked her head to avoid Lillian's gaze and minimize her chance of the older woman suspecting anything wrong. "This is way too early to be having this conversation. But yes, I had a good time."

"That's all I got out of her last night," Eva confirmed. "I nearly broke my neck running down the stairs to peek out the living room window, and all I saw was David walking back to his car."

"Millie, we didn't get here at 5:00 a.m. to see which of us has the worst bed head," Aunt Mimi said. She was clutching a red Dosie's mug in one hand and holding the dog with the other. "Did he kiss you?"

Millie started removing chairs from on top of the tables. "You all have to give me some space."

"When are you going to see him again?" Aunt Keeker fingered the ostrich plume in her hat. "And what will you be doing? I have to know what hat to wear."

"I don't know," Millie replied. "Maybe in a week or so. I don't want him to think I'm too available."

"Don't wait too long," her mother advised. "He'll think you aren't interested."

"Men have fragile egos," Aunt Lillian stated. Her blue eyes peered up at Millie very seriously. "You have to praise them a lot and make sure you flatter them. Even if it's over something silly— like the way they fold their socks. It's the secret, honey, to a healthy relationship."

"They're like dogs," Aunt Mimi added. "Most have to be trained. You give them a cookie when they do something right, and you yell at them when they're bad." She kissed her poodle on the top of its small orange head. "When I met Maurice, he was immediately put into puppy training to learn the basics. Gift giving, sensitivity—that sort of thing."

Millie laughed. "David is well past puppy training. He has great manners and even dances divinely." She remembered the way David held her when they danced and smiled. His body was lean and strong, like a runner's. It'd taken mere seconds for him to adjust to her size and shape, and then it'd felt like they'd been dancing together for years. She didn't know how he'd done that.

Finishing with the chairs, Millie realized Aunt Lillian was staring at her. "Can I get you some hot tea?"

"In a minute." The older woman's sharp blue eyes fixed on Millie. "Something is different about you." She drummed her fingers on the arm of the wheelchair. "I can't put my finger on it, but I feel it. A little sparkle or something."

"That tingle you feel is the circulation returning to your fingers," Millie quipped, but she busied herself with lining up the salt and pepper shakers that were already sitting side by side, like an old couple.

"Don't you think something's different about Millie?" Lillian asked Keeker.

"Absolutely," Keeker agreed. "She's a girl with a secret in her eyes. It was like that for me, too, when I met Roland." She smiled at Millie. "I understand, honey. When something special comes along, you have to protect it. So stop looking at her like that, Lillian, and come help me decide if I should spend Easter in Chicago or Denver. Jessica's pregnant and shouldn't travel, and Brianna has all those kids to organize. Not to mention how expensive it would be for her to fly. . ."

Millie recognized her escape and left the two women by the fireplace talking.

"Bart?" David knocked on his son's bedroom door. "Are you up?"

"Yeah. I'll be down in a minute."

He'd been saying this for the past fifteen minutes. David thought about the eggs and bacon sitting on the kitchen table getting cold. He was due at the office at seven thirty to prep for Mrs. Daniels, who was always early and would have an anxiety attack and leave if he wasn't there to coax her into the examination room. And there was still the matter of the instant message Aris had found on Bart's computer. David had hoped to discuss this over breakfast.

Opening the door, he stepped into the room. A boy-sized lump lay in the middle of the bed. "Bart? You're still in bed?"

Bart mumbled something unintelligible.

"It's six thirty," David said. "We're going to be late."

"Why are you waking me up so early?" Bart mumbled sleepily. "The bus doesn't come until eight."

"I made breakfast," David said. "We need to talk." Reaching for the bedside lamp, he clicked it on, and the room exploded with light. Out of her silver frame, Lisa smiled serenely from her spot on the bedside table. He met her gaze for a moment, wondering how she would have handled this. She probably would have known— without asking—who the bully was, called up the bully's mother, retrieved the hat, and set up a playdate, all before Bart left for school.

"Talk about what? Your date?"

Blood rushed unexpectedly to David's face at the thought of Millie in that black silk dress with her dark hair falling around the creamy white skin of her shoulders. "No," he said. He and Bart had a long talk on Wednesday night about David seeing other women and how it didn't mean he loved Bart's mom less. Bart had seemed fine with it, more curious about the logistics than the implications. However, looking down at his son, David wondered if Bart was as fine with him dating as he seemed. "Please get up," he said. "The eggs are getting cold."

Bart stretched but made no move to get up. "Can I have contact lenses?"

David blinked at the unexpected change in topics. "Well, yeah, you can. But you have to take care of your eyes, make sure you clean the lenses every day." The piles of clothing that lay on the floor were mute testimony to Bart's sloppiness.

"I'll do it," Bart said. "And I want karate lessons."

Because of the whole bully thing? *Great,* David thought, *Aris has been talking to him about chop-sueying people.* "Why the sudden interest?"

Bart shrugged. "I just want to stop looking like a nerd."

"There's nothing wrong with the way you look," David pointed out, trying not to think about how late they already were going to be and that they really needed to talk about that IM.

"Dad, I have braces and wear glasses. I'm short, and the only thing I'm good at is computer games. Face it. I'm a nerd."

"That's not true," David said. "You're good at lots of things."

Bart stared at him in silent challenge. *Like what?* his huge blue eyes seemed to say.

"You won the geography and math bee last year, and you're great in science, and. . ." David paused, thinking hard but unable to name a single thing that didn't support Bart's nerdiness. He raked his fingers through his hair. "You can have karate lessons if you want, but don't try and be someone different. I like you just the way you are."

"You're my father," Bart stated. "You have to like me. It's like a law or something."

"Other people like you, as well," David stated firmly.

Bart's mouth took on a tight, pinched look, and his gaze slid away from David's. "Not everyone."

He'd intended to have this discussion downstairs, where Bart would see that David had made Bart's favorite breakfast and understand that David had Bart's best interests at heart. However, it felt like Bart had opened the door to the conversation, and after a brief hesitation, during which David prayed he'd have the right words, he said, "Listen, Bart, I know about your hat. I know you're being bullied at school. We need to talk about it."

Bart's mouth opened and closed. Color flooded his round cheeks. "What are you talking about?"

"Who's GorillaGuy?"

His son's lips shut tightly. "That's none of your business. You've been on my computer, haven't you? That is so low, Dad. I can't believe you would do that." Pushing back the covers, Bart sprang from the bed and marched across the room.

"If you're being bullied, I need to know about it."

Bart grabbed yesterday's blue jeans from the floor and a shirt that hung on the back of his desk chair. "You think *spying* on me is going to help?"

"How I found out is irrelevant," David stated firmly. He wasn't about to throw Aris under the bus. "The point is that some kid at school stole your hat and threatened you. I take that seriously."

Pausing at the connecting door to the bathroom, Bart looked back at him. Defiance flashed from his eyes, and yet he looked vulnerable, too, standing there in checkered flannel pajamas that were just a bit too big for him. "Stay out of this, Dad. And stay out of my computer."

"We need to talk to the principal, Bart, and tell him everything."

"Like *that'll* help." Bart's voice rose. "All it'd do is get me beaten up or labeled a tattler."

"Were there any witnesses? Did this boy do anything else?"

"I can handle this," Bart said. "Why can't you trust me?"

Despite his fears for his son, David felt a small stirring of pride rise up inside himself at his son's determination to handle this problem himself. "I do trust you, but it's my job to make sure you're safe at school."

"I can take care of myself."

"I know, but. . ." David sought valiantly for a response that wouldn't hurt his son's feelings. The truth was, his son was short, kind of round, and apt to trip over his own feet. In other words, the Denvers's genes took a lot of time to mature.

"But you don't think I can do it."

"Of course I don't think that," David said.

"Then stay out of this."

"I'm your father," David said, trying not to get frustrated at the way this conversation was going. "My job is to take care of you the best way I can. Now I'm asking you to tell me the name of this boy."

Bart folded his arms. "No."

"No?" David couldn't ever remember Bart defying him like this. He felt that if he didn't deal with this correctly now, he was setting a new standard for their future arguments. He raised his voice slightly so Bart would know he was serious. "You will tell me the name of this kid, and you'll do it now."

"No," Bart said meeting his gaze levelly. "And you can't make me."

David considered agreeing with his son then grounding him for the rest of his life, but then he realized it probably wouldn't do either of them much good. "Look," he said, forcing himself to stay calm, "we're on the same side here. I'm trying to help you."

"Then stay out of this. Stay out of my computer."

"I'm your father, and I'll do whatever I need to do to keep you safe." David realized that he was grinding his teeth again and forced himself to relax his jaw. He briefly considered bribery—pizza primarily—then steeled himself to finish their argument. "Do you want to lose your computer privileges?"

Before Bart could reply, there was the sound of breaking glass.

As David sprinted to the top of the staircase, he heard more noises, china clinking against china, and a grunting noise. Hurrying into the kitchen, he saw Tank standing on top of the table. She'd knocked over the pitcher of orange juice—that was the crash he'd heard from upstairs—and was currently cleaning off a plate of scrambled eggs floating in an orange pool. The dog grinned happily. *Come on,* her brown eyes invited. *There's plenty for both of us.*

For a moment, David stood there, stupidly surveying the mess and fighting the urge just to leave it. Grunting, he hefted the dog off the table, carried her into his study, and shut the door so she couldn't get cut on the glass before he cleaned it up. Returning to the kitchen, he lifted the corners of the tablecloth and marched the contents of the table to the garbage in the garage and threw it all out. However, when he tried to get back in the house, he discovered he'd locked himself out. On the way to the front door, he spotted Cynthia, who was parked across the street.

She waved at him cheerfully from behind an oversized pair of dark glasses. "You're running a little late this morning, David. Want me to take Bart to school for you?"

David counted to ten then yelled back, "No thanks." As he

turned to go back inside, he thought about fixing another breakfast then decided there wasn't time. They'd talk in the car. He'd stop at Dosie Dough's for some coffee and muffins. It'd be quick and easy and was right on the way to his office and Bart's school. He brightened unexpectedly at the thought.

Chapter 11

Millie almost dropped the double stack of gingerbread pancakes she was balancing on a tray when David and a boy who looked so much like him that it could only be his son walked into the café. What were they doing here? She hadn't expected to see him so soon and especially not with his son. Setting the plates down, she wiped her hands on her apron and hurried up to the front counter.

"David—what a nice surprise." She kissed his cheek lightly then turned to the boy, who crossed his arms and looked as if he'd rather be struck by lightning than be hugged by her. "You've got to be Bart." She flashed her best smile and stuck out her hand. "I'm Millie Hogan."

Bart mumbled something and gave her a jellyfish for a hand. David shot him a warning look.

"We had a breakfast malfunction this morning," David explained. "Tank—that's our bulldog—jumped on the table and ate the eggs and bacon." He glanced sideways at Bart. "I mean bacon and eggs." He laughed uncomfortably.

Bart shifted his weight and completely ignored his father. Millie chuckled politely but didn't quite get the joke. "No worries—we've got plenty of eggs and bacon here." Millie picked up a couple of menus. "Let's get you a table."

"Actually, we don't have time. If you could just get us some coffee and donuts and orange juice for Bart, we'll take it to go."

"Sure." Millie lifted the dome off the glass case with the pastries. "What kind would you like?"

Bart's eyes widened behind his oversized glasses when he spotted the fresh-baked donuts. However, when his father asked him to pick out a few, he shrugged and the sullen look returned to his face.

"We'll have chocolate frosted," David supplied. "And a couple chocolate ones with sprinkles. I usually don't let him have so much sugar for breakfast, but I figure once in a while it's okay."

"Especially on mornings when you have a breakfast malfunction."

David laughed, but Bart didn't. As she placed the pastries in a paper sack, she watched David attempt to meet the boy's gaze. The kid ignored him, pulled out his cell, and started fiddling with the keys. Millie wondered if it was always like this between them or if they'd had an argument. If it was the latter, she hoped it had nothing to do with her. "I'll just get the juice. Back in a minute."

When she returned, Bart was alone at the counter, still punching buttons on his cell. Millie added the bottle of orange juice to a second bag then filled a large Styrofoam cup to the brim with coffee. She threw a couple of creamers and some sugar packets into the bag. "Where's your dad?"

"He had to take a phone call. He said he'd be right back."

Millie took her time arranging the food in the bag, adding napkins, extra creamers, and more wooden stirring sticks than he could possibly use. Eventually she ran out of things to add, and there were only so many ways to fold shut the top. Bart watched her closely. She pretended not to notice and wondered if he was totally freaked out at the idea of his dad dating her.

She wished David would get back. Over the top of Bart's head, she looked through the bay window into the parking lot. She spotted David pacing back and forth with his cell pressed to his ear. He wasn't alone, however. He was being trailed by Cynthia Shively. The blond finally managed to catch him and tap him on the shoulder.

David turned around, saw Cynthia, and jerked visibly. Millie almost laughed as she watched David try to manage a polite smile.

Now that she'd caught his attention, Cynthia went into full manhunting posture. Millie gave the woman full points for her moves: a perfect flip of her long blond hair, a bright smile that showed off excellent orthodontic work, and graceful footwork in the high-heeled boots as she advanced into David's personal space.

David, who was taking one step backward for every one Cynthia took forward, glanced at the café, and even from where she stood it was an obvious cry for help.

Millie looked at Bart, who also was watching the scene in progress. "I guess I should go rescue him."

"He's fine," Bart said. "Can I have a donut?"

Millie watched Cynthia pin David against the side of a red pickup truck. "My goodness she's aggressive. Your poor dad looks like he wishes the earth would swallow him up."

Bart laughed. "Dad always says we should be tolerant of others— even the ones that bug us the most." His blue eyes, so like David's, looked up at her seriously. "We should probably leave them alone to work things out."

Millie looked down at David's son in surprise. He sounded like a mini-adult—a little mini-man.

"We don't have much time before school starts," Bart added. "Maybe I should eat while they're talking."

She gave one last glance out the window. Part of her still wanted to go out there and rescue David, but another part of her thought it would be a good opportunity for David to tell Cynthia that he had a girlfriend now. The message would be better delivered without Millie rushing to his defense.

"Okay," she said and led him to an empty booth then plopped down across from him. "So what grade are you in?"

A long pause, and then he said, "Sixth."

"Oh. Middle school." Millie's nose wrinkled. Those years had been the worst for her. She'd never forget all the rumors and whispers that had followed her around like a bad smell. She pushed aside the thought and focused on Bart's round face. "You like it?"

"It's okay."

"What's your favorite subject?"

There was another long hesitation. "Science."

"Science?" Millie opened the take-out bag and handed him a double chocolate frosted donut. "What kind of science?" She hoped it wasn't biology. She'd nearly failed that one. The terminology had been incomprehensible, and never once had she managed to see the stupid little cell thingies through the microscope.

He took the donut. "Nuclear physics," he said and bit into the donut.

Millie felt her jaw drop. This was even worse than she feared. "Nuclear physics? They didn't teach that when I went to middle school."

Bart snorted. "I studied it at camp last summer in California— at UCLA."

"You went to nuclear physics camp?" She had never heard of any kid going to nuclear physics camp. "Are you a genius?"

Bart swallowed another bite of donut. "I don't know. We called it nerd camp. This is a pretty good donut." It was gone in the blink of an eye, and before she could pull the bag back, he'd grabbed another.

"So what's nuclear physics about?"

"Well," he said, "you study the interactions of atomic nuclei."

Millie swallowed. "That sounds interesting," she said but had no idea what he was talking about. "You want some juice?"

"No thanks," he said and grabbed a third donut.

This is it, Millie thought. *I can't carry on a conversation about nuclear physics, and I doubt he caught last night's episode of* Top Chef. She looked around for help, but no one would make eye contact, although she felt sure everyone had been furiously eavesdropping or staring moments before.

"Who's that?" Bart was pointing to a black-and-white photo on the wall.

"That's my mother."

"She looks like you."

"Yes, she does." In the photo her mother was in her early forties. Her hair was still dark brown and curled to the top of her shoulders in a style similar to Millie's. Eva had yet to gain weight, and her body was slim and athletic looking in a one-piece ski outfit that Millie was pretty sure was still hanging in her closet.

"That's an old photo of her at the Winterfest Snow Carnival box sled races." She pointed to the rectangular cardboard sled just behind her mother. "That's her sled—it's a giant chocolate éclair."

Bart reached for a fourth donut. There were two more in the bag, and at the speed he was eating, she feared he was going to get sick. She didn't think David would appreciate it if his son barfed all over the front seat of his car on the way to school.

"It's an interesting story," Millie said and picked up the Bavarian cream. She really didn't need the calories—if she ever got cast on a reality television show, the cameras would add ten pounds to her weight. However, there was probably only one way to keep Bart from eating it. She stuffed a large bite into her mouth.

"When I was about your age, my mom wanted to start a restaurant. We didn't have much money, and every time she tried to get a business loan, she got turned down. She hadn't had a job in years—and to be honest, we were pretty close to being bankrupt. The owners of Deer Park Mountain were trying to promote the idea of a family fun day at the ski hill and came up with the idea of a box sled race. So my mom basically challenged the owner of the bank to go head-to-head in the race. She wagered him a lifetime of strudel against a loan for her restaurant if he beat her. She pushed him in public, he took the challenge, and well, you can probably guess the rest—my mother won the race and got the loan."

She and Bart split the last donut. Only a few sprinkles were at the bottom of the bag.

"That's so cool," he said. "I've heard about that race at school. A lot of kids are entering it."

"I'm not surprised. It's a very big deal here. Last year we even had people who came down from Canada." She read the interest on his face. "There's lots of categories—most creative and of course the adult and junior race categories."

"When is it?"

"The first Saturday in March."

"When are entries due?"

"Right up until race day." Millie studied his face. "Are you thinking of entering? My mom and I would help if you wanted. Her sled still holds the winning time."

"Maybe," Bart said. "Hey, I see my dad—I'd better get going."

She looked at the entrance, and sure enough David was standing just inside the door. He shook his head when he caught her eye and made a long-suffering face. Millie smiled sweetly at him and waved.

"Hey, Bart," she said, "before you go, let me put in a few more donuts for your dad." She saw some chocolate icing on the corner of his mouth. "Maybe you should tell him you've already had a couple." Maybe she shouldn't have let Bart eat so many. "Then again, maybe you shouldn't."

"Don't worry," Bart said. "He really doesn't care what I eat."

Millie frowned. Bart's face was neutral, as if he'd just reported on the temperature outside, but the remark had a slightly bitter undertone that resonated inside her. Adding a couple of donuts to the bag, she remembered feeling that way as a child when Eva had been so busy starting the café that it seemed like Millie only existed in context to it. She wanted to question Bart more deeply, but he grabbed both bags and headed for the door. She didn't know what she would have said anyway.

David tried to pay, but she told him it was on the house and then changed the subject to what a great time she'd had last night at Ben's. When the last jingle of the bell faded behind them, the café seemed to come to life again. Aunt Lillian proclaimed that "the child was adorable enough to eat," and Aunt Keeker fanned herself with her sombrero and declared David was the best-looking man she'd seen in twenty years. Even Aunt Mimi stroked her dog and declared happily, "And his dog eats off the kitchen table. What could be better?"

Hollywood, Millie thought but was wise enough to keep her mouth shut.

Chapter 12

For their second un-date, David and Millie went cross-country skiing. Millie wasn't too keen on such an athletic date, but she liked the idea of going somewhere private so neither of them would have to pretend they liked each other in front of other people. After some more discussion, they agreed to go on Saturday afternoon while Bart was at the movies with some friends.

At 2:58 the bells on the café's door jingled, and David walked inside. His ski jacket was unzipped to reveal a lean torso, and his black ski pants molded around a pair of muscular thighs. His blue eyes were even a more vivid shade than she remembered. When that gaze came to rest on her, she felt a small tingle but pushed it firmly to the back of her mind.

"Hi." She gave him a kiss on the cheek and breathed in a little of that yummy soap. She let herself linger a minute in his arms. It wasn't that she enjoyed the feel of his arms around her, she assured herself. She was simply getting into character.

Behind her one of the aunts laughed and asked if Millie was planning on introducing him or if she was going to hug him for the rest of the afternoon.

"You can meet him if you promise to behave," Millie warned. Taking his arm, she led him to the table by the picture window.

"These are my aunts—Mrs. Keeker Dupree, Mrs. Lillian Wade, and Mrs. Mimi Decker—that's her dog Earl Gray."

"Technically, we're ABCs—aunts by choice." Aunt Lillian reached out a blue-veined hand and flashed a smile that had earned her the title of Miss South Dakota in 1965. "I'm so glad to meet you."

"The pleasure is mine. Millie has told me so much about you all."

Millie kept her smile firmly in place. She hoped David remembered how carefully he had to act around them. *The aunts have known me since I was born, and all their senses are going to be on high alert when they meet you,"* she'd warned him when they'd planned this date. *"They can smell a skunk a mile off."*

David had been fascinated with the idea of Eva's best friends forming a tight-knit group of aunts and had listened closely as Millie had explained how the circle had started when Lillian had sold Eva her house and then widened as Eva met Keeker in the grocery store and had become fascinated by the plastic fruit in her hat. They'd been interrupted by a small, apricot-colored poodle that had run up to them with Mimi chasing it and the store manager chasing Mimi.

Turning to Aunt Keeker, David extended his hand to hers and gave her a smile that Millie had to admit looked 100 percent believable. "Nice hat," he said.

Aunt Keeker touched the blue-and-white ski cap. "Thank you, David. It's made from the hair of the Tong sheep in China, which graze on herbs that appear to make them exceptionally fertile." Her brown eyes twinkled as she stared at David. "Would you care to smell it? It has a very mild but pleasing scent."

"No," Millie all but shouted. She took a deep breath. "I mean, ha-ha, Aunt Keeker is only joking. Right, Aunt Keeker?"

"I have six children," Keeker replied proudly. "My youngest,

Jessica, just returned the hat a few weeks ago. She lives in Chicago and is having triplets in July. That'll give me fifteen grandchildren." She removed the wool hat and extended it toward them. "Here," she said. "You can keep it as long as you want."

Millie looked at David, who had a wicked grin on his face and looked as if he might actually reach for the hat.

"No," Millie said firmly. "We are not going to smell, touch, or wear that hat." She took David's arm and redirected his attention. "Have you met my aunt Mimi?"

"Nice to meet you," David said. His gaze fell on Earl Gray who was sitting up in Mimi's lap and wagging his tail. "What a cute dog. I love dogs."

Before Millie could warn him that the dog couldn't be trusted, David reached to pat Earl Gray. The poodle gave a death growl and launched itself at David's hand. David jerked his arm away as the dog sank its fangs into the sleeve of his coat. He stepped back, the poodle dangling from his arm.

"Earl, you let go right now!" Mimi tugged ineffectively at the dog, which was still growling through its clenched jaws. "Bad boy!"

The dog held on tightly as Mimi put all of her ninety pounds into pulling him off David's sleeve.

Millie grabbed a glass of water. She dumped half the contents on top of the dog's head. It immediately released David's sleeve, and Mimi snatched it away.

"Are you okay?" Millie asked.

"I'm fine," he said, eyeing the small puncture marks in his jacket.

"I'm so sorry, David," Mimi said. With one hand, she gave him a paper napkin to dry his sleeve, and in the other she clutched her dog to her chest like a football. Her large hazel eyes looked up at him apologetically. "Earl only does this when he likes someone."

"It's true," Eva announced, striding into the room. "He only snaps at the nicest people." She cast the dog a withering glance. "Stupidest animal in creation."

"It's not stupidity," Mimi shot back. "It's a confidence issue. Earl only bites nice people because he knows they won't bite him back. It's actually a very smart strategy." She stroked the dog's curly coat. "Little by little, Earl is learning to believe in himself. Someday his big moment is going to come."

"More likely he's going to hurt somebody and you're going to feel awful," Eva warned.

"Stay back, David," Keeker warned as David moved closer to the table. "The thing jumps like a squirrel."

"You'll see," Mimi said. "Poodles are highly intelligent. When the time comes, Earl Gray will rise to the occasion." She kissed the top of the dog's head. "Won't you, sweet baby?"

"Sweet baby, my foot." Eva turned to David. "I'll sew up your sleeve for you if you give me a minute."

"It's fine," David said. He looked at Millie, who sent him a mental apology. "We really should get going."

"Well," Eva said, "have fun, but be careful. Don't ski into a tree or get lost or eaten by a bear or something." She thrust a pack into Millie's hands. "Don't forget your snacks."

Millie took it from her hands. She'd purposely left her mother alone with it so Eva could inspect the contents. By the smile on Eva's round face, she knew her mother not only had peeked inside, but that she approved the choice of items. "Thanks," she said.

"Millie, it's colder than you think outside. Why don't you borrow Keeker's hat? It would go beautifully with your parka."

The Tong sheep? No way. "No thanks."

"We probably should get going," David said, coming to her

rescue. "Are you ready?"

"Yes," Lillian, Keeker, Mimi, and her mother replied simultaneously.

Thirty minutes later she was half sliding, half jogging behind David. She wasn't very good at cross-country skiing, but she was keeping up. The temperature had risen to a balmy thirty degrees, and the snow was so bright it hurt to look at it. For once the wind had died down, and the great dark mountains covered with the dense ponderosa pines made her feel like an explorer—as if she might be part of a documentary on the Black Hills. She imagined a camera crew from National Geographic following them with cameras perched on their shoulders.

"How are you doing?" David called over his shoulder.

"Great," Millie panted, trying not to sound out of shape, which was impossible because she was out of shape. She tightened her grip on the poles and promised herself to start working out more regularly. She couldn't narrate a documentary if she didn't have the breath to speak.

David slowed as the trail began a slow climb. Millie turned her feet out, tramping upward in a classic V pattern that made her feel like a giant duck waddling up the hill. From the back, it probably was the most unflattering camera angle possible. She decided to stop fantasizing about being filmed.

David waited for her at the top. His eyes were hidden behind mirrored sunglasses, but his smile was wide and open. "I haven't done this in years," he said. "Next time I'm going to bring Bart. He needs to get out more and spend less time playing video games."

Millie leaned heavily on her poles. She was too out of breath to do anything but nod. The man had lungs like Lance Armstrong. He wasn't even sweating. How far had they gone? Five miles? Ten? A hundred?

Just as she was about to call it quits, she spotted a small log cabin a short way off. The rest station. She sighed in relief and steeled herself to ski the remaining distance. When she got to the picnic area, she popped her bindings gratefully and stepped out of the skis. Dusting snow off a bench, she flopped down.

David shrugged off his backpack and stepped out of his skis. Still looking pretty fresh from their skiing, he unzipped his jacket and sat down across from her. "No way is Cynthia going to follow us here."

"Don't be too sure," Millie said, still sucking an embarrassing amount of air into her lungs and trying to pretend her heartbeat wasn't off the charts. She was sweating and unzipped the front of her parka.

"She is pretty persistent," David agreed. He began to unpack the contents of the backpack. Pulling out a checkered wool blanket, he laid it over the top of the table then pulled out a silver thermos and two cups. "She came by the office this morning, and guess what her latest scheme is."

Millie watched him pour the coffee into one of the Styrofoam cups. Small curls of steam released into the air. "What?"

"She's thinking of becoming a dental hygienist and wants to be my assistant so she can observe what dentistry is really like."

"What'd you tell her?"

"That I was afraid you wouldn't be comfortable with the idea of me spending so much time with her. And I offered to make a phone call or two into Sioux City to see if another dentist could use her help."

Millie laughed. "Good answer." She took a sip of the hot liquid. "You don't think she's dangerous, do you?" An image of Glenn Close in *Fatal Attraction* flashed through her mind.

"Oh no. She's just lonely and confused. She'd probably have backed off already if my mother wasn't encouraging her."

Now that her breathing had slowed, Millie went to work helping David unpack their picnic. She opened a container of a fruit and cream cheese chutney and began spreading it on some crackers.

"That looks really good."

"Hope so," Millie said, biting into the cracker. "It's a new recipe. I invented it for our date."

"Really?"

She nodded, pleased that he seemed impressed. "I knew my mother would be interested in the food messages I was sending you."

David helped himself to another cracker. "Well, the food message I'm sending you is that I'm about to make a total pig of myself."

Millie laughed. "In our food language, if you eat everything, then you're saying that you like me as much or more than I like you."

"What?"

"The food, David. It's a conversation. The amount of food and the effort that went into preparing it says I'm very interested in you. The kind of food says that it's a romantic interest."

David studied the cracker with interest. "It says all that?"

"Absolutely," Millie told him. "If I was trying to express doubts about our relationship, I would have made baked brie and cheese."

"That's good, too."

"No it isn't. Not in my dating language. Baked brie is a safe choice to serve. I would never serve that to a guy I really liked." She nibbled a cracker. "The mango and coconut flavors in the chutney are supposed to invoke an image of tropical islands. You're supposed to taste something exotic and slightly seductive." She frowned a little. "But not too seductive. More like something you want to have a little more of."

"Well it's working. I do want more of it," David said, polishing off another cracker. "What else is in the backpack?"

"Oh," Millie said. "Prosciutto and Jarlsberg cheese on baguettes with butter lettuce and tomato. Some sweet potato chips—and dessert."

David brightened. "Dessert?"

"Mini-carrot-cake muffins with cream cheese frosting."

"Carrot cake is one of my favorite desserts."

"I know." Millie beamed. "Your dad told me. I tried calling your office to ask your mom what you liked, but she kept putting me on hold, and then"—she made quotation marks with her fingers—" 'accidentally' hanging up on me."

"Sorry about that," David said and wiped his mouth on a crisp white linen napkin. "She's been in a horrible mood ever since we went on our date last week."

"That's good—it means she's taking our relationship seriously."

"She is." The sandwich was gone in a couple more bites, and he was reaching for another. He wasn't a tall man, or a heavy one, and watching him pack away the food made Millie wonder where he put it all. "She was so desperate to prove that Cynthia is the right woman for me that she went to the Saint Francis cemetery and photographed graves to prove my family and Cynthia's were friends as far back as in the 1800s."

Millie put her sandwich down and frowned. "Well, I hope it doesn't mean I'm about to get visited by the ghosts of your relatives who want you to marry Cynthia Shively."

David laughed. "Don't worry. No family ghost would want me to marry Cynthia. She's nice, but she isn't for me." He shook his head. "I was lucky once. My wife, Lisa, was an amazing woman—I don't think I'll ever feel the same about any other woman."

Something in Millie's gut clenched. What about her? Why didn't he think she'd ever be good enough for him? She almost asked, but then she remembered it wasn't a real date. She flushed, realizing she'd almost overreacted. The point was that David was talking about his dead wife and that had to be painful for him. She touched his arm. "I'm sorry. Really sorry."

"Yeah—me, too," David said in that same matter-of-fact voice. He took another bite of baguette, but the expression on his face suggested he no longer tasted it.

Millie studied her half-eaten sandwich. She wanted to find out more about David's late wife but knew it was none of her business and a clear violation of the spirit of their plan. It didn't stop her, however, from thinking about David's wife. She remembered seeing a photograph in the local paper shortly after David had gotten engaged. Lisa had been lovely—a petite California blond with delicate features and a lovely smile. She'd been a pediatric dentist, and Millie remembered thinking David had done well.

"Oh, by the way," David said. "Tomorrow morning you're going to get a dozen white roses from me. I arranged for them to be delivered to the café."

Millie sipped her hot coffee slowly. "Nice touch," she said. "I'll call on Monday to thank you, but if you don't hear from me, it means your mother is putting me on hold again. By the way, that background music is really, really annoying. All it plays is a string rendition of 'My Heart Will Go On.'"

David chuckled. "I didn't know—it was one of the things I

left the same when I took over my dad's practice. I'll do something about it." His grin widened. "What do you like? When I have the music changed, it'll be one more example of how I'm really falling for you."

"More likely, I'll never get through on the phone." She smiled though. "You should change it to something *you* like."

Millie thought of her mother's stubborn determination to hold on to the past. It was as if change, even a small one, would upset the balance of the universe and end in disaster of epic proportions. Eva stubbornly refused to redecorate either the café or their house. Even small stuff—like Millie suggesting some changes to the menu—was met with resistance. *"Good idea, honey,"* Eva would say. *"I'll think about it."* But nothing would ever happen.

"Try this," she urged, handing him a mini-carrot-cake muffin. "The frosting got a little smushed, but it should be pretty good."

He chewed slowly, swallowed, and looked at her. "You made this?"

Millie nodded. "I thought about making you something chocolate, but thought it was a little too soon. I decided we should work up to it. I'll make you cheesecake next."

"I hope there's a lot of working up to do," David said happily.

Millie nodded but let silence creep into their conversation. They weren't supposed to be engaging in so much small talk. They weren't supposed to be enjoying themselves—they'd come here so they wouldn't have to pretend in front of other people. She was glad David got the hint when a few moments later he pulled their books out of the backpack. He handed her a copy of *Acting in Television Commercials: For Fun and Profit* without comment.

Millie started the first chapter—"The Million-Dollar Minute."

"Did you know," she read, *"that most people make their first impres-*

sion of another person within the first three seconds of meeting them?"

That seemed far too short. There was even the five-second rule for food that fell on the floor. She glanced at David, intending to ask his opinion, but stopped when she saw the title of his book: *HELP! My Child Is Being Bullied.*

Millie frowned. Bart bullied? She pictured the boy's pale complexion, thick glasses, and chubby cheeks. *Do not get involved,* she ordered herself. *Do not ask why he's reading that book.* She forced her eyes back to the page.

"How do you make that first impression be a good one and clinch that role? First you have to do your homework. Before you even step into the room, you have to decipher the meaning behind the commercial script."

Millie looked up. David's brow was creased. It seemed a long time before he turned the page. She looked back down at her book.

"How do you decipher the meaning behind the commercial script? How do you. . ."

She glanced up. Bit her lip and looked down at her book again. The words on the page blurred. She reminded herself firmly that whatever was happening in David's personal life was none of her business and venturing into those waters was a very bad idea. And then she heard a voice that sounded very much like hers say, "Is your son being bullied?"

David looked up. "Uh, sort of. I'm meeting with the principal on Monday to talk about it."

"Oh."

Rex Woody was a tall, thin man with a bad comb-over who wore black suits and a perpetually sad expression. He was a nice guy but had trouble making up his mind about things. Whenever he came into the café, he would spend long moments with his gaze fixed to the menu board then end up ordering a plain cheeseburger.

"Oh what?" David prompted.

"Oh, probably nothing," Millie murmured. She turned back to her book. "It's just, well, Rex can be a little wishy-washy."

"I've been thinking the same thing," David admitted. "He had a very hard time deciding if Bart should skip a grade or not when I enrolled him. In the end, he gave me the choice, and I thought Bart would be happier with kids his age. Maybe that was a mistake."

"I'm sure you did the right thing," Millie assured him. "This kid, whoever he is, he isn't hurting Bart physically, is he?"

"No. So far it's just a prank, a note, and a stolen ski hat."

"It's still bullying." Millie curled her hair around her finger. "The chief of police eats lunch at the café. The next time I see him, I could ask him to talk to this kid for you."

David shook his head. "I don't want to involve the police at this point."

"Well, how about calling the kid's parents?"

"Bart won't tell me the name of the kid. All I know is that he goes by the alias GorillaGuy."

"How'd you find that out?" The little voice in her head warning Millie not to get involved made a weak protest, but she drowned it out with a swallow of coffee.

"It's a long story."

"I like long stories." She set her book on the table. "Maybe you should start at the beginning."

The light was beginning to fade by the time David finished his story. "He thinks I spied on him—and he's pretty upset with me right now." David turned his empty coffee cup absently in his hands. "He's pushing me to let him handle this himself, but I'm afraid he's going to get creamed if he gets into a physical fight."

Millie pictured Bart's sweet round face and agreed with David. "Maybe he could figure out a way to stand up to this kid but not actually fight him."

"I don't think a kid who goes by the alias GorillaGuy is going to accept a challenge to take on Bart in the Math Olympics."

She thought hard but was distracted by a crunching sound in the woods. "Maybe the solution is to find out if this girl Lauren likes Bart back. You could ask him to have one of his friends ask one of her girlfriends. That's the way we used to do it." She remembered just a little too late that David had been the exception to the rule. He'd just walked up to her one day in the cafeteria line and asked her out—and she'd simply said no.

"And if she says no, then Bart would stop trying to get up his nerve to ask her out, and the bully kid might back off." David stroked his chin. "Not a bad idea."

Something snapped in the woods. It sounded like a branch. Millie paused, listening, but the vast woods once more went silent. "Did you hear that?"

David held up his hand, indicating for her to be silent as another cracking noise popped loudly in the woods, followed by smaller but nonetheless unmistakable sounds of something picking its way through the underbrush.

It's Cynthia, Millie thought. Who knew the woman had the nose of a bloodhound? More branches popped, and Millie had the uncharitable thought that Cynthia might have a nice figure and face, but she wasn't very light on her feet. Either that or she'd brought Mrs. Denvers along with her. Even as she thought it, she glimpsed a large shadow moving between the trees. This was much bigger than a human.

"David," she squeaked.

Chapter 13

David began stuffing things into the backpack. "Come on," he said. "We've got to get going."

Millie strained to see the dark shape in the woods. Whatever it was, it had four legs. And it was *big*. She froze on the seat, hoping that whatever it was, it would go away. Instead, she glimpsed massive branches moving toward them then realized a tree wasn't moving—the branches were a huge set of antlers.

"Millie," David said quietly. "We need to get out of here."

Move? She could hardly breathe. Moose, especially bull moose, could be aggressive if they felt threatened—if they thought their territory was being invaded or they were protecting their young. Quite possibly she and David were sitting in the moose's favorite feeding ground. Quite possibly it was deciding between death by impalement or death by trampling. She had the sudden strong urge to pee and felt every ounce of the dark Colombian coffee pressing urgently against her bladder.

"Millie," David whispered more urgently, "let's go."

This might be true, but from the state of her limbs, she wasn't going anywhere. The moose was staring right at her. It could probably smell her fear.

"Move slowly, and don't look it in the eye."

Millie reminded herself that she'd dealt with worse than a moose. She'd had to knee a guy in the crotch on a date that had gone terribly wrong and once had chased down a tourist who'd tried to run out without paying his check.

Very slowly, very deliberately she climbed to her feet. Because David had told her not to look the moose in the eye, she found her gaze being drawn right to the beast's luminous brown eyes. "Now what?" she whispered.

"We retreat." He had moved to her side of the picnic table and placed himself between her and the moose.

Millie crept even closer to David's back. Leaning over him, she felt his back move with his breathing. "Maybe it's hungry," she whispered. "Maybe we should give it something to eat."

"Shhh," David said. "It's trying to decide what to do."

As if it'd heard, the moose lifted its heavy, gargantuan head and snorted. The sound blasted like a trumpet through the quiet woods, sending a shiver of fear down Millie's back. "I think it just decided," she whispered. "And it's not good news for us."

"Stay behind me," David ordered. He lifted the cross-country ski pole high into the air and placed his other hand on his hip, imitating a fencing position. "If it charges, run for the restrooms and I'll hold it off."

"David." Millie tugged his elbow. "You're holding a ski pole, not a saber."

"I'm going to count to three. When I say go, you run as fast as you can."

Millie tightened her grip on his elbow. "I'm not leaving you."

"We don't have time to discuss this."

"Give it some food, and then we'll both make a run for it."

"That's just going to make it madder," David whispered harshly. "One, two. . ."

"David, you cannot challenge that moose to a duel and think it's going to end well for you." She tightened her grip on his arm. "We both go, or no one goes." She took a small step backward and tugged at David's arm. Although he wasn't a lot taller than she was, he was significantly stronger. Moving him was like pulling at the branch of a heavy oak.

"Stop that," he hissed.

"I'm not letting you get killed by a moose," Millie said, planting her feet and pulling harder. Years of carrying heavy food trays and hours on her feet had given her pretty strong muscles. She felt his feet slip a little, but the few inches she gained were immediately lost as he caught his balance and snapped back into the same position as before.

"Millie—let go." He tried to break free of her grip, but she set her jaw and held on tightly.

The moose let loose another trumpet blast, stopping them both in their tracks. Over David's shoulder, Millie watched it stomp its front hoof and toss its head. It backed up a few steps as if giving itself more room to build up speed to trample them.

"Oh no," Millie gasped.

"Just go!" David ordered, pushing her toward the restrooms.

Just in case he had any crazy ideas about holding his ground, she grabbed his hand and held tightly as she fled for the building. It was less than a dozen strides away, but they were knee-deep in snow, and it felt like a dozen miles. David's voice burned in her ear, encouraging her to go even faster. She didn't dare glance in the moose's direction for fear that she'd see it charging to intercept them.

They skidded around the privacy wall and slid into the ladies' room. Millie came to a screeching stop in front of the sinks. Wheeling around, she saw David right behind her, snow dripping off his boots and his brown hair standing nearly upright. His nostrils were slightly flared, his eyes were a flinty blue, and the plume of his breath hung visibly in the cold air.

He spun around and used his body to block the exit. She read his intent to fight if it came down to it in the taut lines of his body. She found herself staring at the breadth of his shoulders, the way the muscles in his thighs strained against the fabric of his snow pants, and felt something very primitive, very cave-womanish tingle inside her.

When he turned around, she was aware just how small the room seemed. There were only two stalls and two sinks. The two of them could easily have joined hands and spanned the width of the room. In the soft light filtering from the skylight in the roof, she studied the shadows on his face.

"We're safe," he said, and her eyes watched in fascination the rise and fall of his chest, visible beneath his unzipped parka. It almost, but not quite, distracted her from the more immediate problem of the moose.

"You think it's gone?" she asked.

David shrugged. "I'm not sure. Probably."

Probably meant possibly. She leaned back against the sink. There wasn't even a window they could look out to see if the moose had left. "There's no cell signal out here either," she said. "I wonder how long it'll take the rangers before they come looking for us."

"We won't be here that long," David said confidently. "It's probably long gone. Most wild animals are much more afraid of humans than we are of them."

Millie folded her arms. "They obviously didn't count me in that survey."

"Don't worry," David said. "I'll just go take a quick peek around the privacy wall."

"What if it's just waiting for you to do that? Don't be like the person in horror movies who investigates the scary noise in the basement and then gets killed."

He just laughed. "Millie, I'll just be a second."

When he returned moments later, he wasn't smiling. "You're not going to believe this," he said. "But there's two of them now. A male and a female."

Millie blinked. "You've got to be kidding."

"I wish."

"So we're stuck here, in the ladies' room, in the middle of nowhere, being held hostage by two moose."

"Basically," David agreed.

Millie shook her head. "I can't believe this is happening."

"At least we have shelter," David pointed out. "And I managed to grab our backpack, so we have a blanket and food."

"You think we'll be here that long?"

"No," David replied. "I'll look again in a few minutes, and if they aren't gone, I'll throw some snowballs and make some noise to scare them away."

"Maybe there'll be three of them the next time you look," Millie said glumly. "And the next time you go out there. . ." She lowered her head, formed antlers with her hands, and pantomimed a charging moose.

He smiled confidently. "Don't worry, Millie. I was first alternate on the fencing team at UCLA."

She nodded. "I'm sure you're very good at fencing, but I think we're better off with my plan."

"Which is. . . ?"

"Feeding it."

"Feeding it?"

"Yes. Once I realized that we were dealing with a moose and not your mother and Cynthia, I came up with the idea of distracting it."

An incredulous smile played along David's lips. "Hold on a second. You thought that moose was my mother?"

"Well, actually I thought it was your mother *and* Cynthia. And I thought they were both a little heavy on their feet."

David laughed. "How could you mix up my mother and a moose?"

"It was easy," she replied. "It sounded like two people tramping around in the woods. And who else would want to spy on us? I was not expecting a moose."

"I know. I was beginning to wonder if I was ever going to get you moving. You were stiff as a statue."

"I was trying to decide if we should give the moose the fruit chutney or the leftover carrot-cake muffins. But then you went into the fencing stance. I knew we had no shot of convincing it that we came in peace."

He walked a few paces closer to her. "You seriously thought throwing carrot cake at a moose would be taken as a gesture of friendship?" His eyes sparkled, and he was grinning hugely.

Millie lifted her chin a notch. "Offering food is a universal gesture of friendship. Think Pilgrims and the Indians."

"I don't think the Indians lobbed corncobs at the Pilgrims."

"Who knows? Maybe the history books have it all wrong."

David laughed. "I don't think so."

Millie didn't think so either. But the thought of the Indians standing on one side of a field and throwing corncobs to the Pilgrims who screamed and ducked for cover was so absurd that she started to laugh. Once she started, she couldn't seem to stop, and then suddenly David was laughing, too, and every time they looked at each other, they burst out in fresh humor. She'd never seen David's face so bright red, and the sound he was making was really funny—a string of *ha-has* that just kept going and going until it left him breathless and doubled over.

She hugged herself hard, but her ribs were shaking so hard she could feel the points jutting into her stomach.

After several failed attempts, Millie came up for air and managed to stop laughing. She didn't dare look at David and concentrated instead on wiping her eyes and blowing her nose. She was breathing hard from the exertion of laughing, but it felt good—like a poison had been cleared from her system. She couldn't remember feeling so light inside in a long time.

When she looked up, she caught him staring at her intently. She felt a tingle inside. A very definite tingle. She ordered the part of herself that was tingling to stop immediately. It didn't. She faked an easy smile. "Maybe we should check and see if the moose is still there," she said. "It's getting late, and we should probably head back before the park rangers get worried."

"We definitely don't want to be in the park after dark."

He returned a moment later. "Coast is clear."

After a brief and necessary pit stop while David waited outside, they gathered their equipment and headed out on the trail. The light was fading as they skied back to the rental shop, and Millie had to concentrate on following David's tracks. She wasn't scared though. She'd had an adventure—which was something she hadn't had in years. She couldn't wait to tell her mom about getting trapped in the restroom by two moose. Eva would laugh herself silly then say something like, "He defended you from a moose, Millie. How romantic!"

It was almost pitch black by the time they'd turned in their equipment and headed for the parking lot. Stepping down the stone steps from the building, David glanced sideways at her. "I'm really glad you didn't surrender our carrot cake. I'm kind of getting hungry again."

She punched him lightly on the shoulder. "Like you're getting the leftovers," she scoffed, but they both knew he was. They crossed the parking lot, almost empty now and lit by a smattering of tall light posts. A few thin patches of black ice gleamed in the darkness. They were hard to see, and it seemed the most natural thing in the world when David slipped his arm around her shoulders as they walked to the Lexus.

Chapter 14

Your mother called twice," Aris said in greeting as David stepped through the garage door into the kitchen. It was just before six o'clock, and she jiggled her keys impatiently. "She wants you to call her immediately."

David threw his parka onto the back of a chair. "Okay. Thanks. How's Bart?"

Aris's face softened. "Doing well. He ate peanut butter cookies when he came home from the movies. That's a good sign." She gestured toward the oven. "Tuna casserole for dinner. I've got to run. Garden Club business."

She stuck her hat over her long silver braid and was out the door a moment later. David picked up the mail on the kitchen table and absently sorted through it. He saw the message light blinking on his phone but decided to call his mother back later.

"Hey, Bart," he called loudly enough to be heard over his son's music. "I'm home." In response the volume of the music coming from upstairs increased. The bass was so loud that it sounded as if at least a dozen heavy people were in Bart's room jumping up and down. Obviously his son was still angry at him about the breach of trust. David felt all the good feelings stored up from his date with Millie begin to fade.

Frowning, he started up the staircase. "Hey, buddy," he yelled, "turn it down." He paused outside his son's door. *Keep your cool,* David coached himself as he knocked. *It's going to take time to regain his trust.* He knocked a bit louder then, despite his determination to remain patient, tried the handle of the door. To his surprise, he found it locked.

This had never happened before. David knocked harder on the door. "Open. . .the. . .door. . .*now!*"

The music abruptly ceased, and the door swung open. "Dad," Bart said, blinking owlishly up at him. "I didn't hear you."

"Because you're playing your music at top volume." David put his hands on his hips. "It's time for dinner." He ordered himself to lower his voice. "I want to hear about your day."

Bart's face closed as if David had just asked him to divulge Batman's identity or the arm codes to the nation's nuclear weaponry system. His face said it would be a long time before he trusted David again. David squared his shoulders. He was Bart's father, and if this was what it took to keep his son safe, so be it.

In the kitchen, he pulled out the casserole and set it on the kitchen table. "Aris cooked your favorite again," he joked. "Tuna casserole." As he placed some on Bart's plate, he thought of the mini-muffins Millie had given him and perked up a little. Bart loved carrot cake.

Bart plunked down at the kitchen table and took a long drink of milk.

"So how was the movie?" David handed him a plate.

Bart poked at the mound with his fork and shrugged. "Good."

"Did your friends like it?"

"I guess."

"Did you see anyone else there you knew?" *Like GorillaGuy*

or that girl you like? David forced himself not to ask. After several unsuccessful attempts to draw out Bart, he changed the topic to his date with Millie. However, when he told the story about the moose chasing him and Millie into the restroom, it didn't sound nearly as funny. Although he laughed in the retelling, Bart didn't even crack a smile.

Twenty minutes later, David scraped the remains of tuna casserole into the garbage. He could have counted the number of words they'd exchanged during the whole dinner on his hands. At the sink, Bart rinsed the dishes and placed them in the dishwasher. The *clink* and *clank* of the dishes replaced conversation.

Finally, Bart turned off the water and wiped his hands on a dish towel. "Can I be excused now?"

David decided to grab the bull by the horns. "Look," he said. "I know you're upset about your privacy being violated, but you have to understand, Bart, that sometimes it's necessary."

"How would you feel if I spied on your date with Miss Hogan?"

"That's not the point. I need to know if anything else has happened at school."

"Why don't you just log on to my computer and read my e-mails?"

David blinked at the sarcasm. Had he ever spoken to his father like this? What would his dad have done? More like what would his mother have done? She was the disciplinarian.

His father had been more passive about discipline, more interested in teaching him how to play chess or tie a bow tie than he was in reprimanding David for not cleaning his room or for staying up late at night reading. His father had taken him on long hikes and taught him the names of all the trees. David realized that he wanted this same relationship with Bart. He'd thought he'd had it, too, until recently.

"One more word like that," David said, amazed at how calm his voice sounded when his heart thumped in his chest, "and you lose computer privileges for a week."

It was like telling his son that he was losing his right arm. Something like hurt flashed across his son's round face. "You'd do that?"

"Yes," David said, praying that he wouldn't have to. "I'm your father. You have to respect me even if you don't like what I tell you."

"Even when you spy on me?"

He hadn't spied on Bart; Aris had. But he refused to throw Aris under the bus just so Bart would like him. "Even if I have to do things that you don't like," David said. "I'm meeting with your principal on Monday, so if this boy has harassed you again, I need to know."

"You're meeting with the principal?" Bart's voice jumped up an octave. "Dad, you can't do that! Seriously—don't do that!"

"I have no choice."

Two splotches of angry red darkened Bart's normally pale cheeks. "I'm telling you. I'll handle this. I've got a plan."

David thought of Aris's plan to have an instructor teach Bart to chop-suey people. "I hope it's not taking karate classes."

The comment earned him a dark look. "It isn't, but I don't see why you wouldn't let me learn karate."

"It's not karate I mind," David said. "It's the fighting. You know how I feel about that. Violence doesn't solve anything. Bart, you need to tell me the name of this kid so I can talk to his parents."

Bart's chin came up a notch. "First, learning karate doesn't mean I'm going to fight someone. Second, I'm not five years old. I can handle this kid. He's just a cocky jerk. Third, I have a plan."

"Let's hear it."

"Well, you know how everyone in town is so big on the box sled race? If I beat this kid in that race, he'll leave me alone. I know it."

David frowned thoughtfully. "What makes you think he would even go in the race?" More likely, Bart would get stuffed in a locker for even asking the question.

"This kid likes to shoot his mouth off about how great he is at everything," Bart explained. "And last year he sort of won it. So when we're at lunch, I'll start talking about maybe entering it. I'm sure he'll start bragging about being the best to everyone—and that's when I'll challenge him to beat me."

"Bart, what if he takes you on your challenge and beats you? Won't that make things worse?"

Bart's face clouded over. "You don't think I'm good enough to win?"

David wished he'd expressed his fears differently. "Of course you can. It's just a possibility."

"All I have to do is sit in a cardboard box, Dad. Even I can handle that."

"It's more than that. I entered this race about twenty years ago, and my sled didn't even make it to the bottom of the slope. I had to get out and walk it down the hill."

"You don't have to design it," Bart pointed out. "I've been playing with some designs on the computer. All I need is a box, some duct tape, and paint."

David shook his head. "We need to let the principal know that a kid is bothering you."

"All that'll do, Dad, is make me look like a tattletale."

He sighed, caught between his need to protect his son and desire to please him. "How about we compromise? I'll talk to the principal, and you enter the sled race?"

"That's not a compromise," Bart pointed out. "A compromise would mean you gave something up—like talking to the principal—and I would give something up, like, say, trying to do everything on my own."

David's mind raced for a counterpoint. He heard himself say, "Well, that's the best you'll get. I'm your father, and I have your best interests at heart." It was lame, and he knew it. Yet he couldn't very well say, "I'm scared you'll get hurt."

Bart might be smart, but he was small for his size and had been a sensitive kid who cried easily. Until kindergarten, his best friends had been two girls who liked to play Barbies and watch Disney movies.

"What if I found someone who knows about building sleds and could help us? Would you agree to hold off on talking to the principal and let me enter the race?"

"My meeting with the principal is on Monday morning. I don't see how you'd find someone in time."

Behind his oversized glasses, Bart's gaze was rock steady. "But if I could, would you agree?"

"Maybe." He sensed a trap. "It would have to be someone I trusted."

Bart gave what sounded like an involuntary snort of triumph. "How about Miss Hogan? Her mother won the race awhile ago, and her sled still has the fastest recorded time."

David's expression froze. He couldn't very well say he didn't trust the woman he was supposed to be dating. Although he could still overrule his son and go to the principal, he hesitated. He was going to look pretty lame going to the principal without one shred of evidence or Bart to back him up. Besides, he couldn't protect Bart from everything—Lisa's death a case in point—and sadly his son already had figured this out. "You can ask," he conceded, "but if the Hogans say no, we do it my way."

Bart grinned as if it were a done deal and extended his hand for David to shake.

Chapter 15

Millie balanced the refrigerator box with one hand and tapped the garage door with the other. Behind her, her mother grunted as if in pain.

"Go on, hun," Eva urged. "Move. Before I drop everything."

"Stop pushing," Millie complained. "We can't move until David opens the garage door." It was late afternoon, and she and her mother had come to David's garage to begin work on the sled. She shifted her grip then nearly dropped the load as her mother gave another push.

The door rumbled then slowly rose. It had taken them a couple of days to find the exact right box. Several of the café's regulars had tried to help, but her mom had rejected box after box until finally Nelson Ridley had come up with the name of a friend of a friend who worked at Home Depot in Sioux Falls. A few phone calls later they were the proud owners of a Frigidaire side-by-side refrigerator box.

The garage door rumbled open, revealing what had to be the cleanest garage Millie had ever seen in her life. Tools neatly hung on Peg-Board, shelves held labeled plastic tubs, two bikes hung from the wall, and an enormous dry-erase board held a schedule for rotating tires and fertilizing the trees.

"Good grief, David," Millie said as she and her mother deposited their load in the middle of the floor. "You could operate in here."

David laughed. "When my dad needs to escape my mother, he comes here and organizes my garage."

"Well, send him over to ours the next time," Millie said. "But you'd better warn him that we have so many layers it's like an archaeological dig." She spotted Bart seated on the steps between the garage and the house. "Hi, Bart. You ready to build a box sled?"

Bart stood up and adjusted his glasses. "I guess," he said.

"Great," Millie said. "This is my mom, Mrs. Hogan—the current box sled record holder."

"Nice to meet you," Eva said. Instead of shaking the boy's hand, she simply enfolded him into her embrace and held him there, squashing him between her breasts. "We're going to build one heck of a sled, honey."

Bart emerged from her arms with his glasses askew and a look of dazed horror on his face. "Uh, nice to meet you."

Millie winked sympathetically.

"You look just like your dad when he was your age," her mother declared. "He and Millie were in a community play together. Remember, Millie? You and David were in *The Muffin Man*. David was Mr. Muffin, and you were Mrs. Muffin."

"Mom," Millie said. "That was like a hundred years ago."

"I've got pictures at home. Bart, you'll enjoy seeing your father dressed as a blueberry muffin," her mother said. "Oh, hold on a second. Almost forgot—one more thing in the car."

Her mother's absence seemed to leave a gap in the room. Eva was like that. She could produce a certain energy that attracted other people to her like a magnet. She couldn't go anywhere without someone stopping to hug her and talk. Her mother always had just the right word or touch. People laughed easily with her and walked away with a lighter step. Sometimes Millie studied herself in the bathroom mirror to see if her mother's spark could be seen in her own gray eyes. Other times she searched her reflection, afraid she'd see her mother looking back.

The silence lengthened. Both Denvers were studiously not looking at each other. Millie sighed and pulled at the thread of conversation her mother had started. "Your father was a really good singer in that play, Bart." Reaching into the box, she began pulling out supplies and handed Bart a couple rolls of duct tape. "You can stack these along the wall." She gave David a box cutter and a pair of heavy-duty sheers. "And he danced well, too—for a guy in a muffin suit."

"It wasn't dancing," David said. "We kind of ran around the stage a few times. I remember Karl Kauffman trying to trip me when I passed him."

"Karl was jealous because he wanted to be the muffin man," Millie said, continuing to unload the box. "Were you in any school or community plays, Bart?"

"I was the Stink Bug in our first-grade play called *Bugz*."

"He did great," David said.

"Dad," Bart said, "I stank."

"Wasn't that the whole point?" Millie met Bart's gaze, and they both smiled.

"Okay," Eva said, walking back into the garage with a blast of cold air through the side door. "This is for you." She handed Bart a white bakery box. "Go ahead," she urged him. "Open it. There's a batch of double chocolate brownies inside. I just made them."

They'd fought about it—Millie arguing that Eva would ruin Bart's appetite for supper. Eva had gotten red-faced and loud.

"Double fudge brownies are one of life's pleasures. Besides," she'd added more gently, "I want him to like me."

Bart tore into the box and wolfed down a brownie. "These are really good," he said as he chewed.

Eva helped herself to a brownie, looked at Bart, and said, "Ummm-umm—like I died and went to heaven."

Millie folded her arms as Bart helped himself to another brownie. "Hope we don't ruin Bart's appetite for dinner."

"Oh, it's fine," David replied. "We don't worry about that stuff."

"It's true," Bart said. "Our stomachs are really strong from digesting the food Aris makes."

"That's not being respectful," David said.

"Have one, David," Eva urged. "I separate the two layers of brownie with a thin coat of peppermint bark."

"Mom," Millie said, "maybe he wants to have one later."

"But they're still a little warm." Eva continued to hold the box out to David, who took one, bit into it, then grinned.

"These are fabulous." He smiled at her. "Almost as good as the carrot-cake muffins Millie made."

Millie smiled back at him. "Thank you."

"Millie," Eva said. "Aren't you going to have one, too?"

Translation: *Let me love you, too.*

"I know they're fabulous, but maybe later." Millie busied herself organizing the supplies they'd unloaded from the box.

"Next time I'll bring you chocolate éclairs, Bart."

Translation: *I like you a lot, Bart.*

"I love chocolate éclairs," Bart said.

"Me, too," David declared.

"Tomorrow," Eva promised and gave Millie a triumphant look. *You see,* her shining eyes said, *food makes people happy.*

Millie bit her tongue. "Let's get to work. What do we do first?" She directed the question at her mother.

"Well," Eva said, wiping her hands on her jeans, "we need to agree on a design. I sketched something the other night. It's in the red spiral."

Millie opened the notebook as David and Bart gathered around her. On the first page there was a pencil drawing of various rectangles that looked as if they'd been cut with pinking shears. Her mother had arrows pointing, half circles bisecting angles, and notes penciled in the margins. Millie turned the page. More crinkle-cut pieces— these looked like wings—and more incomprehensible notes. On the third page she saw a rough construction of something that might or might not have been a sled. The whole thing was very narrow, much narrower than the refrigerator box they'd brought with them.

"Mom?"

"Isn't she a beauty?"

"What exactly is it?" Millie didn't want to say that it looked like a coffin with funny cutout edges. "Aren't the sleds supposed to look like something—like a pirate ship or SpongeBob SquarePants?"

Eva sighed heavily and turned to Bart. "Millie nearly failed geometry. Couldn't do a proof to save her soul—but I blame the principal for moving the home ec teacher into the class after Albert Nevers had the heart attack. Idiot, spineless man, that principal. Spouted school policy without caring one bit about the kids. I'd like to have whacked him on the side of the head with my skillet."

Millie could laugh now, but at the time her mother's protectiveness had been a source of embarrassment. She hadn't wanted Eva flying to the school to argue a grade she'd gotten on an essay or challenge the teacher to defend the wording on an exam question. "What does my geometry grade have to do with the sled?"

Eva smiled at Bart. "She can't see what I've designed—but I think you can."

Bart looked up. Behind his glasses, his blue eyes were as clear as marbles. Millie could almost see the power of his considerable brain working away. "Is it a winged french fry sled?"

"Exactly! The wings fold in though. They're design elements."

"What?" Millie tried not to sound horrified and failed. "A french fry with wings?"

"I had a dream the night we talked about building the sled," Eva explained. "In my dream, there was a storm. Only instead of lightning bolts coming out of the clouds, it was giant french fries with wings."

Millie glanced at David, whose polite smile looked firmly frozen on his face. She didn't blame him. Her mother sounded like a lunatic.

"Now some people would say that dreaming about flying french fries was simply because I work in a café and we fry out a good hundred pounds a day, but I know the dream meant something."

"It means you went to bed hungry," Millie suggested.

Her mother shot her a dark look. "It was a sign," she insisted. "About the race. I think we're supposed to call the sled the *Flying French Fry*."

"Mom—that's a terrible name. Bart could get beat up for having a sled named the *Flying French Fry*."

"Nonsense," her mother replied with a dismissive wave. "We don't want anyone taking Bart seriously." She pointed her finger at Bart. "When people underestimate you, it gives you an advantage and you end up wiping the floor with them. I'm living proof of that. Everyone laughed at me for entering a sled shaped like a chocolate éclair—especially that cocky loan officer at First National. But he wasn't laughing when I sailed past him." She shrugged. "Of course it's up to you, Bart, what we name the sled."

"Uh, maybe we could brainstorm," David suggested. "How about *White Lightning*? That way we would use the object in your dream."

"I like the *Flying French Fry*," Bart immediately stated and shot his dad a challenging look.

Millie wondered if he only liked the name because David didn't.

Her mother grinned. "Good. It's all settled." She motioned to Bart. "Now I want you to lie inside the box so we can customize it to your measurements."

"Why didn't we just get a narrower box?"

Eva sighed at Millie's question. "We'll cut it so we can double the cardboard on the bottom layer. That way the sled will be stronger. The bottom will hold up when Bart has multiple heats."

"How am I going to see," Bart asked, "if I'm lying flat on my back?"

"Good question," Eva said approvingly. "You'll lie feet first. We'll bank the cardboard just a small amount to raise your head and lower the cardboard at your feet so you can see over the top. But we want you as flat as possible—that way you'll be more aerodynamic."

Bart lay down on the cardboard. As Millie's mom began to trace his body with a piece of chalk, he called out, "This is so cool. It's like a crime scene, and I'm the body."

"You'll be a body if you don't hold still," her mom said, but cheerfully. "You're the perfect size for this, Bart. You wait and see. You're going to win that race. Millie, please hand me the yardstick."

Eva made some measurements then referred to the sketch again. "We're going to need to take six inches off the width, graduate the slope of the sides, and lose about a foot off the top."

Millie hovered with a pencil, ready to mark the lines, but her mother waved her away. "I've got this," she said. "Relax. Talk to

David and have a brownie, hun."

In other words, *Go away.*

Her mother loved projects and could not be stopped from stepping in and assuming control. In high school, Eva had practically snatched Millie's projects from her hands. More than once Millie had awakened to find some model or poster-board project magically enhanced overnight. It was the same thing in the kitchen. Everything had to be done exactly as Eva wanted it. No variation to any recipe. Although Millie tried not to let it get to her, sometimes it felt that her efforts never measured up to Eva's.

Millie stepped back a few paces and folded her arms across her chest. Watching her mother and Bart banter back and forth made her a little uneasy. When she'd agreed to help build the sled, she hadn't pictured her mother and Bart bonding. He'd seemed too old for the infant her mother fantasized holding in her arms.

She noticed David squinting through one of the side windows and walked over to him. "What are you looking at?"

He drew back with a guilty look. "Just checking to see if she's there."

She, of course, meant Cynthia. Millie edged forward to look through the ice patterns etched onto the glass pane. The street was dark. Two cars were parked on the street. "Is she there?"

"No," David replied. "I think we're making progress."

Millie smiled. "That's great news." She lowered her voice. "We should probably go to the next step. I should give you something small but personal to display in your office." She thought about it. "A photograph of me—an eight-by-ten so she won't miss it."

David's eyes lit up. "Great idea. But how about two so I can put one in my office and one in my examination room? More people will see it."

"Perfect. And I'll need your photograph for my desk. Hold on. I've got another idea." She retrieved her cell from her purse then stood next to him. Holding out the phone, she estimated the center of the shot. "Smile," she said and snapped a picture. A moment later she held out her cell "Look—we're my new background."

Actually it was a pretty cute photo. She was snuggled comfortably against David's chest, and her smile looked genuinely happy. David had his arm around her, and his head tilted toward hers. His smile was open, his eyes crinkled at the corners. Studying the photo more closely, she noticed something different about his hair, too. He'd styled it differently. It was a little messier, a little more contemporary. She decided she liked it.

"You should send me a copy of that," David said. "I'll save it as my background as well."

Millie nodded. "The more evidence everyone sees of us together, the better. I should give you a Dosie's take-out menu. I've got one in my car. I'll give it to you before I leave."

"And I'll give you a magnet with my practice's information on it to put on your refrigerator."

"I'll need a couple. One for home and a few others for the café." She glanced at Bart, who was laughing at something Eva had said. They had their heads bent closely together. Eva was quoting some physicist Millie had never heard of, and Bart was spouting some mathematical equation at her.

"They're sure getting along," David commented.

"Maybe a little too well." Millie stuffed her hands in her pockets. "It might be a good idea to set a time for us to break up. You know, we don't want to give them too much time to get attached."

David nodded. "I've been thinking about that as well. What do you think about doing it right after the Winterfest Carnival?"

"I think that's perfect." Millie paused as the wind pushed a cold breath of snow beneath the garage door and frost danced across the floor then disappeared like a ghost. This would give her a little over a month to plan everything. Because after she broke up with David, she was heading for Los Angeles and auditioning for any acting job she could find. She looked over at her mother and wondered if she'd really have the guts to go through with this.

David seemed to misread her hesitation. "We could do it sooner."

"Oh no," Millie said. "I'm fine with waiting. One thing though." She inched closer to David and lowered her voice even further. "You're going to have to break up with me. And it has to be public. Preferably humiliating for me."

David frowned. "Can't it just be mutual? I really don't like scenes."

"Well, I'll have to cry," she explained. "But I'll keep it to a minimum—no screaming and thrashing around or breaking things. It'll be tasteful, I promise."

"I'd rather be dumped than the one to dump you."

Millie glanced over her shoulder to make sure neither her mother nor Bart were listening. "I'm sorry, but it has to be you. I won't bad-mouth you or anything. But you need to break my heart. That way everyone will understand why I need to get away. I'll just happen to pick California, and while I'm there"—she shrugged—"who knows what might happen? An audition, a small part in a movie, a spot on a reality television show. You just never know."

"You've been thinking about this a lot," David said quietly.

Millie kept her gaze steady on his. "Pretty much my whole life."

Chapter 16

David's mother dropped a black-and-white photograph of a weathered gray headstone onto his desk. "This is a photo of your great-great grandmother's grave." Another photo landed beside the first. "Now here's the marker for Cynthia's great-great grandmother." His mom's jeweled fingers tapped the first photo. "The two of them are buried right next to each other. So you see, David," she concluded triumphantly, "the bond between our two families goes back generations."

David raked his hands through his hair. All morning he'd successfully avoided his mother and her photos taken from the Saint Francis cemetery. Unfortunately, when the office closed for lunch at noon, his mother pinned him down.

"Mom, I'm not interested in Cynthia. I don't care if our families came over together on the *Mayflower*."

His mother laughed. "Who knows, maybe they did. You could discuss that over lunch. She happens to be free today."

"You should be encouraging her to see a counselor, not me." David picked up the photos of the headstones and handed them back to her. "Did I tell you that Bart is entering the box sled race at the Winterfest Snow Carnival? The Hogans are helping him build his sled."

His mother's smile thinned. "Is that really a good idea, David? Letting the boy get attached to that family will only hurt him in the long run." She fingered the long bead of pearls that hung atop her blue cashmere sweater. "I know you think you're too old to get advice from your mother, but relationships need a solid base. You get that through faith. Neither Millie nor her mother is a believer."

"You don't know what she believes," David said sharply. "It's not up to you to judge her."

His mother leaned forward. "David, they don't go to church."

"It doesn't mean they *won't* go to church."

"I love you, David," his mother said. "More than my own life. I want you to be happy. Cynthia is a good Christian woman. Our families have strong ties. She'd love you, David. She'd make a good mother for Bart."

His muscles tensed. "She's not the right woman for me."

"She could be if you'd give her a chance. You've been gone a long time, David. I'm not going to gossip, but there are things you don't know about Millie Hogan. I'd be very careful about how much time you let Bart spend with that family."

"The Hogans are good people." David found himself leaning over the desk. "Honest, caring, and hardworking—they're *exactly* the kind of people Bart should be hanging around with." He crossed the room in three strides, aware of the shocked expression on his mother's face but too angry to care.

He marched to the door. "I've put up with your silly matchmaking because I knew you were trying to help. But I *will not* put up with you insulting Millie. Is that clear, Mom?"

"Where are you going?"

Until she'd asked, he hadn't been sure himself. His only thought was to get away before he said something that he regretted. But now, looking at her, he knew. "To lunch. It's Thursday. The special at Dosie Dough's is meat loaf, mashed potatoes, and green beans."

His mother sucked in her breath as if he'd announced he was having lunch with the devil himself, but then David was out the door. He nearly knocked down Cynthia, who had her ear pressed against the door.

David steadied her with one hand then strode past her. Outside the January afternoon was painfully bright and clear. On the sidewalk, he took a deep breath of the cold, pure air, released it, took another, and then another.

He drove straight down Cumberland, clenching the cold steering wheel in his bare hands, past Ed's Market, the First National Bank, Unique Antiques, Monica's Beauty Salon, and Ready, Aim, Fire Hunting Supplies.

Small town, small minds. He'd never thought that way before; he had always been proud of Deer Park's Old World charm and was secretly grateful that it hadn't become as upscale as other towns in South Dakota that were closer to Mount Rushmore or the hot springs or all the amenities that Rapid City offered.

The biggest draw here was the Black Hills, which drew their share of vacationing families looking for skiing, hunting, or bargain shopping for gold jewelry that came from local mines. The tourism kept the town going, but it wasn't enough to make anyone rich.

The clock tower in the town square rang its hourly chime as he passed. As little as he liked it, his mother had spoken the truth. The Bible stated very clearly that a relationship between a believer and nonbeliever was doomed. Not that he intended to marry Millie—but it was the principle of the whole thing that bothered him. Every person had value. Every person was equally loved in God's eyes. People didn't crawl out of the womb praising Jesus. Following Christ was a choice. It was Millie's choice and not up to him or anyone else to judge her.

Soon the giant éclair on the top of Dosie Dough's roof came into sight. He found a parking spot on the street and headed for the building. A CLOSED sign hung in the dark window, and the front door was locked. Puzzled, David stood in the freezing cold and wondered what'd happened. His breath hung in the air, and he was aware of a bad feeling forming in the pit of his stomach. Getting back in the car, he turned back onto Mail Street and fishtailed a little on the sleety street as he headed for Millie's house.

She met him at the front door. Something inside him stirred at the sight of her in a pair of Levi's worn soft at the knee and a red flannel shirt that looked about two sizes too big. Without any makeup and her hair pulled back into a loose ponytail, she looked younger, almost exactly the way he remembered her in high school.

"David?" She blinked up at him, all big eyes and soft curves. "Is everything all right?"

"That's what I want to know. I went by the café. I got worried."

"Oh." Millie pulled the door wider, letting warm air escape from the house and with it the barest trace of the scent of something cooking. "Come in."

Stamping his feet free of a crust of snow, he walked inside. Millie raised her fingers to her lips, indicating for him to be quiet. "Mom's upstairs sleeping," she whispered and led him back to the kitchen.

"Have a seat." Millie gestured to the ladder-backed chairs that surrounded a battered-looking wooden table. Piles of mail and magazines, at least four cookbooks, and an assortment of prescription medicines covered half the tabletop. "Sorry everything's so messy," she said, clearing a spot for him. "I'm making chili. Can I get you some?"

"First tell me what's going on with Eva."

Millie sighed. "Her blood sugar went crazy." She moved a stack of books and papers next to an equally tall stack on the kitchen counter. "Last night it dropped to 45, and then it shot up to 250. We've been trying to stabilize it, but so far we haven't been able to."

"Shouldn't you call a doctor?"

"I already did. If she's not better in a few hours, I'll take her to see Dr. Wong."

David studied the dark circles under her eyes and the paleness of her lips. The scrubbed-down version made him feel like he was seeing a more vulnerable Millie. "What can I do to help?"

"Nothing—but thanks for asking."

"Are you sure it wasn't something she ate at our house? Or too much activity with building the box sled?"

Millie pulled a brick of yellow cheese out of the refrigerator and began to grate it. "Are you kidding? All she could talk about was how smart and cute Bart was and how much she enjoyed building that sled."

A small mountain of cheese appeared, but Millie continued grating.

"So when she came home, her blood sugar was fine?"

"Yeah, we tested it, and then she said she wanted to bake some red velvet cupcakes for Aunt Keeker—it's her half birthday today. I sat in the kitchen, working on my essay for *Chef's Challenge*—that's a new reality TV show on the Food Network."

She finished the last shreds of the brick and then, pulling out a white bowl from the cabinet, filled it to the brim with piping hot chili. Placing it in front of him, she asked, "How about some avocado or onions?"

David picked up the spoon. "This looks great. I don't need

anything else." He looked at her. "Aren't you going to have some?"

"I'm not that hungry," Millie said.

He took a bite of the chili. It tasted pretty great, but Millie was giving him a funny look. "It's excellent," he pronounced.

"Do you taste the cinnamon? I tried to hide it with extra cumin and chili powder."

David shook his head. "No," he said. "I like it." He spooned up another bite. "Does cinnamon have special meaning in your talking-with-food vocabulary?"

"No," Millie said. "Cinnamon is good for people with diabetes. But if my mother suspects that I'm trying to get her to eat healthier, she'll get mad."

As he put down another bite, his gaze fell on a piece of paper sitting on top of a *People* magazine. He realized it was an application for that reality TV show Millie had been talking about—*Chef's Challenge.* The printed handwriting covered every inch of the page. The lettering was slightly rounded, and he imagined her taking her time, trying to make it look as neat as possible.

"So you were working on your application and Eva was cooking," David prompted. "What happened next?"

Millie set down her mug of coffee. "I went outside and shoveled the driveway. By the time I finished, the cupcakes were ready to be frosted. We did that together then cleaned up the kitchen and went to bed. A couple of hours later, she knocked on my bedroom door and said she wasn't feeling so great."

"Did you see her take any medication?"

"Just the pills she took at dinner."

David watched the rooster clock on the wall twitch its tail with each passing second. Pictures stuck on the refrigerator spoke loudly of the closeness between Millie and Eva. He could see nothing that would have caused Eva's blood sugar to drop so unexpectedly. Nothing—unless. . . His gaze returned to Millie. "You don't think she could have doubled her medication by accident?"

Millie frowned. "No. She hates taking her medication. Usually I have to remind her to take it."

David stirred the chili. "You sure? Maybe she got overexcited building the box sled, or maybe she ate too many brownies and was trying to balance things."

Millie shook her head. "I'm sure. Her blood sugar was fine when she tested it before she went to bed. I saw her do it."

He chewed on another mouthful of chili. He couldn't accept that Eva's blood sugar had dropped so suddenly without there being a medical explanation. An accidental overdose seemed the most likely, but Millie felt the chances of this were extremely low, and he believed her.

His mind jumped to another possibility. What if Eva had deliberately overmedicated herself? He immediately rejected the possibility. Eva Hogan was not a stupid woman, and overmedicating herself was a pretty dumb thing to do. He would not even voice this thought to Millie.

And then his gaze seemed to go of its own volition to the application on the table. He wondered if Eva had watched Millie fill it out while she baked the cupcakes. If Eva had seen something in her daughter's face that said Millie wasn't as ready to settle down as Eva wanted her to be.

"Can I read this?"

"Sure."

He picked up the paper.

Hi! My name is Millie Hogan. I am thirty-one years old

and live in Deer Park, South Dakota. For most of my life I've worked at Dosie Dough's, which is a breakfast and lunch café. My mother owns the place. We sell a lot of burgers and sandwiches, but we specialize in breads and cakes. Once the Deer Park Reporter *gave us a four-star review, which is pretty good considering we don't advertise in that paper.*

I should be on your show because I am not afraid of any challenge. I think it would be fun to ice fish and then make a meal on a bonfire started from sticks and tinder. I would be happy to swim in a tank of eels or forage in the woods and create a gourmet meal out of berries and tree bark.

Education-wise, I took a few accounting classes at Sioux Falls Community College. Mostly, though, my education comes from the school of real life.

You want other qualifications? I was runner-up in the 1998 Miss Pronghorn Antelope beauty contest and played Blanche DuBois in my high school production of A Streetcar Named Desire.

In conclusion, you should pick me because I have restaurant experience, an adventurous spirit, and acting experience. I am including a three-minute audition tape and a recent head shot. I will be in the California area in mid-March and would be glad to come in for a screen test.

David read the short essay twice. His gaze remained fixed on the paper even after he finished reading. He didn't like what he was thinking.

"It's terrible, isn't it?" Millie stated. "I'm not much of a writer."

"It's fine. Great, I mean." He fingered the application. "You think she read it while you were out shoveling the driveway?"

Millie blinked. "Maybe. I didn't try and hide it. Why?"

David put down the paper. "Maybe that last line about you going to California upset her," he said as tactfully as he could. "Have you ever mentioned an actual date in your other applications?"

"No. But even if my mother read my essay and it upset her—which is a big if—I still don't think it would have caused her blood sugar to crash." She sipped from a mug with a big chocolate M&M on it. "My mother doesn't think I'll ever get selected to audition. Trust me. She doesn't believe I have a shred of talent and thinks it's a waste of time for me to even think about going to Hollywood."

"Maybe you've got it wrong," David suggested. "Maybe she's afraid that you'll go to California and be so successful that you won't come back. Or maybe she's just trying to keep you from getting disappointed." He thought, given the timing of Eva's attack, the former was more likely than the latter. However, he hoped Millie would make the leap to that conclusion herself. He was only speculating, and suggesting her mother was manipulative enough to use her diabetes as a weapon was a pretty strong statement. And it really wasn't any of his business.

He checked his watch. It was close to one o'clock. "I'm sorry, Millie, but I'd better get going."

"You haven't finished your lunch."

He was about to suggest she pack it up for him to eat later when a familiar voice said, "Going? I finally drag myself out of bed to say hello and you leave?"

Eva strode into the kitchen. She was wearing a thick fleece bathrobe the color of an eggplant. There were dark circles under her eyes of the same color, and her skin was puffy and blotched as if she'd been standing outside in the cold.

David jumped up to give her his seat. "I'm sorry to hear you had a bad night."

Eva dismissed his concern with a wave of her hand. "I'm fine now. What time can we come over and work on the sled?"

"Mom," Millie said firmly. "You need to rest. The sled can wait."

"I need to get off my duff," Eva corrected. "I'm really feeling much better. I made some extra cupcakes for Bart—and you, too, David."

"Let's see what your blood sugar level says." Millie unzipped a small black case. With the ease of someone who had done this hundreds of times before, she inserted a fresh lancet into the tester and wiped Eva's finger with a small pad of alcohol. Eva didn't flinch as Millie triggered the blade.

"You're still a little low," Millie said, reading the result. "I'll get you some orange juice."

"Thank you, honey," Eva said. "I don't know what I'd do without you."

"Oh you'd probably do fine, Mom."

The corners of Eva's mouth tugged slightly downward. "I think the Eskimos had the right idea. When someone got old and it was their time, they'd send them off on their own little iceberg. That way they were never a burden to their people."

"That was in the days before cable television," Millie joked, setting a glass down in front of her mother. "Now they just park people in front of the Game Show Network and turn up the volume. Have a sip, Mom. You'll feel a lot better after you've eaten."

"It's excellent chili," David added.

Eva gave him a penetrating look. "You sure? Last time she tried to make it healthier for me, and it gave me terrible gas. I'm telling you, David, I went *rat-a-tat-tat* for days."

Millie set a bowl down in front of her mother. "Just eat this and be quiet," she ordered, but David watched her squeeze her mother's shoulder affectionately.

"Well," David said, pulling his keys from his pocket, "anything I can do, just call." He grabbed his coat off the back of his chair and hesitated. Leaving suddenly seemed wrong.

He looked into Millie's large gray eyes. *Who looks out for you?* he wanted to ask and had to remind himself again that it wasn't his place to ask. But it still bothered him, and he found himself lingering at the front door. "If you need me, just call," he said. "I mean it, Millie—even if it's in the middle of the night."

Climbing into his Lexus, he thought about how tightly Eva clung to Millie and understood for the first time why Millie might dream of a different life. He had always thought of love as the best possible way to be bound to someone. Its presence alone was a God thing, something to be thankful for. Although Lisa's death had taught him that love could hurt, he'd never had to hurt someone else in order to be happy.

He backed the car slowly down the driveway. There really wasn't any other instinct stronger than the one to protect your children, and if Eva had deliberately taken the wrong medication, he felt sure Eva was acting out of love, possibly misguided, but love all the same.

He thought a parent could donate a kidney, empty a bank account, or step in front of a speeding car to save his child, and yet the hardest thing a parent might ever have to do was stand back and let go. When it came his time, he prayed Bart would never see just how hard this would be for him.

Chapter 17

It started to sleet as Millie drove with her mother to the café. A travel advisory was posted, and she gripped the wheel more tightly as small pellets pinged off the Subaru's windshield. The wipers swept rhythmically back and forth, noisy on a salt-splattered windshield.

"That was nice of David to stop by," her mother commented.

"Yes. It was."

Her mom snorted in agreement. "That boy of his is so cute I could just eat him up."

Millie tapped the brakes lightly so the car wouldn't skid as they came to a four-way stop. She hadn't planned to question her mother any further about the incident with her blood sugar, but the opportunity had presented itself, and she couldn't quite dismiss David's words. "Speaking of eating," she said carefully. "I've been thinking about last night—the way your blood sugar dropped so low. I was wondering if maybe you might have taken a double dose of Glucophage last night by accident."

"You think I'm that senile?"

"I'm just trying to understand what happened. It was busy last night. You could have been tired."

Her mother sighed. "Honey, just worry about your driving. Whatever it was, it's gone. I'm fine now."

Millie cast a sideways glance at her. "We don't want that to happen again. It's scary, Mom, when your blood sugar goes down like that."

"There's more danger that we're going to skid off the road if you don't look where you're going. I don't want to talk about this anymore."

Something in Millie wouldn't let it go. "Maybe we should keep that appointment at four with Dr. Wong. Run some blood tests and make sure you're really okay."

"I'm fine. I have an appointment in two weeks. We can talk about what happened then."

"Mom," Millie said, "if you don't go see him, I'm going to worry every night when you go to bed that your blood sugar is going to drop and you'll go into a coma."

"I'm not about to kick the bucket, so you can stop worrying. Besides, if I go, all Dr. Wong is going to do is run an A1C test and tell me that I need to be stricter about my diet, lose weight, and exercise more. That's all he ever says. And he charges a fortune."

This was true, but Dr. Wong also warned Eva that her casual approach to managing her diabetes was a big mistake, that with her disease came an increased risk for heart attack, stroke, and a host of other serious conditions.

Miles of wire fence line marked fields covered with snow. Millie sped past Burial Hill Road, which led to the cemetery where her grandmother was buried. After Grandma Gert passed away, she and her mother used to go there daily. That first summer, they planted black-eyed Susans in fat clay pots that flanked the small flat marker and lugged over gallon containers of water. While Millie tended the grave, her mother stared down at the plot with such grief in her face that Millie could not bear to look at her. No words could help, so Millie brushed dirt off the engraved letters, the weight of the vast blue sky bearing down on her shoulders. That summer, Eva's diabetes had required her to be hospitalized twice, and Millie remembered it as being the hardest summer in her life.

Dr. Wong had explained that grief could wreak havoc on the body and to expect fluctuations in her mother's health. He advised Millie to minimize any further stress and to watch for signs of depression. By the end of July, Millie was managing the café full-time and had decided to defer her admission to the University of South Dakota. The next summer, however, had been no better. Lightning had struck a tree, which had toppled onto the café's roof. Although insurance had picked up most of the expenses, Millie had needed to help her mother handle the paperwork and oversee the renovations. That fall Millie had started courses at the local community college, but caring for her mom and running the café proved to be more than she could handle, and she'd dropped out before the semester ended.

Ahead the hanging traffic light marked the entrance to Deer Park's business district. Cars and trucks parked in slanting lines filled both sides of the road. Stores stripped of their Christmas decorations now sported murals of ski hills, sleds, and banners advertising the coming Winterfest Snow Carnival.

She turned at the next light and pulled around to the back of Dosie Dough's. As she stepped out of the car, a gust of wind blew the sleet sideways, striking her face. She ducked her head into the collar of her parka and thought about how warm it must be in California right now. How people drove around in convertibles or sat at outdoor cafés sipping cool drinks and eating wraps made with sprouts and avocados. She pictured herself there, watching the world from behind a pair of dark glasses, an expensive silk scarf tied around her neck, the air warm and silky on her bare shoulders.

They came in through the back door, and Millie flipped on the lights. The stainless steel counters gleamed with near-surgical cleanliness, the twin refrigerators hummed in the background, and the vast grill sat empty and waiting, the fry basket sitting beside the covered tub of oil.

Millie tied on an apron then had to wrestle the forty-pound bag of flour from her mother's arms. "I've got this," she said. "You sit at the counter and supervise."

Eva shook her head. "I'm not a supervising kind of woman. I'm a doing kind of woman."

"Then work on the starter," Millie suggested as she emptied half the bag into an industrial-sized mixing bowl. A cloud of fine white dust rose into the air. "What kind of bread are we making anyway?"

"Sourdough," her mother said as if this were obvious. "We always have sourdough on Thursdays. Goes well with tomato basil soup."

She felt her mother's gaze as she gently stirred salt into the flour and then attached the dough hook to the machine. Eva was near fanatical in the handling of the dry ingredients prior to the addition of the starter sponge and water. She claimed overworking the dough made it tough and always watched to make sure Millie didn't stir too many times.

As a preteen, Millie remembered some of their worst fights had stemmed from baking bread. Eva had insisted she learn the proper way to bake, and Millie had been equally determined that she wouldn't. As her mother had gone over and over the way to knead the bread, round it, and proof it, Millie had let her mother's words flow through her brain like water down a drain.

Instead, she'd stared at Eva's broad face and mentally given her a makeover—a foundation so her skin would not look so pale and washed out and a concealer to hide the dark shadows beneath her eyes. She'd restyled her mother's thick curly hair into a neat, straight bob like the one her English teacher wore. She'd changed her mother's outfit from the shapeless black stretch pants and red sweatshirt with the oversized chocolate éclair into a sleek wrap dress. She imagined Eva as a slim, stylish mother who turned heads when she came to Millie's school plays, instead of the Eva who always was running late and more often than not showed up with her clothing dusted with flour or shirts stained with oil from the fryer.

Once Millie had told Eva that her appearance was an embarrassment.

"You're a teenager, and I'm your mother," Eva had retorted. "I'm supposed to embarrass you." And she'd laughed heartily at her own joke. But she'd stayed away at the next performance, and her absence had left Millie feeling gutted—like the jeweled bellies of the fish her mother slit open and emptied before baking them.

Eva walked over with the starter sponge and pitcher of tepid water. She began mixing the ingredients with a long, wooden paddle and the ease of someone who'd done it hundreds of times before. "This is nice—a quiet afternoon, no customers, no hustle and bustle—just you and me."

"It is," Millie agreed. The forming ball of dough smelled yeasty. She couldn't deny that there was something soothing about watching the hook chase the ball of dough around the metal mixing bowl and listening to the sound of sleet on the roof.

"I was thinking, after we finish the sourdough, maybe we could whip up a batch of apple tarts."

They were Millie's childhood favorite, and her mother had made them both to celebrate her accomplishments and console her failures. Today the tarts said, *Sorry I kept you awake most of last night. Let me make it up to you.*

Millie wiped her hands on her apron and left ghostly flour prints on the tomato-red fabric. *I don't want apple tarts*, she wanted to say. *I want you to tell me to go to Hollywood and do something amazing with my life—that you believe I can. I want you to look me in the eye and tell me that you don't need me.*

She bit her lip. Here she was again, still trying to remake Eva. She supposed it was impossible for her not to—just as Eva could not help trying to make Millie into the daughter she wanted.

"I don't need apple tarts," Millie began and was about to add that television cameras added ten pounds. But then she stopped at the look of disappointment that deepened the lines in her mother's face and killed the light in her eyes. Eva had essentially heard, *I don't accept your apology.*

Millie turned off the mixer and lifted the hook from the dough. "I don't need apple tarts," she repeated. "But you know I can't resist them."

Eva beamed at her. Apology made and accepted. "Excellent," she said.

Chapter 18

"So why did you become a dentist?" Millie lay in bed with the cordless receiver tucked to her ear and the down comforter pulled high around her. It was nearly ten o'clock, which was late for her to be awake, but ever since Eva's blood sugar had plummeted so inexplicably three days ago, David had been calling after he finished putting Bart to bed. *Just to check on you and Eva,* he'd explained.

Although initially Millie had bristled—she didn't need anyone checking on her—when David suggested that their talking on the phone was a natural part of the dating process, even if they were un-dating, she had agreed.

"I don't know," David's deep voice rumbled pleasantly in her ear. "I guess it seemed like a really cool job. I remember going with my dad to the office and him showing me the tools. I liked making the chair ride up and down."

Millie laughed. "But did you feel pressure to be a dentist because your father was one?"

"No. In fact, he wanted me to be a lawyer. An environmental lawyer so I could protect trees. He was very big on trees."

"Trees," Millie repeated, smiling. "Was it hard then, telling him that you weren't going to be a tree lawyer?" She pulled her knees up higher. In the very back of her mind, a small voice warned her that their phone conversations were getting longer every night, and these questions had ventured into personal waters.

"No. He said he understood. *His* father wanted him to be an architect. He said that God gave everyone a gift and a purpose and that to deny it was to waste it. And then he said he was proud of me, no matter what profession I chose, and that was it."

"Seriously? He didn't go into a decline?"

"No. But he sent me a ficus tree the day I opened my practice in Los Angeles."

Millie laughed then pressed the phone a little closer against her ear. "Tell me what it was like there," she said.

"Well, it was very nice, but not as nice as here."

The answer wasn't what she expected. "Why not?"

"It wasn't home," he said.

"In the old days," her mother explained, ripping a length of duct tape off the roll, "they used to let you use chicken wire to support the body of the box sled. But then they decided to simplify things and only use cardboard, duct tape, glue, and paint." She cut the tape. "If you ask me, the more people try and simplify things these days, the more complicated they get."

The propane heater warmed David's garage, chasing away the chill of a late-January afternoon. They'd discarded their coats and gloves and squatted on an old quilt near the cardboard carcass of what was slowly becoming the *Flying French Fry*.

Under the naked lightbulb hanging from the center of the garage's ceiling, Millie's mother's eyes sparkled, and her movements were fluid and purposeful. "Take the computer for example. Does anyone truly believe it's made their life any easier?"

"Maybe not easier," Bart agreed, "but a lot more fun. Have you ever played Sims?"

"Sims? What's that? Sounds like a respiratory disease."

Millie rolled her eyes and cut into a square of cardboard. "That's SARS, Mom."

"Sims is a cool computer game. I could teach you how to play it, Mrs. Hogan."

"Thank you, Bart, but you-know-where will freeze over before the computer makes any sense to me."

Millie and David exchanged smiles. Although her mother would never admit it, part of her dislike for computers came from her fear of pushing the wrong button. As if a single erroneous keystroke could take down the power grid in several states.

"You want some help?" David asked Millie.

She was cutting the cardboard in order to reinforce the hull, but the material was thick and hard to cut. She kept stopping to rest her hand.

David leaned over to pull the cardboard taut to make it easier for her to cut. The fabric of his wool sweater stretched over his lean torso. His face was close to her own, and she could feel the warmth in his blue eyes peering at her.

"If you tear the cardboard," Millie cautioned, "Mom will kill us."

"And bury you in the backyard," her mother confirmed and tapped her yardstick against her UGG boot like a military sergeant. "We don't want to compromise the integrity of the structure. Bart, have you seen the protractor? I'm wondering if we could shave off another degree or two from the front of the sled."

"It's in my pencil pouch in my room. Want me to get it?"

"Please," Millie's mother said. As the boy ran to retrieve it, she turned to Millie. "While you and David finish cutting the hull support, I'm going to discuss some race strategy with Aris."

"What race strategy?" Millie asked.

"You know," her mother said vaguely. "Ways we can help Bart." She was talking as she walked, and it was obvious to Millie that her mother was simply trying to give her an opportunity to be alone with David.

Millie snuck a peek at David to see if he realized. Of course he had. His blue eyes were laughing. "Take your time, Mrs. Hogan." He scooted a little closer to Millie. "Honey, let me help you with that."

When she handed him the scissors, their hands touched, and the heat of his skin sent a shiver through her. She glanced up to see if David had felt the same jolt. He hadn't moved, but the laughter had disappeared from his face. The easygoing, intellectual David was gone, and a man with a strong jaw and intense blue eyes was looking back at her.

Correction. Looking into her. It wasn't a staring contest kind of look at all. It was strong, and it was penetrating, and she felt it all the way to the tips of her toes.

She tried to remind herself of just why she'd given up men. Words like *trapped*, *dependent*, and *weak* floated through her mind as insubstantial as ghosts. His eyes continued to hold her, and the look was undoing something that had been tightly knotted inside her. She forced herself to look down, but it didn't help. The sight of his tapered fingers, the skin as pale as sand, made her skin burn.

The steps creaked. Startled, Millie's head jerked back. Her mother? She felt a flush of anger. Why was her mother standing there watching them? What was wrong with her? She clenched her fists, furious. *Go away*, she wanted to shout.

But she wasn't as mad at Eva as she was with herself. She'd wanted to kiss David—and that would have ruined everything. As soon as the door closed behind her mom, Millie released her breath. An instinct she hadn't known she possessed seemed to take control of her.

"You were amazing," she said. "The way you were looking at me just then was totally believable."

David flexed the scissors. His eyes said he wasn't fooled. "You were pretty believable yourself."

She didn't want to be reminded of any longings that he might have glimpsed in her eyes. "Well, you know me. I've had a lot of practice." She laughed as if this was funny, but David remained silent, and after a moment he began to cut the cardboard.

As the scissors hacked through the thick layers, Millie sat cross-legged, wondering why she'd felt the need to make herself sound cheap.

Beneath her lashes, she studied his profile. Usually she preferred tall, muscular men with craggy faces, steely eyes, and six packs. Her fantasy men were Navy SEALs, secret agents, and occasionally a Scottish laird with wide shoulders and a deep lyrical brogue.

She'd never fantasized about a dentist of average height and build.

To be fair, David had probably never dreamed of falling for a waitress. His first wife had been educated; they'd gone to dental school together. Millie had only a semester of college. Lisa had been blond, tiny, and beautiful; Millie was dark-haired, tall, and strong.

David finished cutting and placed the rectangle of cardboard inside the hull. Sitting back, he studied the sled. "One side looks a little higher."

Millie could have cared less. She still was thinking about her earlier remark and wishing she hadn't said it. She thought she might have hurt him, although this was more of a sense than a fact. She plucked at the fabric of her sweatshirt.

"I didn't mean that the way it sounded," she said.

"Mean what?" He picked up the yardstick and measured the lowest point of the sled.

He had to know exactly what she meant, and his politeness was only going to make it harder. She fingered the remains of a piece of cardboard. "Look," she said flatly. "I've dated a lot of guys, but. . ."

"What difference does that make?" David interrupted, studying the lines on the yardstick as if they were hieroglyphics that required immediate translation. "There's a quarter inch discrepancy between the sides. We should fix it." He picked up a pencil and marked the spot.

"One quarter of an inch isn't going to make a difference," Millie stated. "And I know I don't have to explain everything to you, but I want to."

He looked up. "Do you know that when I set a crown in a person's mouth, if it is as much as one one-hundreth of a centimeter off, the person's whole bite will be affected?" He picked up the scissors and cut the piece he'd just installed in the hull to make it fit better. "One side will bite down first. Every time that person chews something, he'll feel it. It could cause terrible problems down the road. TMJ for one."

"It's a sled," Millie argued, "not a dental appliance."

"It's an easy fix."

"That's not the point." Millie placed her hand over his, preventing him from cutting the cardboard. She felt the same tingle as before. She clenched her jaw. "David, I'm trying to tell you something about myself. Things maybe you need to hear."

"I appreciate that. And I'm trying to tell you that you don't have to tell me anything. I like who you are, and the rest doesn't matter."

The words stung in a way he probably hadn't intended. She lifted her hand off his and looked at him in astonishment. Why wasn't "the rest" important? "The rest" was her past. Wasn't he curious about the rumors he must have heard about her? Or was he trying to tell her that what happened in the past had no relevance because they had no future?

She wanted to ask but couldn't. She bit her lip and tried to find the way to express her feelings without actually risking anything. She couldn't get past the truth—that when they'd touched, she'd come alive in a way she never had before. And when she'd looked into his eyes, she felt him inside her.

At the same time, all this was terrifying. She'd always called the shots in the relationship. She always managed to stay at arm's length emotionally, if not physically.

What if she told David she wasn't just pretending to like him? What if he didn't like her back? And maybe, just maybe, she wasn't good enough for him.

Even scarier, though, was the thought he might like her in the same way she liked him. Where would that leave them?

In a relationship, she decided, that wasn't right for either of them.

Chapter 19

Millie played it cool when she kissed David good-bye. Walking out to the car, she straightened her shoulders against the frigid January night. Men complicated things. They made strong women vulnerable. If you let them, they would break your heart. If she had any doubt about this, she had only to look at her grandmother and mother, both single parents.

She backed down the driveway. In the passenger seat, her mother was uncharacteristically quiet. Eva looked out the window, and her profile was serious. Maybe old memories were kicking around in her head, too.

It'd been a rainy, chilly morning in April when Max Hogan had stopped being Millie's father.

She'd hurried down the stairs, grumpy because she'd overslept and was going to be late for school if she didn't hurry. She had a math test, which she was probably going to fail, and that would probably start another war with her mother, who thought she spent far too much time rehearsing the lines in her play and not enough time studying.

The house was uncharacteristically quiet when she walked into the kitchen. Eva was seated at the kitchen table with her head folded into her hands as if it were a weight her neck could no longer carry. She'd lifted her head long enough for Millie to glimpse her chalk-white face and scary red-rimmed eyes, and then her head crumpled back into her hands.

"*What's wrong?*" *Millie whispered. She'd never seen her mother cry, and the sight was terrifying.* "*Mom?*"

Grandma Gert padded silently into the room in her fluffy blue robe and slippers. "*Your father's gone.*"

"*Gone to work?*" *Millie asked.*

"*Gone,*" *Grandma Gert repeated, and her face twisted.* "*I'm sorry, child.*"

Her mother made a deep guttural noise that sounded as if it had been torn out of her chest. Millie's skin turned to ice. Dad's dead. Impossible, *she thought,* I just saw him last night. *But there was her mother, bent with grief at the table.*

I'm never going to see Dad again. *The thought sliced something wide open inside. Flinging herself into Grandma Gert's big chest, she closed her eyes and wept.*

It was only later that evening, when she'd gathered her courage to ask Grandma Gert how her father had died, that she learned he had packed his suitcase and left in the middle of the night. In a way, this was worse, because it opened up all sorts of questions in her mind. Why had he left? Where had he gone? And why hadn't he asked her if she wanted to go with him?

She couldn't ask any of those questions though. Her mother stopped speaking and started spending long hours in the kitchen. When Millie came home from school, Eva would be at the speckled blue linoleum counter stirring a bowl of batter. Evidence of the day's baking would be lined up along the counter—German chocolate cakes with flaky coconut icing, heavy loaves of lemon pound cake drizzled in a raspberry glaze, and trays of brownies frosted in pink peppermint icing. Breads in various stages of rise battled for space with the sweet cinnamon rolls topped with sticky pecan glaze.

Each night Millie and Grandma Gert wrapped up the baking and gave it to neighbors. But when they awoke in the morning, the countertops were again filled with breads and pastries.

Eva couldn't stop, and as cakes and pies and cookies overflowed the kitchen into the dining and living room, out of desperation Millie wrote Free Pastries on a piece of poster board and stuck it at the end of the driveway. Word spread quickly, and it wasn't long before a steady stream of people came for the baked goods. Millie never charged anyone for the food, but people left money on the counters, under the front-door mat, and in the mailbox. It wasn't long before Millie began finding handwritten orders on scraps of paper, "a dozen raspberry Danishes," "an apple-strudel coffee cake," and "a Black Forest cake."

Pulling into her garage, Millie turned off the car's engine and tried to push back the memories. She thought of her mother's brokenness—buried deep now but still part of her. Millie suspected it always would be.

She barely tasted the baked potato soup that Eva heated for dinner and hurried to her bedroom straight after dinner where she spent an hour on the PC, searching for auditions and cheap airfares to New York and California. At nine o'clock, she took off her makeup, brushed her teeth, pulled on her pajamas, and climbed into the cold bed.

A little after nine, she turned off the lights. She rolled onto her side so she wouldn't watch the clock. She wasn't sure if David would call or not, but if he did, she didn't plan on answering. She'd let him slip past her defenses just a little, but it had been a wake-up call. She needed to pull back before she lost control of the situation.

When the phone rang at 9:25, she jerked. Placing the pillow over her head, she waited as the phone jingled loudly once, twice, three times.

Finally, the answering machine kicked in, and the room went silent. She sat up, turned on the light, and fought back the panic that said maybe she'd done the wrong thing. Taking a sip of water from the glass on the bedside table, she tried to swallow the unexpected lump in her throat. Had the house always felt so quiet? Her room so tomblike? Her life suddenly seemed so inescapable, so dreary in its predictability, that she almost wanted to throw her glass against the wall just to see it break.

She didn't want to feel anything for David Denvers. She didn't want to miss the sound of his voice, the nightly conversations. She didn't want him in her head, her heart, or anywhere else. He did not belong in the life she wanted, and she certainly didn't belong in his. She turned off the light and laid her head on the pillow.

Suddenly there was a soft knocking on her door. "Millie?" Eva said, poking her head inside. "David's on the phone."

Millie concentrated on staying still and keeping her breathing smooth and even, although her heart was racing.

"Millie?" her mother whispered more loudly. "Are you awake?"

She clenched her jaw and lay corpselike on the bed. There was a long pause, and then the door clicked quietly shut. Millie heard the floor creak as Eva retreated down the hallway. She lay awake for a long time thinking about David, wondering if she'd done the right thing and what they might have said to each other if she'd picked up the phone.

Chapter 20

For years Gunderson Park had been a local hangout for teens. In the winter, the town roped off a portion of the lake and cleared the surface with a Bobcat. For ten dollars and a trip to the town hall, a skating pass could be bought for the season.

When she was fourteen, Millie had come here as often as she could find someone to drive her. It kept her out of the café and away from her mother. Millie didn't understand how Eva could be talking and giggling one moment, and the next she would be shrieking at a vendor or sitting at the counter too depressed to lift her head from her hands. Daily, it seemed, Eva was changing, gaining weight, and becoming more emotionally unpredictable. Grandma Gert whispered to be patient, but Millie discovered the only solution was to stay out of Eva's way as much as possible.

So it shocked her one sunny afternoon at Gunderson Park when Aaron Hughes skated up next to her. He was two years older and towered over her, although she was already the tallest girl in eighth grade. "Hi," was all he'd needed to say to start her heart thundering.

She kept her gaze firmly on the ice, because if she even glanced at his face, she'd have fallen flat on the ice.

"I was wondering," he said, "if maybe you'd like a hot chocolate."

Millie had practically swooned with importance. "Sure," she'd managed.

They'd wobbled their way up to the concession hut. He'd bought her a hot chocolate, and they'd stood beside a fire burning inside an oil drum and talked. It wasn't long before he said he wanted to show her something and led her to a grove of pines. He'd shaken the snow off the bough of one of the larger trees and pulled her beneath. Smiling, he'd looked down at her. "You're a really pretty girl. Did you know that?" he'd whispered and lowered his cold lips onto hers.

She hadn't liked the kiss, but she'd liked bragging to her friends about it. Although her relationship with Aaron hadn't lasted a week, Millie had discovered something about herself. She had power, and with a little practice, she began to know how to use it. By the time she was old enough to drive herself to the park, she was never without a boyfriend. And if other girls whispered behind her back, Millie ignored them. She liked the attention and wasn't giving it up.

Although Millie hadn't been ice skating in years, these thoughts were very much on her mind as David turned the Lexus into the entrance of Gunderson Park. She stiffened at the sight of the white van with the Methodist church bumper sticker. All her misgivings came rushing back, and she wished she hadn't given in to David's insistence that she attend the church's skating function.

Bart hit the ground running as soon as David parked the car. "Not cool to be seen with your father," David remarked wryly as they watched the boy speed toward the group of boys who were sitting on plank benches and putting on their skates.

Millie slung her skates over her shoulder. "We ditched our parents when we were Bart's age, remember?"

"I remember you had a white parka with a fur-trimmed hood, only you never wore the hood up. You had a white headband, and you wore your hair in the thickest, longest braid I'd ever seen."

She glanced sideways at him. Her eyes were nearly level with his. "You remember that?"

"Well it wasn't *that* long ago."

She felt her cheeks pink up as she remembered all those little trips behind the concession stand. David probably remembered them, too—although he was too polite to admit it. Plunking down on one of the cold plank benches, she pried open the ancient figure skates.

Sticking her foot into the cold, stiff leather, she crossed the laces tightly. Laughter and the sound of children yelling to one another filled the air. Knotting the laces, she sat up and scanned the ice and began recognizing people.

"Are you worried?" she finally asked.

"About what?" David finished lacing one skate and was working on the other.

Millie's stomach tightened as she continued to study the stream of skaters passing, circling the ice. She feared being judged and found not good enough to be dating David. "About being seen with me."

"You mean you're worried that people won't believe we're dating?"

She gave a small, brittle laugh. "No," she said, shaking her head. "The exact opposite. I'm worried that they will."

The ice was rock hard, uneven, and black as night. A slice of wind reduced Millie's eyes to slits, and her skates immediately began to rub her ankle. A group of kids whizzed past her, and she had to throw her hands out to catch her balance and ended up hitting David across the chest.

"Sorry," she apologized.

"Don't worry about it," he replied. "You want some help?"

"No, I think I've got it." Next to her, David barely needed to shift his weight to keep pace with her. "How come you look like this is easy?" she asked.

"It is. You just have to relax."

Relax? She'd never felt more uptight in her life. Over there was Henry Belltown, an ex-boyfriend. He was married now, as was Robert Sanders. She dropped her gaze, afraid of recognizing anyone else.

About halfway around the rink, it got a little easier. She made herself concentrate on how sweet the cold air smelled and the feel of her skates cutting across the ice. Her spirits lifted. None of the skaters they passed gave them anything but a friendly wave.

"You know, we should probably hold hands."

"Right." Her heart gave a little jump as her fingers inside her cashmere glove wove together with his leather-encased hands. It seemed all at once masculine and feminine—her softness to his strength—and it made her tingle.

They skated more closely together. He could have skated faster without her, but she appreciated the careful way he guided her around the rink. Glancing sideways at him, she started to thank him then found herself admiring the way the sunlight brought out the highlights in his dark hair and the clean, strong line of his jaw.

He caught her staring at him. She looked away so fast that it threw her off step. The blades of the skates clapped sharply against each other. David laughed a little. "You trying to trip me?"

"You're onto me," Millie deadpanned. "I was hoping to knock the wind out of you and then have my way with you in front of the members of your church. That way everyone will know I'm serious about you."

He shot her an amused glance. "I'm sure they'd enjoy that," he said. "Particularly Reverend Stockman." He gestured to the tall white-haired man in an oversized black wool coat who was skating a short distance ahead of them.

Millie groaned.

"He's a good guy—but maybe we should say hello to him," David suggested innocently, "before you tackle me. It'll make a better impression."

"David!" She hit his arm lightly with her free hand. "I was joking about tackling you, and I don't want to talk to Reverend Stockman."

"Why not?"

"Because," Millie murmured, unsure how to express what she felt. She measured the distance between them. It wouldn't be long before they intercepted the man. "I just don't want a lecture about Jesus, going to church, or the salvation of my immortal soul."

"He wouldn't do that," David stated firmly then shot her a sideways grin. "At least not on your first meeting."

Millie rolled her eyes. "I'll save him the lecture. Church isn't for everyone."

"You don't know that until you try it."

She gave him a hard sideways look. "I have tried it. My father used to be an usher in the church, remember? And it didn't stop him from walking out on my mother and me."

David's body swayed gently with the movement of his skates. "He might have done something wrong, but it doesn't mean you and your mom should stay away from church."

"You have no idea what it was like after my father left. People talked. It was awful."

"People can be pretty thoughtless, but I'd hate to see you give up on the idea of God and a church family."

"I don't want to talk about it anymore. And I really don't want to talk to Reverend Stockman. Whenever he comes in the café, he always looks at me as if he can see everything I've ever done wrong my entire life."

"He looks at everyone that way," David said dryly. "I think it's an occupational hazard."

Millie refused to see the humor in his words. They had almost caught up with the reverend. "Please."

He gave her a funny look but then cut across the ice and away from the reverend.

"Thank you."

"You're welcome."

She could have dropped it, but something in her felt compelled to add, "It'd hurt Eva if I went to church. It'd reopen everything for her. I can't do that."

"Sometimes the only way to heal something is to talk about it. Pastor Chris—he was the senior pastor back at my church in California—helped me a lot after Lisa died. I didn't want to talk about her, but he prayed with me and helped me understand that it was okay to be angry at God—the important thing was to talk to Him."

"I'm not saying that I don't believe in God, David. To me, God and church are two different things." She lurched a little as they hit a rough patch of ice, and he steadied her arm.

"So you believe in God?"

"Of course," Millie said. "I believe in heaven and hell and all the rest. I just don't believe in going to church." She didn't want to explain that she also felt that while God existed, she didn't think He loved her or wanted her to talk to Him. Like her father, God had long ago moved on to other people, other places. As a child, she'd learned to depend on herself. She didn't want to go to church with all its false hopes and phony promises.

"And Jesus—do you accept Him as God's one and only Son?"

Millie shot him an angry look. "Look—I avoided Reverend Stockman just to avoid a conversation like this. Don't try to save me, David." She skated a little faster, clipping the steel blade of her skate's edge against his in the process.

"I'm just trying to understand what you believe." David gripped her arm and used his body weight as a drag to slow them down. "Faith is important to me. I'm not judging you. I want to know."

She struggled against his arm and then against his weight slowing them down. Then she steeled herself to finish the conversation. Slowing to a stop, she turned to face him. The wind sliced across her cheeks, and she drew her hand through the hair that had fallen free and angled across her face. "It feels like you are—judging me."

His eyes were kind but steady, bright blue in the cold air. "I'm sorry it feels like that. But I'm not. I promise."

She crossed her arms. "Why does it matter what I believe?"

A group of kids whizzed by them so closely that Millie held her breath until they were safely past.

"It matters," David said when they were alone again, "because you matter." His gaze peered intently into hers. "I know we have a plan, so don't take this the wrong way, but the more I get to know you, the more I like you—as a friend of course."

She lifted her chin. "You mean the more you want to do your Christian duty and save me, right?"

"If you believe in Jesus, you're already saved," he said. "I just want to encourage you to give church another try."

Fat chance, Millie thought and shifted her weight. "It's just not for me. I'm sorry."

David nodded as if he understood, but his gaze stayed steady on hers. "I'm not going to tell you that everyone who goes to church is perfect and always does the right thing—but I will tell you that for me, after Lisa died, our church family were the ones who stepped in and helped. For weeks, maybe longer, I don't remember, I'd come home and someone would have cut my grass or left a basket with cookies on my doorstep. People invited Bart over for playdates or just called to ask how I was doing." He paused. "One of Lisa's friends—Lynn—bred English bulldogs, and she just showed up one Saturday morning with a little brindle puppy. It was the last thing I needed, but Bart's face—it lit up like a Christmas tree. The dog licked his face, wiggled all over, and then peed on him. Bart thought that was hilarious, and suddenly we were all laughing." He paused. "It didn't mean we missed Lisa less, but we felt loved. It helped. That's what a church family does."

His expression softened. "Just think about coming to church, okay?"

Millie shrugged and looked away from the hopeful look in his eyes. She didn't have the heart to tell him that the probability of changing her mind was low. More troubling to her was the snapshots that had formed in her mind of David's life in California, the obvious love he had for Lisa—perfect Lisa, whom Millie disliked without even meeting and for no good reason.

And why shouldn't David still love Lisa? Lisa was probably as beautiful on the inside as she'd been on the outside. Millie would probably look like a giant next to her, and there'd never been any question that God loved Lisa—that He'd chosen Lisa to be on His team. David had loved her deeply. She'd seen it in his eyes.

Millie clenched her fists. The truth was that she didn't dislike perfect Lisa as much as she was jealous of her. She drew an angry line across the ice with the blade of her skate. She didn't want to imagine David loving another woman.

Chapter 21

The mood had changed. Maybe David shouldn't have gone on and on about the church family and how good they'd been to him and Lisa. He'd seen something in Millie's face close down, and yet he'd kept talking, hoping that she'd reconsider her position on going to church. If she would only try it, she'd see for herself how it could be a source of comfort and strength.

The wind whipped off the ice. Millie shivered and hugged her arms around herself. She looked unhappy standing there, and yet he couldn't regret what he'd said. She believed in God—that was a good start. They'd continue the conversation later, and he would talk less, listen more, and hopefully address her fears.

"You want to get some hot chocolate?" he asked.

"Yeah, I'm ready for a break."

He steadied her by the elbow—not that she needed it, but it felt good to hold on to her as they wobbled off the ice, unlaced their skates, and put on their boots. At the concession hut, he bought them both cups of hot chocolate and then led her to one of the burning oil drums near the shoreline.

"Just as watered-down and lukewarm as it was fifteen years ago," David commented as they stood in the warmth of the flames and watched the parade of skaters glide past them.

"I'd be disappointed if it wasn't," Millie said. "It's part of the whole Gunderson Park experience."

David laughed. She was right. One sip and he was instantly transported to a nerdy, short teenager who played ice hockey every winter on the town's least competitive team. The games they'd won could be counted on one hand, but he'd had fun and made some good friends.

He remembered seeing Millie skating. She'd been tall and graceful and always surrounded by friends. He'd watched her because he couldn't help it and wished he was the one skating next to her. He sipped the hot chocolate and recognized the irony of the situation. Here they were, all these years later, skating together, and she was still just as unattainable to him.

"I was reading in the paper the other day about a new play opening up in Sioux City. It's a murder mystery, and the audience gets to vote on the ending. I was thinking maybe you'd like to go with me."

Millie's face lit up. "I'd love to," she said. "I know exactly what play you're talking about. It's about a woman who gets poisoned, and there's like five suspects and a twist. It's supposed to be fabulous."

"How about we make it a Valentine's Day date?"

Her eyebrows shot up. "Oh right—I almost forgot Valentine's Day is a week from Saturday. Get ready for something big and chocolaty."

David smiled. "You think everyone is ready for us to move on to the chocolate stage in our relationship?" He was partially teasing. He hadn't forgotten that in Millie's world food spoke a language of its own. Making him something chocolate had implications.

"They'll not only accept it," she said, "but they'll expect it. How do you feel about cake? Or are you a brownies kind of guy?"

"I'm not quite sure," David said, pretending to be serious and working to keep from smiling. "But if you made me both, I'm sure I could decide."

Her nose crinkled as she looked up at him. "You know, if I make you two desserts, people might jump to conclusions."

"What kind of conclusions?"

"That I'm chasing you."

David laughed. "I like that idea," he said and leaned even closer to her. "Now I definitely want the two desserts."

"Okay," Millie said, and her eyes were so clear and bright he could see the speckles of gray in her irises. "But be prepared—the aunts are going to razz the both of us about this."

She sipped her hot chocolate, and his gaze lingered on her lips. They were slightly more red than pink and invitingly full. His gaze lingered. He imagined himself moving closer, lowering his head, and kissing her. Immediately the heat burned inside him, as if he were already doing this.

Suddenly Millie frowned a little, and a small furrow appeared between her brows. "Uh-oh. Cynthia Shively, twelve o'clock. I think she sees us."

He started to glance over his shoulder, but Millie's hand on his arm stopped him just in time. "Don't look at her," Millie whispered. "Look at me."

He braced himself, dreading the encounter and wishing Cynthia would just go away so he could admire Millie's lips a little more.

"David, you're clenching your jaw, and you've stopped blinking. We're supposed to be having fun. Pretend to steal my hat or something."

When David did, Millie's curly hair tumbled to her shoulders. This was the way he liked her hair best, and for a happy moment he almost forgot about Cynthia.

"David," Millie prompted, smiling, "give me my hat."

It was a soft piece of red yarn with a large pom-pom. "Is this one of Aunt Keeker's hats by any chance?"

"It was my Christmas present from her," Millie admitted, standing on her tiptoes to reach for it. "The yarn is infused with the scent of forget-me-not flowers. When I wear this, you're not supposed to think of anyone but me."

David sniffed the hat and inhaled the smallest trace of something floral. He smiled and let himself look long and hard into her eyes. "It's working," he said, and although he'd meant to say it lightly, it didn't come out that way at all.

Millie's big gray eyes locked on his, and for a moment he felt something strong and real pass between them. He jumped when a hand tapped him lightly on the shoulder.

"Hello, stranger," Cynthia said brightly. "Feels like forever since I've seen you!"

He turned slowly and forced a smile. "Hello, Cynthia."

"Hi," Millie added.

Cynthia was dressed all in white—a fur-trimmed white parka, white stretch pants, and a white headband. The only color was her eyes, large and blue. "Well, Millie Hogan." Cynthia's smile widened. "I didn't expect to see you here. This is a wonderful surprise!"

Why wouldn't she expect to see Millie here? He and Millie were dating, and this was a family function. And then he saw the comment for what it was—a dig at Millie for coming to a church function when she wasn't a member. He slipped a protective arm around Millie's waist. "She's a pretty good skater."

"Well, I'm a little rusty," Millie said. "But I haven't taken out anyone yet." She smiled up at David. "Although we've had a couple of close calls."

Cynthia laughed. "I'm sure." She looked at David. "Have you introduced her to everyone? I know everyone will want to welcome her—especially Reverend Stockman." Her blue eyes sparkled as if they held a thousand secrets. "He loves meeting new people."

"Actually, I already know Reverend Stockman," Millie said.

"You do?" Cynthia looked at David as if to confirm this was true.

"Of course. My family were members at this church a long time ago."

"I didn't know that," Cynthia said.

"You were probably already at boarding school," David said. "Well, it's been very nice running into you, Cynthia, but Millie and I probably ought to get going."

She nodded. "Of course, but first, I was wondering, Millie, if I could borrow David for a few minutes."

Borrow him? He wasn't a book at the library that could be checked out. He restrained his irritation. "Maybe another time would be better."

"It's okay," Millie said. She flashed an encouraging smile at him and then gave him a quick kiss on the cheek. "Take your time."

It wasn't much of a kiss, but he smelled the very lightest trace of something floral—maybe it was the forget-me-not hat—and then she was gone. His gaze followed the sway of her hips as she walked up the hill.

"So I need your opinion, David," Cynthia was saying. "I'm thinking of taking on some volunteer work with the church."

This was what she needed to get him alone to ask? "That's great," he said.

"Well, it would mean I wouldn't have time to help your mom at the office with your files."

David tried not to grin and refrained from pointing out that she hadn't been hanging around his office in a while. "That's okay."

She frowned. "You say that, but you need someone." She pursed her lips hard, looked away from him, and seemed to wrestle with herself. "I could be that person, if you'd let me."

"We'll be fine," David assured her. "You go ahead and take that volunteering opportunity." He could hardly wait to tell Millie the good news.

"I will," she said. "One more thing—I don't know how to say this, but please be careful." Her voice was barely louder than a whisper. "She isn't one of us."

"You mean Millie?"

Cynthia nodded.

"What do you mean she isn't one of us?"

"You know what I'm saying."

"No, I don't."

She looked him long and hard in the eyes. "The whole church thing. If you aren't raised in a church, the chances that you will attend church as an adult are greatly reduced." Cynthia's eyes were flat and cold. "I didn't make that up, David."

"So what?" he snapped. "Not everybody gets to grow up in a churchgoing family. What are we supposed to do, ostracize those who aren't?" *Just the opposite should happen,* he thought angrily. *Just the opposite.*

"People are talking," she said. "I thought you should know."

"If people are talking, they should be saying how nice it is to see Millie here today—and they should mean it."

"You just don't want to hear the truth."

He planted his hands on his hips and then made himself count to ten. "The truth is that you need to get yourself another dentist."

"David—what?"

"Until you can be nice to Millie, we're done."

"You don't mean that."

"I mean it with every breath in my body," he said. Turning, he left her standing there and began making his way up the hill in the direction Millie had taken. He put his anger into each footstep and felt better as the distance between himself and Cynthia widened. Scanning the wooden plank benches, he searched for Millie's red parka.

She wasn't hard to find—she was in the back row, lacing her skates. All he could see was the fat knot of the yarn ball on top of her red hat. Something in him came alive, and he realized suddenly that he was no longer dating Millie because it buffered him from Cynthia or any other woman. He liked her for who she was—and those feelings were growing stronger. His step quickened. Despite Cynthia's warning, he felt strongly that being with Millie was a good thing, that he had not so much turned away from his faith as he had trusted it.

"Hey," he said and slid onto the bench next to her.

She looked up and smiled. "Hey, you survived the whole one-on-one with Cynthia."

"You had doubts?"

"Only a few," she said.

Chapter 22

Is there any more duct tape?" Eva asked from her spot at the hull of the box sled. "I'm still not satisfied with the strength of the hull. Racing can get ugly. People will ram you on purpose, Bart."

They were inside David's garage working on the sled, just as they'd done every night that week.

Millie handed her mother a thick roll of the silver tape then returned to outlining the winged french fries on the side of the sled. Next to her, David was cutting out a crinkle-cut piece of cardboard, which would serve as a rudder. Finishing the final cut, he held it up for Eva's inspection.

"Perfect," she declared. "But we'll want it double strength, so cut two. When you're finished, we'll wrap the pieces together with more duct tape."

"Maybe we should test to see if it'll fit in the hole first," Bart suggested.

He took the rudder from his father's hands. Crawling into the sled, he threaded it through a narrow slit in the cardboard right above where his head would be. "Cool," he said. "How does it look?"

"Perfect," David said. "Try moving it back and forth."

Bart managed to steer the rudder a few inches both ways.

"Now it looks like the sled is wagging its tail," Millie said. "It's a happy sled."

Bart sat up and peered over the edge of the cardboard. "It looks like poop," he said. "Like the sled is pooping a lightning bolt."

"Bart," David said sternly. "Please don't say things like that in public."

Millie giggled, earning her an equally stern look from David.

"I can't help it," Bart said. "And you know you're thinking the same thing."

"It'll look much better when it's painted," Eva promised. "You'll see."

They worked awhile longer, the topics ranging from Eva's advice on how to get the sled to slide faster to Bart's story about the sixth-grade teacher, Mrs. Mills, who had decided someone in class had stinky feet. "She made everyone take off his shoes, and then she smelled them one by one until she found the guy."

"Who was it?" David asked.

"Me," Bart admitted. He let everyone laugh for a moment, and then he said, "I'm only kidding. It was this kid, Roger Blanit."

Millie grinned at Bart. She liked his dry sense of humor and the ease with which he spoke to adults. He wasn't a bit shy, and she supposed part of it was because Bart was an only child. She wondered if, like her, being an only child was making him grow up a lot faster. Millie had only been a little older than Bart was now when Eva started turning to her to unburden herself. Millie remembered feeling extremely adultlike and proud during those discussions.

She also recalled the weight she'd carried. Millie had been her mom's friend, coworker, and at times, even a parent. This had been particularly true in the early stages of Eva's diabetes.

It would be different for Bart though. David was a very different sort of parent than her mother had been. Eva never would have let Millie handle this bully situation by herself. She would have assumed total control.

David's way was better. He was concerned but not hovering. Involved but willing to step back and let Bart help build the sled. David's confidence in Bart would give Bart confidence in himself.

"So, what do you say, Millie? You up for it?"

She jerked a little and studied Eva's face for clues. "Huh?"

"We're finished, and there's still a little time before dinner. The moon's out. And it's a perfect night for it."

Perfect night for what? Millie didn't want to admit she'd been in her own world, dwelling on Eva's shortcomings as a parent. "Do you want to?"

"Of course," Eva said.

"Then yes," Millie agreed.

"Super," her mother said.

Bart cheered, and even David looked pleased. "Let's get our coats on."

"Why?" Millie asked, wondering just how much of the conversation she'd missed and what she'd just agreed to do.

"We're going sledding," her mother answered. "We're going to help Bart practice racing."

The snow crunched under Millie's boots as David led them into the backyard. The temperature had dropped, and the air felt cold and wet against her skin. Her eyes teared as a gust of wind lifted a veil of snow from the ground and whipped it through the air.

Millie wiped her eyes with the edge of her mitten. She felt the deep quiet of the country settling into her bones. Lights twinkled from distant houses. As a child, she remembered walking past houses like these and straining for a glimpse of the families inside. Once she'd seen a father and daughter sitting at a kitchen table. They were bent over a book, and it was obvious he was helping with the girl's homework. Millie had stood for an hour watching them, longing to be that girl.

Beside her, David marched along, dragging the sled behind him. "My parents gave us the sleds for Christmas, but this is the first time I've gotten to try mine out."

"That's because you always say you're too tired, or you have to work, or the snow's too deep to be any good," Bart complained over his shoulder. He was walking next to Eva, who was dragging an aluminum saucer.

"Or you have to do your homework," David added unsympathetically. "Which you still have to do later."

Bart groaned.

"It's okay," Eva assured him. "We'll have plenty of time to get in some runs." She began walking more quickly, and they soon reached a fairly steep slope flanked by thick groves of ponderosa pines. The moonlight illuminated a sparkling blue-white hillside, unbroken except for the places where three large hardwoods had clawed through the surface and a scattering of prickly, waist-high bushes.

"You doing okay, Mom?"

"Just great." A touch of defiance edged into her mother's voice.

"When the *Flying French Fry* is done, we can test run it here," Bart suggested.

"No test runs," her mom stated. "It'll only weaken the structure. You build the sled the best you can, and then you have to have faith that it will be the fastest thing on the hill."

"Slow down, Mom," Millie warned. Her mother was noticeably huffing and puffing. "*You* don't have to be the fastest thing on the hill."

Her mother kept up the brisk pace. Despite her bulk, she climbed gracefully, her movements fluid and strong. Watching, Millie glimpsed a much younger, much more athletic Eva—an Eva that she'd seen in photographs but could not remember.

Moments later they all stood on the crest, breathing the thin, cold air and staring down at the climb they'd just made.

"Okay, Bart, I'm going to make a track now." Her mother placed the flying saucer at the lip of the hill and lowered her bulk into it. The snow crunched as the saucer sank into the snow. "Push," she ordered as the sled stalled.

It took Bart, Millie, and David's combined efforts to get the saucer started. However, once over the edge, the saucer began to slide. It immediately spun around so that Eva was facing backward as she slid down the hill. She began to laugh and shout. "Yell if I'm aiming for a tree!"

They watched her progress. It was slow but steady, and when she reached the bottom, Eva yelled triumphantly up at them. Bart sank to his knees and jumped headfirst onto his sled. Whooping, he pushed off and sailed down the hill. Millie watched him glide straight down, his knees bent toward his back to keep his feet from dragging. The Flexible Flyer moved much faster than her mother's flying saucer, and it wasn't long before he reached the bottom. They watched him jump off the sled and pump a triumphant fist in the air.

Millie gazed at the remaining sled then at David. "You go first. I'll go next time."

"That's silly," David said. "There's room for both of us."

Millie worried her bottom lip. Sled with David? That would mean being close to him, physically holding on to him—actually touching him. She felt her heart jump a little.

"You want the front or the back?" David asked.

It was easier to climb onto the sled than explain why she didn't want to ride with him. Sitting on the wooden slats, she wiggled forward as far as she could and put her feet on the steering bars. David climbed on behind her, and immediately the sled shrank. He moved closer and settled his boots on the outside edges of the steering bar next to hers. His chest pressed hard and solid against her back.

"You ready?"

"Yeah." His arms wrapped around her waist, fitting her against him. She wondered if he could feel the way her heart was pounding. Her head was almost level with his, and she knew if she turned they would be face-to-face. She wouldn't let herself do that, but the possibility of what might happen if she did seemed to crackle in the air between them. Her heart began to pound, and she was breathing faster.

David briefly released her to push with his hands. Their combined weight made the blades stick in the snow, and they had to rock the sled with their bodies to gain the necessary momentum to move forward. Finally, they managed to hop the sled to the lip. They paused. She didn't know why.

Far below, she could see her mother and Bart waiting for them at the bottom. They were small shapes, currently engaging in a snowball fight. Her mother ran behind a tree in an effort to avoid Bart's dead-on aim.

"Millie," he said, and his voice rumbled soft and low-pitched in her ear. "You smell really, really good."

"I baked chocolate muffins this morning," she said. Her voice sounded unfamiliar. She couldn't seem to help herself from leaning a little harder into him.

Start the darn sled, she turned to say, but his face was even closer than she thought. The words were lost as her mouth brushed the cold roughness of his cheek. He jolted briefly as if her touch had stung him, but then his lips lowered, grazing the corner of her mouth. She shifted a little, and on the next brush he found her lips.

Her hands seemed to rise of their own accord to wrap themselves around his neck. His lips moved lightly, unhurried, asking, making her heart beat faster. Her eyes closed. He was going so slowly, agonizingly slowly, and every pass was loosening something tightly wound inside her. Couldn't he feel the ache in her? Didn't he know each second the need got worse and worse?

He pulled her closer and finally deepened the kiss. She nearly groaned with relief and pushed herself more tightly against him. She was falling, tumbling through a dark tunnel, and she couldn't stop herself. But as long as she was holding on to him, it was okay. More than okay—it was as if she was coming alive in a way she never had before. All her senses sharpened, but she wasn't just Millie anymore.

Gripping him more tightly, she kissed him until she was lost to herself and there was only him and the growing realization that she'd been incredibly stupid. She'd thought she'd known what it was like to be kissed, how it felt to lose herself without losing her head, and how to walk away before things got out of hand. But kissing David, Millie understood how wrong she'd been. All these years, and it turned out she knew nothing at all.

Chapter 23

The next morning, Millie gave Mrs. Ellison caffeinated tea by accident then felt guilty when the librarian's hands shook so hard she dropped the change when Millie rang her up on the register. Millie also forgot to add the Tabasco sauce to Jeff Gulden's scrambled eggs and plunked down a jelly donut instead of a Bavarian cream in front of Lou Pinella's plate.

She mistotaled Chief Glugan's bill then snapped when Lillian accused her of daydreaming about David. By ten o'clock she had to flee to the ladies' room to avoid the speculation on the cause of her mental state. Staring into the mirror above the sink, Millie tried to make sense of the woman who gazed back at her—the one who couldn't stop thinking about David. The one who'd made a total fool of herself last night, practically whimpering in his arms for him to kiss her.

Do you really want to let yourself fall for a dentist—a guy who fights tooth decay and gingivitis for a living? The woman in the mirror looked steadily back. *Yes,* the woman said. *I'd follow him anywhere— to the ends of the earth. I'd climb mountains and ford rivers. I'd trek across deserts. I'd sleep in a tent or go hungry. Because when he looks into my eyes, when he kisses me, when I think about him—he's all I want.*

But what if being with him meant going nowhere at all? Would you stay here, in Deer Park, to be with him?

I don't know, Millie thought and watched the light die in the eyes of her image.

When the pink roses arrived at noon, she read the card then stuffed it in the pocket of her apron. At least a dozen times she picked up the phone to call him then hung up before the call went through.

She was relieved when finally the last customer left for the day. She locked the front door and turned the OPEN sign to CLOSED. As her mother cleaned the grill, Millie put the chairs up and mopped the floor. Aunt Lillian, who was waiting for Eva to finish closing up, had climbed up on a stool to close out the cash register. The sound of the clanking coins jangled Millie's nerves.

"I'm going for a walk," she announced, jerking her parka off its hook.

"That's fine," Eva called back. "Don't forget we're meeting David at six. Lillian can drop me off after we get our hair done."

"Be careful. It's supposed to sleet later," Millie warned. Lillian was known for having a lead foot and liked to joke that her van not only had been modified to accommodate a driver in a wheelchair, but also that its engine had a couple of extra cylinders.

"We're fine. Have a nice walk," Eva said.

Millie grunted a reply and stepped out into the gray afternoon. Stuffing her hands into her pockets, she began walking. She had two hours to herself and needed to figure out what to say to David about the kiss. He would have expectations now. It was always best to deal with these things head-on.

She walked with her head down, not looking where she was going and not particularly caring. It was her thoughts she wanted to get away from.

The distances between the buildings became greater. She kept walking until she found herself in front of the Methodist church, and she realized this had been her destination the entire time.

She studied the white clapboard building with massive oval-shaped double doors and a tall steeple with a bell that still rang each Sunday morning. People who worshipped here probably didn't doubt God like she did. They probably didn't wonder why He helped some people and not others. Why some prayers were answered and others seemed to pass through Him like wind through the trees.

She wondered if inner beauty was something you were either born with or not. If the purity of a soul was decided before birth, like height, hair color, or the shape of a person's lips. If this enabled some people to have faith while others would have doubts.

She thought about the night her father had left—if he had crept into her bedroom and tucked the blankets more tightly around her or whispered that he loved her. Or if maybe he'd stared at her sleeping face and seen something exposed that wasn't visible during the day. If in the stripes of moonlight slanting between the blinds and across her face, he'd seen an ugliness to her features that reflected the imperfections of her soul.

Why did he leave me, God? Was I so unlovable?

She flinched, as if she'd touched the tip of an inner pain so hot and fierce and deep it burned all the way to her soul.

Do You love me, God?

Why should He? She hadn't been to church in years, never read the Bible, and openly challenged Him when she wasn't doubting that He existed at all.

David believed. She was sure of it.

Millie clasped her mittened hands and thought of David with equal parts of longing and fear. Their relationship had come to a turning point, and from the way he'd kissed her, she was pretty sure what he wanted. But what if she opened herself completely to him? What if he turned out to be like her father, and once he knew her—all her faults and all her weaknesses—he couldn't love her? She didn't think she could handle that. You couldn't keep breaking a heart and have any hope left at all. And without hope, without dreams, what was left?

Nothing.

She felt the cold penetrating the warmth of her coat and knew it was time to head back to the café. It'd grown darker, but the light was still more blue than black as she picked her way over the snow-glazed sidewalk. She heard a car on the road behind her, and when it didn't pass, she glanced back over her shoulder and groaned. Karl had a black Ford Ranger truck just like that one. She hunched her shoulders and walked faster. The last thing she wanted right now was to deal with her ex-boyfriend.

The truck pulled alongside her, and the tinted window on the driver's side slid open. "Want a ride?"

Sure enough, Karl sat in the driver's seat. A smile softened his craggy features.

"No thanks." She waved him off.

He paced her a little longer. She tried to ignore him, and in the process paid less attention to her footing. When her boots hit a patch of ice, she slipped and just barely managed to catch her balance. Karl immediately pulled to the curb and got out of the truck. "You okay?"

She crossed her arms tightly around herself. "Yes." He was standing right in front of her, and when she tried to walk around him, he blocked her path.

"Millie," he said gently. "Let me drive you home."

He was a large man, older than her by a few years. He'd always reminded her of a grizzly bear with his thick muscular body, jet-black hair, and large, strong features. The first time they'd kissed, he'd lifted her off the ground and held her suspended as if she weighed nothing at all. She'd felt the strength of his arms and known he'd protect her to his last breath. She remembered that now.

"No thanks." When he didn't move, she added, "Come on, Karl. It's freezing."

"We could go somewhere warmer," Karl suggested. Although he was dressed in nothing more than a thick red flannel shirt and a pair of jeans that looked barely able to contain his muscular legs, he didn't seem cold at all. She remembered looking into the lines fanning out from his eyes and thinking that he wore his age well. She liked that he was older. It made her feel young, girlish—safe. She craved the feel of his arms around her even as she recognized that she didn't love him in the same way he loved her.

"Or not," Millie said.

"You're being silly," Karl stated calmly. "Just because we broke up doesn't mean we can't be friends. Haven't you been getting my notes?"

"The parking tickets?" Millie lifted her chin. "I'm seeing David now."

He looked around and lifted his eyebrows innocently. "I don't see him now."

Millie crossed her arms. The crooked smile on his face was getting to her. It also told her that he still had feelings for her. That with one word they could go back to how it was before. "Shouldn't you be on patrol?"

"Got off at three. What do you say I buy you a steak over at the Blue Moose?"

"Thanks, but I have plans."

"I miss you, Millie. Do you know that? Things didn't work out the way I hoped they would, but I accept that. What bothers me, though, is that you avoid me like the plague."

"Not the plague," Millie replied. "More like chicken pox."

He laughed. "I happen to know you had chicken pox when you were four years old, same as me. I'm not contagious." His voice softened. "Let's have coffee."

She shifted her weight, weighing her answer carefully. She didn't want to lead him on, but part of her wanted to say yes. It was cold. Coffee sounded good, and being around him reminded her that he was a good man. Besides, she'd broken up with him, hurt him, and now that she knew what it was like to care about someone, she realized how hard it must be to stand here now and ask for something as small as coffee, to be reduced to asking for scraps of friendship.

She checked her watch. There was time for a quick cup. "I'd like that," Millie said. She stepped closer to him and held out her hand. "I've been an idiot," she said. "There's no reason we can't be friends."

"Friends," Karl echoed, shaking her hand. The lines in his face seemed deeper, his skin reddened as if scraped by the cold. "Now let's go get you warm."

"I'm due at David's at six."

"I'll have you there in plenty of time." He walked her to his truck and opened the door for her. Offering his arm, he settled her protectively into the interior of the truck. Cranking up the heat, he tuned the radio to a rock station that she liked. She felt herself relax into the leather seats. He kept the conversation light, mostly about mutual friends Hilly and Tom Mengalo who had just bought a new Expedition. The car was a gas hog, Karl said, but with five kids in the family, there wasn't much choice.

Kids had always been part of Karl's picture of the future. She could tell by his tone they still were. She'd been far less enthusiastic about the prospect of motherhood. *"Why have kids when I've got Eva?"* she had joked.

They reached a four-way stop at the same time a taupe-colored Taurus navigated the intersection from the other direction. It wasn't until the cars crossed in the middle of the street that Millie recognized Mrs. Denvers at the driver's wheel. For a split second their eyes met. Millie ducked, but it was too late. Her heart sank at what David's mother must be thinking. For a moment, she thought of asking Karl to turn around or stop the car, but she didn't. The moment flashed past, and the ability to change anything slipped past her.

I'm only having coffee with him, she reminded herself and kept her mouth firmly shut and her eyes on the black strip of road in front of her.

David swung the door open and looked down into the warm brown eyes of Eva Hogan. All afternoon he'd been watching the clock, looking forward to seeing Millie. He wondered if she liked the flowers, if she'd been thinking about their kiss as obsessively as he had.

Eva Hogan stood on his doorstep. A puffy powder-blue coat the shape of a down comforter fell to her ankles. It made her seem almost as wide as she was tall, but when she smiled it was warm enough to take the sting out of the February night. The smile, he realized, was almost exactly like Millie's.

"Come on in," he urged, all the while peering over her shoulder at the empty driveway and wondering why there wasn't a battered-looking red Subaru parked in his driveway. "Where's Millie?"

"On her way," Eva said cheerfully. "Lillian dropped me off. Millie should be here any minute."

He pulled the door wider and motioned Eva inside. "Come on in. Did you get your hair done? It looks very nice."

"Oh." Eva preened, patting the tight white curls. "Thank you."

He took Eva's coat and asked if she wanted something to drink. As he walked to the closet, the down jacket felt bulky and too light in his arms. It wasn't cherry red with the fur trim, and it didn't have the faint smell of cinnamon. He shut the closet door with a deliberate click of the latch.

"Hey, Mrs. Hogan," Bart said, trotting down the steps. "I was surfing online last night and found this neat racing car blog that talks about calculating the slope of the car's hood in order to make it the most aerodynamic. We need to give our sled a 27.333 slope. We're at 34 degrees right now. We can glue another layer of cardboard in the back to raise it up."

"Hold on," Eva said, stepping forward and squeezing Bart's shoulder with affection. "Blog? What's a blog?"

"It's an online journal," Bart explained. "People set up a website where other people can read their journal."

"Why would anyone want other people to read their journal?" Eva's short white curls stayed firmly in place as she shook her head. "In my day, we kept diaries under lock and key and threatened to kill anyone who read them."

"Because it's fun," Bart replied. "You learn all sorts of cool stuff. Lots of kids my age blog." He paused to shoot David a significant look. "And they're all on Facebook. I've asked my dad, but of course my dad won't let me have my own page."

Eva patted his shoulder. "I don't know what those things are, but a blog sounds awfully close to *The Blob*, which was one of the scariest movies of the 1950s. It looked like a huge pile of sludge. It crept out of the darkness, slid across the floor, and ate people. I had to sleep with the closet light on for months."

"My dad and I watched *War of the Worlds* together," Bart offered. "The aliens were cool."

"Millie and I watched that, too. We had to hide under our blankets when the scary parts happened."

"You hide under blankets?" Bart asked with equal parts of skepticism and glee in his voice.

"Yes. We pull them over our heads so we can't see," Eva confirmed. "Then we argue about who has to look first to see if it's safe to come out. Usually I win."

David swallowed laughter. He would love to see that. Although he and Bart didn't watch scary movies often, when they did, they were of the man school, which meant that neither admitted to being scared. Other than an occasional involuntary grunt or flinch, both he and Bart made their way through scary movies with their lips tightly sealed and their hands securely wrapped around the respective arms of their chairs.

The stairs creaked under his feet as David led the way into the garage. He flipped a switch, and the room burst into light. The *Flying French Fry* lay on a tarp, its cardboard body looking more than ever like a baked potato wrapped in duct tape.

"It looks fantastic," Eva exclaimed. "Once Millie paints those french fries and stencils the name, it's really going to be a beauty." She tested the hood with her hand.

"What about the slope?" Bart's eyes were sparkling and focused behind his wire-rimmed glasses. "Are we going to bring it up to code?"

"Oh right," Eva said thoughtfully. "What were you saying about the extra cardboard?"

They settled into an easy work rhythm. Eva called out the orders, and David and Bart executed them like well-trained soldiers. Eva and Bart bantered back and forth, both seeming to enjoy the wide generation gap that lay between them. Bart had a good relationship with David's parents, but there was a certain stiffness, a formality that was absent with Eva. She had an unfiltered way of speaking that was relaxing. You never had to wonder what she was thinking about.

David stepped aside to give Eva and Bart more space. Standing beside the frost-etched side windows, he gazed out at the night. Where was Millie? He tried not to worry. The garage door rattled, and a whisper of cold air blew along the concrete.

He wondered if the kiss more than any errand or work at the café explained Millie's absence. He hadn't meant for it to happen, but she'd been scrunched up against him on that sled. His arms had been full of her soft curves, and when she'd turned her head, it'd just happened.

He hadn't kissed anyone since Lisa, but recently he'd been thinking a lot about it. About Millie, he amended. What it would be like. *Was it just me being lonely or ready, or was it something more?* He'd prayed about this, and again, having a relationship with Millie felt right. At the same time, he realized that faith-wise they were in different places. He really wasn't sure what she believed, and she wouldn't talk about it either. While he'd gotten angry at Cynthia and his mother for judging Millie, what if Millie never wanted to explore or deepen her faith? He couldn't see a future for them if this was the case. He needed to talk to her about it tonight if possible. He checked his watch.

It was nearly seven o'clock—an hour past when Millie was due to arrive. He glanced at Eva. "I think we should try calling her."

Eva nodded and rose heavily to her feet. She retrieved her cell from her purse and after squinting at the receiver, punched in some numbers. A moment later, the lines in her face deepened, and her lips tightened. She left a message then hung up.

When they still hadn't heard from Millie by seven thirty, David offered to drive around and look for her. "Make sure she didn't have a flat tire on the way."

"I'm sure she's fine," Eva said. "Maybe there was a problem with the meat delivery and she drove over to pick it up herself. Although why she can't pick up the phone is beyond me."

"Maybe she's in a noncell zone," Bart suggested. "We should go look for her, Dad."

David nodded. They left the supplies on the garage floor, turned off the space heater, and put on their coats.

It was a cold night, probably in the teens, but clear. Only a few flurries spotted the windshield as David wound his way through their neighborhood and onto Route 7. It was the way Millie would have come if she'd headed from town, and he was relieved to see there were no accidents on the side of the road. Eva sat in the front seat next to him, uncharacteristically quiet. He could feel tension radiating off her and tried to put her at ease by turning on the radio to the Christian rock station he preferred. "Maybe she went home and took a nap and is still sleeping."

"And maybe she got kidnapped by aliens," Eva snapped then sighed. "I'm sorry, David. I know you're trying to help."

They backtracked to Dosie Dough's. They saw Millie's Subaru parked in front, but she wasn't inside. "She's got to be somewhere close," David said. But where? Most of the stores around the town center had closed. All he could think of was the movie theater, the

CVS, and the grocery store. He glanced at Eva. "Let's ask around."

To his surprise, however, Eva shook her head. "She said she was going for a walk. I'm sure she just ran into an old friend and lost track of time."

It still didn't explain why she hadn't called. He found himself picturing car accidents, kidnappers, and muggers, although he knew none of these were likely. Wherever she'd gone, she'd gone on foot. "Maybe we should call the police."

"No," Eva said sharply. "I want to go home and phone a few of her friends. If you don't mind, David, I think you and Bart should go back to your place in case she shows up there. Whoever sees her first will call the other."

"You're all right being alone?"

"Oh yeah. It's Millie you need to be worrying about. When she comes home, I'm going to kill her for scaring us like this."

David gave one last peek into the dark interior of the car. "Call me," he said. "No matter how late it is, I'll be up."

Chapter 24

The lights were blazing in the house when Millie pulled into the driveway around ten o'clock. She hurried up the porch steps, but before she could stick her key in the lock, the door swung open. Eva stood in the doorway as if she'd been watching out the window for her to come home. Millie felt a flush of irritation. She wasn't a teenager breaking curfew.

"Mom," she said, unbuttoning her coat. "You didn't have to wait up for me."

Her mother folded her arms and glared at her. "Just where have you been? I've been worried sick all evening."

"Didn't you get my message?"

"What message? I've been calling you every hour on your cell."

Millie hung her coat on the rack. For the first time she noticed the haggard cast to her mother's complexion and the fatigue and worry in her brown eyes. "You didn't get a message from Karl Kauffman?"

"Why would I have gotten a message from Karl Kauffman when I was calling you?" Her mother's brows pushed together. "What's going on?"

"I ran into Karl, and we went out for coffee. We were having a good time, and time sort of got away from us. I tried to call, but my cell died." Millie kicked off her boots. "Karl left you a message. I heard him do it."

"I never got any message," her mother stated firmly. "And I checked my phone a hundred times. I even had David check in case I was doing it wrong." She planted her hands on her hips and stared at Millie unhappily. "Do you know how scared we were when you didn't show up at David's house? Do you know where we've been? Backtracking. Making sure you hadn't driven into a ditch."

Millie shook her head. There had to be some mistake. She'd seen Karl dial the phone, talk into it, and leave his phone number. It occurred to her then that he'd been pretending, purposely dialing the wrong number. "I'm sorry you were worried. I really thought Karl called you."

Her mother looked even more upset. "What in the world were you doing going out with Karl?"

"He needed to talk to me, Mom. I felt like I owed him." She had a quick flash of Karl's craggy face softened in the dim lights of the bar. "You don't look happy," he said. "Let's see what we can do to fix that." She hadn't protested when he'd drawn her onto the dance floor.

"I'm sure he wanted to *talk*." Her mother snorted in disgust. "All this time we've been worrying, and you were out gallivanting with Karl Kauffman?"

"Coffee, Mom," Millie said tightly. She bit her lip to keep herself from telling Eva to back off. It wasn't any of her mother's business whom she saw or what she did. Yet here she was, having to justify her actions.

Her mother shook her head and walked back toward the kitchen. "I've got to call David and let him know you're safe. He was worried, Millie. We all were. I don't know what was so important that you had to stay out until ten o'clock."

Millie stiffened. Another rush of anger burned through her. "Oh for Pete's sake, Mom, Letterman isn't even on yet."

"The point is that you stood up David and Bart. I thought I raised you better than that." She picked up the cordless phone, grimaced, and then cocked her arm as if she might hurl the receiver against the wall. "Why is it that every time something good starts to happen in your life, Millie, you sabotage it?" She lowered her arm and tried to punch numbers, but her hand was shaking, and she slammed the phone back into the cradle. "I can't stand it, Millie," she said passionately. "I just can't stand it."

"Stand what?" Millie snapped. "I had coffee with an old friend who wanted to talk. What's the big deal?"

But it was a big deal, and she knew it. She could give herself a hundred reasons for what she'd done, and it wouldn't change the basic fact that she'd messed up. She knew it. She didn't need her mother throwing it in her face.

Her mother pointed her finger at her. "David is the best thing that's happened to you in a long time. You're a fool if you let him go."

"Stop pointing at me." Millie dug her fingernails into the palm of her hands as she remembered the strength of Karl's arms holding her as they danced. She'd flirted with him, gave him her best smile, laughed at his jokes. For a couple of hours, she'd hid herself in the safety of Karl's arms. With Karl she didn't have to think too much or talk too much or feel too much. He never saw past the Millie she gave him.

"You call that man right now and apologize."

She had intended to do just that but wasn't about to admit it to her mother. "Have you checked your blood sugar lately?" It was a comment on her mother's behavior more than her health, and they both knew it.

Her mother's face turned dark red, and her arm sliced the air. "My blood sugar has nothing to do with what's going on. And I've had it up to here with you asking that." Her gesture accidentally knocked over a glass of water, which crashed to the ground and shattered into pieces. Millie started to clean up but then stopped. She was sick of cleaning up her mother's messes. She turned to leave, but Eva grabbed her arm.

"I married a man who spent his life looking out the window and wishing he were somewhere else. Nothing made him happy. All he could think about was what he was missing in a place that probably only existed in his imagination." Her chin quivered, but her gaze was steady on Millie. "I see the same look in your eyes, and it scares me to death. Be honest, Millie. You're planning to break up with David, aren't you?"

"If we're being honest," Millie snapped, "then maybe you should admit why you really want me to settle down in Deer Park with David. It's for your sake, not mine."

Her mother's head jerked as if Millie had struck her. "How can you say that? How *dare* you say that?"

There were tears in her mother's eyes, but Millie was too angry to back down. All the hurt and resentment had been bottled up for too long. "I say it because it's true." Her voice rose. "Tell me you've never used your health as a way to get me to stay in Deer Park."

"I most certainly did not," Eva shouted. "You're the one always harping on the diabetes. It's *my* health. *My* decision. I've never wanted to put that on you."

"But you have," Millie snapped. "You do. If I don't bug you about checking your levels or taking your medicine, you forget."

"So what? That's *my* business."

"And I'm what? Supposed to step over your unconscious body on my way to the car?" Millie heard her voice get shrill but couldn't seem to help herself. "You think I can just stand there and watch you kill yourself?"

A range of emotions washed across her mother's face—anger, fear, then simple resignation. In just those few short sentences, she seemed to shrink before Millie's eyes, aging almost visibly.

"Maybe I've been selfish," she admitted at last, "wanting you settled here in Deer Park. But what I've done for you, Millie, has always been done out of love. Your grandmother raised me by herself, and I've raised you by myself. Two generations of single parenting is enough. I want better for you."

Millie had heard this statement more times than she could count. "Mom," she said sharply. "Don't."

"Children are your guarantee." Her mother stared into Millie's eyes. "I haven't needed a man," she continued, "because I've had you. But when I die, what will you have, Millie?"

Normally Millie would have told her that she wasn't going to die for a very long time, and then she would have hugged her. Tonight the words coming out of her mother's mouth sounded like fingernails on a chalkboard. Her nerves jangled—they had since the moment when she'd realized she wasn't with Karl for his sake, but her own—to make her forget about David. But no matter how hard Karl made her laugh or how tightly he held her when they danced, it was David's voice she wanted to hear. David's arms she wanted to feel around her. She kicked a broken piece of glass and watched it skate across the linoleum.

"What am I supposed to say, Mom? That I'll live my life the way you want so you can die happy? I can't do that."

"No, you ninny." Her mother's voice rose in frustration. "You're supposed to *learn* from my mistakes. You're supposed to do *better* than I have." She scowled fiercely. "You're not supposed to throw your life away."

Millie felt a rush of hurt. She had dreams, but her mother dismissed them, just as she dismissed the idea that Millie had any talent other than waitressing. "Maybe someday I'll have an amazing career. You'll turn on the television to the Food Network and there I'll be on my own show—*Millie's Magnificent Meals* or *Marvelous Menus with Millie Hogan.*"

Her mother rolled her eyes toward the ceiling. "If you really believe that, then God help you," she said. "Because I can't."

For once, would it kill Eva to see things as Millie did? Would it be so hard just to say, "You'd be fantastic on a cooking show, Millie." Instead, her mother looked at her as if she pitied Millie for wanting something so far beyond her reach. Millie's heart pounded, but she couldn't tell if it was from rage or hurt. It didn't matter.

"You think I'm wasting my life dreaming about something that isn't going to happen. What about you?" Millie felt herself growing taller and taller until she seemed to tower over her mother. "Do you honestly think Dad is going to come back?"

Eva drew in a short, quick breath as if the mention of Millie's father had cut her to the bone. For a moment she just looked at Millie, and then she widened her stance and placed her hands on her hips. "I wouldn't take him back if he came crawling on his hands and knees." Her chin trembled, and she paused to steady herself. "The day he comes back is the day I take a skillet to his head."

Millie hadn't come this far to back down. "You've never dated since he left. You haven't changed anything in the house—if something breaks, you replace it with something that looks exactly like the one you had." She couldn't seem to stop herself. "And you overeat because you miss him."

"That is just hogwash." Her mother was breathing heavily, and her cheeks were flushed. "I eat because food tastes good, and I'm not going to let diabetes or anything else steal that joy from me." She pointed her finger at Millie. "I've made a good life for us here, and if you weren't so incredibly dense, you would see that. You wouldn't be so quick to throw it all away." She strode purposefully past Millie. "I'm going to bed." She glanced over her shoulder. "You call David. Tell him whatever you like, but remember there's a child inv—" The rest of her sentence was lost as her foot slipped in the puddle of water on the tile floor.

Millie jumped forward but couldn't catch her mother, who fell to the floor with a small cry and sickening thump. Kneeling, she leaned over her. "Mom!"

Her mother lay on her side, moaning.

"Mom!" Millie bent over her frantically, checking for injury. "Where does it hurt?"

Her mother moaned even louder, the deep guttural sounds coming faster and louder.

Dear, God, Millie thought, fighting panic. *She's broken something.* "Hold still, Mom. Everything'll be okay."

She didn't remember rising from the floor, but then the phone was in her hand. With hands that trembled so badly she could barely hold the receiver, she dialed 911.

Chapter 25

At ten o'clock there still was no word about Millie. David stopped pacing and paused in front of the kitchen window. Through the pitch darkness, he could make out the towering shapes of the trees and the lights of a neighbor's house. He didn't like waiting, and he didn't like feeling helpless. Ironically, it was precisely the combination of these two elements that reminded him there were a lot of things he couldn't control. He closed his eyes and prayed.

"Dad?"

David turned around. Bart was standing a few feet from him, and somehow he looked younger and more vulnerable as if each hour of the night had stripped a year from his son's face. "Hey, buddy. You finish your homework?" As if either of them cared.

"Yeah. It was stupid." He paused. "You hear anything?"

"No." Almost involuntarily David glanced at the telephone and resisted the urge to pick up the receiver, if only to hear the dial tone. "You should probably start getting ready for bed."

"I'm not tired," Bart stated.

"It's a school night," David reminded him.

"I want to stay up. I want to wait with you—make sure she's okay."

"You don't have to do that," David said. "I'm sure Millie's fine."

"What if something bad happened to her? Maybe someone kidnapped her."

David crossed the space between them to tousle Bart's hair. "Nobody in the history of Deer Park has ever gotten kidnapped. More likely she ran into an old friend and lost track of time."

Bart shook his head. "I don't think so. And I don't think you do either." He met David's gaze firmly, and suddenly Bart didn't seem so much like a little kid. "I'm not going to bed."

David considered enforcing his parental authority then realized he wasn't up for an argument. "Eleven, but no later."

Bart glanced at the clock and then nodded.

"How about some coffee for me and some hot chocolate for you?"

Bart shrugged. Although David felt the same ambivalence, it was an action. Neither of them spoke as David turned on the kettle, set out two mugs, and emptied cocoa mix into one and instant coffee into the other. There was something comforting about the presence of his son, and David found himself grateful that Bart had wanted to wait with him.

"Dad?"

He looked up from pouring the hot water.

"I know you weren't the person who spied on me."

"What?"

"Aris broke into my computer, not you."

David set the mug of hot chocolate in front of his son. "What makes you say that?" He poured himself a cup of coffee and anticipated Bart's response with a small amount of smugness— *because you trust me completely.*

Bart scooped a teaspoon full of marshmallows off the top of the hot chocolate. "Because Aris asked to borrow my cell, and I caught her checking my messages. I started thinking about how she's home more than you, and then it all made sense."

David groaned. "I'll talk to her again about snooping. I'm sorry, Bart. I know she loves you and is trying to help."

"I know." He stared into his hot cocoa. "I'm sorry I blamed you."

"It's okay." David wished his son would look at him. "You know you can tell me anything, right?"

"Yeah," Bart agreed, but his voice lacked conviction.

"I'm serious. You could have told me about the bullying. I would have listened."

Bart chased the melting marshmallows around the surface of the hot chocolate. "You were really sad in California, Dad, and then we came here and that woman started stalking you, and you got even more unhappy. You said if you had to handle one more problem you'd lose your mind."

David couldn't remember saying that, but it did sound a little like him. "I didn't mean it."

"And then you met Miss Hogan, and you started getting happy again."

David frowned. "What are you talking about?"

"You laugh more now."

"I do?"

"And you're funnier."

"I am?"

"Except for tonight," Bart pointed out. His gaze cut to the telephone. "Maybe you should call Mrs. Hogan and see if she's heard from her."

"In a minute," David agreed, registering that the leap from his improved parenting skills to the whereabouts of Millie had been a short one. "You like Miss Hogan, don't you?" What he was asking but couldn't bring himself to voice outright was whether it hurt

Bart to see him with another woman. If it was okay for his dad to like someone—to be with someone other than Lisa. He wanted permission, and yet he didn't want the giving of it to be another weight for his son to carry. He sipped his coffee with a casualness he didn't feel.

"She's funny," Bart said. "So is her mom. I like it when they pretend to argue."

"So you like Millie, I mean, Miss Hogan." He was pressing but couldn't seem to help himself. His gaze dropped to the contents of his mug in case the answer he wanted was obvious in his eyes. It occurred to him that now might be a good time to talk about dating relationships. How fragile they could be. How it didn't always work out. He realized, though, that he would be saying this for his own benefit, not Bart's.

He looked up. Bart shrugged. "She's cool," he said.

Cool was good. Maybe cool wasn't the answer he'd hoped for, but it was a good start. He drew a breath then folded his hands around the warm curve of his mug. Across from him, Bart copied his pose right down to the slight hunch of his shoulders. When their gazes met, David was surprised by the quiet strength reflected in his son's blue eyes. Despite his worry over Millie, he felt tremendous pride. He saw himself getting old and Bart gaining everything that David would lose as he aged. It was almost as if they each stood on one side of a scale that would always balance. He thought how God made the world like that and how right it was.

And then the telephone rang.

When David walked into Eva's hospital room, Millie nearly cried aloud in relief. His eyes locked onto hers, and she felt something inside crumble. She walked straight into his arms. All the tears she'd been struggling to hold back began to slide down her cheeks.

From the bed, her mother said, "Oh for heaven's sake. I'm not dead, you know. Where's the chocolate?"

David chuckled, and his arms remained tightly around Millie. "I'm a brave man, Eva, but not so brave that I'd bring you candy while Millie was around."

"Darn right," Millie confirmed, surreptitiously wiping her eyes before she let her mother see her face. "He'd end up in the bed next to yours, and you'd have matching broken bones."

Releasing Millie, David walked over to her mom's bed and kissed her cheek. "You don't look too bad, Eva," David commented, "for a woman with a broken hip."

"Thanks."

"What'd the doctor say?" David asked.

"Which one?" Eva shifted then grimaced. "Had a whole parade of them come through. Looked at me as if I were already lying on the autopsy table."

It wasn't true. While there had been visits from the attending doctor, the radiologist, and the anesthesiologist, all of them had been kind and respectful. Her mom was simply performing again, trying to make the whole situation seem funny so David would forget the reason that her mother was there in the first place.

"They need to screw her hip together," Millie explained. "She's scheduled for surgery at 8:00 a.m. tomorrow morning."

"Is it Dr. Irwin?" David asked. When Millie nodded, he added, "I've heard really good things about him. He'll fix you up, Eva."

"I'm more worried about Millie." Her voice was losing its normal vitality, and she seemed to gather herself with effort. "Would you please take her home? She looks like someone dug her out of the ground and propped her up."

"Thank you for that flattering observation," Millie said, "but I'm staying here tonight."

"Stubborn as a mule," her mother said, but her voice was hardly more than a mumble. "David, please make her go home."

"Just stop talking and rest." Millie locked eyes with her mom. She saw the deep weariness and the pain barely masked by the painkillers.

"How about a quick cup of coffee?" David asked Millie then turned back to Eva. "Why don't you rest for a moment? I'll take care of Millie."

Millie started to protest then saw the relief in her mother's eyes. She realized that if left alone, Eva would stop performing for everyone. She might even sleep a little while.

As they wound their way through the maze of corridors, Millie thanked David for coming. "I know it's late," she said.

"I know, but I wanted to make sure you both were okay."

They weren't—although Millie said they were. She was lost. Not only in the physical maze of the buildings, but also in the flow chart of decisions about her mother's care. Her mother had deferred almost every decision to her. All Eva wanted, she'd said, was to go home. "Too bad I didn't break a leg," she'd muttered when the X-ray results returned. "They could just cut it off then." The radiologist had laughed politely, but Millie had felt a crushing weight of guilt and worry settle over her shoulders as she directed her mother to sign one form after another.

In the cafeteria, as Millie was sipping hot coffee that tasted as if it'd been made out of ash, it occurred to her that it was after eleven and David had arrived alone. "Where's Bart?"

"Home with Aris. He wanted to come, but we figured they wouldn't let him upstairs. I got in with my medical credentials. But he'll be worried. I need to call him pretty soon." His voice softened. "What happened?"

Millie peeled an edge of the Styrofoam coffee cup. The memory of the accident was so fresh she couldn't speak for a moment, and she focused on ripping the cup until the liquid threatened to spill. Even then it felt like her throat was in a vise. "My mother and I were arguing, and she knocked over a glass of water. Both of us were too busy being mad at each other to clean it up. I said some things I'm not proud of, and then my mother started to storm out of the room and slipped on the wet floor." Millie's throat closed up. She'd never forget the sickening thud her mother made as she hit the tile floor. "It was totally my fault."

"It was an accident, and thankfully a broken hip can be fixed."

"I hope so." She continued peeling the Styrofoam and could not look directly at him. He didn't ask what they'd been fighting about or where she'd been earlier in the evening, and she was grateful for that. She owed him explanations for both, but she couldn't bring herself to tell him—not now. If she had to handle one more thing, she'd break into a million pieces, just like that glass that had shattered on the kitchen floor. *Later,* she promised herself. *Later.*

David covered her hand to stop her from mutilating the cup. "This is a good hospital, and they're going to give her the best care possible. There is one thing we can do for her though."

Millie looked up. "There is?"

"We can pray for her."

"Right now? Here?" Millie didn't like the sudden panic that shot through her. "I wouldn't begin to know what to say."

"That's okay. I'll do it for us."

Millie looked around uncomfortably as David reached for her hands. The cafeteria was pretty empty, but the lady at the cash register was in direct view—and so was that older man and what had to be his son and those doctors seated at nearby tables. She tried to tell herself that nobody would think anything of two people sipping coffee and praying, but she couldn't get her mother's warning out of her head. *"Be careful of people who lift their hands to the sky in public and every other word out of their mouth is 'Praise God this. Praise God that,' "* Eva had said. *"They hide behind religion, Millie. They hide their true ugliness and say and do horrible things. Trust me, Millie, I learned this the hard way."*

She felt the warmth of David's hands penetrating her icy fingers and wondered if he could feel her fear.

"Heavenly Father," David began, "we thank You for the doctors and nurses and all the people tonight who helped Eva Hogan. We ask that You lay Your healing hand on her and see her safely through her surgery and recovery. Please, Father, restore her to full health and let her know that You heal her through Your love and Your desire for her to know that love."

For a moment, Millie felt a small light struggling to penetrate the guilt and worry that clouded her thoughts and actions. As David continued to pray, she found herself leaning forward, absorbing every word, and feeling a small amount of comfort spread through her. Even as she held tightly to his hands, something inside whispered to keep up her guard. A long time ago she and her family had regularly attended church. She had been told that God loved her, that He would always be there for her.

But He hadn't. Neither had her father. Both of them had long since moved on, and Millie was on her own.

David said, "Amen."

Millie looked at her mangled coffee cup. David would be moving on as well when he discovered that she'd stood him up to be with Karl Kauffman. What had she been thinking?

Just for a second she felt a stab of regret and the sense that she had let something precious slip through her fingers. She tried to tell herself that she always would have been David's second choice—he'd said very bluntly that no other woman would ever measure up to his wife. But it didn't help. She would give anything to rewind the clock.

She felt the tears pool, and before she could stop them, they overflowed. Instantly, David came around the side of the table and put his arms around her. "Shhh," he said into her hair. "She's going to be fine."

He didn't realize how selfish she was. Her tears were not only for her mother, but also for herself—for the part of herself that had deliberately messed up and the fear that she'd fail over and over again and never understand why.

"It's okay. Millie, it's okay," David whispered. He said her name like a caress, and she felt it moving through her, gently soothing the aching places. She firmly silenced the voice that wanted to tell him about Karl Kauffman and told herself that truth could wait without going bad, that omission was not the same as lying. She let herself hold on to him and tried to believe it when David whispered that they would get through this together.

Chapter 26

The surgeon operated on her mother at eight o'clock the next morning. For the longest forty-five minutes of her life, Millie sat in a waiting room watching CNN. No matter how she tried to reassure herself, she feared there would be complications to the surgery. Eva might never fully recover, and it would be all Millie's fault.

David sat quietly next to her. He'd picked her up at six that morning and had insisted on waiting with her through the surgery. She shot a sideways glance at him, more grateful for his presence than she knew how to say. "It's taking a long time," she said.

"She's going to be fine," he said for probably the tenth time that morning.

"How do you know?"

"Because I heard her tell the doctor that if he messed up, she'd come back and haunt him."

This was true, but it didn't help. She flipped through a dog-eared magazine and replayed the argument with her mother over and over in her mind. She had been wrong, so wrong to think that going out with Karl would help her feel in control of her life. Instead, more than ever, she felt helpless and vulnerable. She sensed strength from David but was reluctant to lean on him too much. She didn't think she deserved it.

It seemed an eternity before the door between the surgical and waiting area opened and Dr. Irwin stepped into the room. His thin aristocratic features gave away nothing. Suddenly he was standing in front of her, and Millie was on her feet.

"She did great," Dr. Irwin said and smiled. He pulled out an X-ray and pointed to some scary-looking screws implanted in a grainy white shape that was probably her mother's hip. "Do you have any questions?" he concluded.

"Will she set off the alarm when she goes through security at the airport?" It was a stupid, stupid question. It wasn't as if Eva traveled.

Dr. Irwin chuckled. "Possibly."

About an hour later a nurse brought Millie into the recovery room. Eva's body was covered to the chin, and an IV dripped into her arm. Millie cautiously touched her mother's shoulder. "Hey," she said when her mother blinked groggily up at her, "you did it."

Eva murmured something unintelligible. Around lunchtime, they wheeled her to a semiprivate room where she continued to sleep. It was a restless sleep interrupted by bouts of moaning and half sentences. "You have to return it," Eva insisted. "You can't keep it. It's not right!"

Millie caressed her mother's forehead. "It's okay," she said. "You're just dreaming. Everything is okay."

Her mother opened her eyes and looked very clearly into Millie's. "I'm so, so sorry," she said. "I didn't know, Sarah. I swear I didn't know."

Sarah? Who was her mother talking about? Millie leaned forward. "Mom," Millie said gently, "you're in the hospital, and the doctor just finished operating on you."

Her mother blinked. "It hurts, Sarah." She turned her head away. "I hate what he did."

Millie charged to the nurse's station. "My mother is in pain," she told the nurse, who checked Eva's chart and saw that it was time for more pain medication.

When Millie returned to the room, her mother was semi-conscious, twisting her head from side to side, and softly groaning. Leaning over the bed rail, Millie curled her fingers around her mother's. "Shhh, shhhh," she said. "The nurse is coming."

Eva's eyes stayed shut. "Please don't tell anyone."

"Tell anyone what?"

"I'm so sorry. I'll make it up. I promise."

Millie wished the nurse would hurry. "Mom, it's okay," she said. "Everything is going to be fine." A few moments later the nurse walked into the room.

Later, as Eva slept, Millie wondered who her mother had been talking about and why Eva had been apologizing. The only person she could think of was Sarah, the reverend's wife, who rarely came into the café. If Eva spoke of her at all, it was to dismiss the idea of going to church. Obviously the pain medication had confused her mother, and most likely Eva had been talking about someone else. Millie picked up another magazine. She wondered what David was doing right now. She'd told him not to come back after he finished work, but she couldn't help wishing he would.

Hours passed as her mother slept, rousing only when a nurse or doctor came into the room. Dinner came, but Eva managed only a few sips of soup. When Millie finally left to go home, she kissed her mother's pale face. "I'm so sorry," she whispered. "I'm so sorry for what I said."

Eva struggled to open her eyes. She smiled a little then went back to sleep.

Millie stroked back her mom's mop of white bangs. "Night, Mom. I love you, and I'm going to be a better daughter. From now on, things are going to be different." She kissed Eva's forehead. "I promise."

When Millie returned to the hospital the next morning, her mother was awake and eating breakfast. Her hair lay matted, but there was more color in her face, and her eyes were bright and focused.

"The eggs taste like cardboard," Eva complained. "And I've already been seen by two vampires."

"So you're feeling better."

"I'm telling you, Millie, it's a miracle anyone survives a stay in the hospital. They won't let you sleep for more than two minutes—and they've taken enough of my blood to start their own bank."

Millie smiled. For the first time in two days she could breathe again. A complaining Eva was a healing Eva. She settled into the chair next to her mother's bed. "So you're feeling better."

"You should go," her mother said. "Who's running the café?"

"It's closed."

Eva frowned. "Go open it, or people will think I'm dying."

"Shhh, Mom," Millie said. "The café can stay closed another day."

"I don't need a babysitter."

"I know. I want to be here."

Her mother lapsed into silence. The morning passed in a blur of game shows and talk shows. Eva perked up whenever a doctor or nurse came into the room. Almost instantly she would transform herself into a lively entertainer who knew how to make everyone—even the sour-faced physical therapy assistant—laugh. As soon as Eva and Millie were alone again, however, the twinkle in Eva's eye faded and her eyes returned to the television set.

By the end of the day, it was clear that her mother was doing well but would need a few more days in the hospital before she came home. They couldn't afford to keep the café closed—and Eva made it clear she didn't want Millie's company—so the next morning at 3:30 a.m. Millie headed for the café. It was earlier than she and her mother usually arrived, but without Eva, she'd be shorthanded, and Millie intended to do most of the extra work before Lottie arrived.

Flicking on the lights, she glanced around at the tables carrying their load of chairs and the gleaming stainless-steel countertops. Her gaze slid over the walls with the old black-and-white shots of stiff-lipped pioneers, saloon scenes from Deadwood, and prospectors panning for gold in the shallow streams of the Black Hills. As she moved to the kitchen area, she could almost feel people in those photographs watching her reproachfully. It was her fault Eva wasn't there, they said, and Millie was a poor substitute.

She pulled a bread starter out of the refrigerator and set it on the counter to breathe. Retrieving supplies from the pantry, she began adding flour, salt, and sugar to the industrial-sized stainless steel mixing bowl.

As the mixer whirled, she thought of the countless mornings when Eva had driven her crazy with her early morning high spirits. How Millie would stare into the mixing bowl and wish she were in Hollywood studying a script in preparation for a morning audition. How daily she wondered if she would always live in the shadow of her mother's exuberant personality. She thought about the long recovery ahead for Eva and worried about her ability to nurse her mother back to health. The house had no downstairs bedrooms or bathrooms. It would be difficult to accommodate a wheelchair. The thought of bathing her mother, of seeing her naked, scared her.

At the same time, she loved her mom. She knew that now clearer than ever before. Lifting the hook from the dough, Millie resolved to do whatever she needed to take care of her mother.

Millie set the rye dough in greased pans for the first rise. There was still pumpernickel, sourdough, and the baguettes to make. She glanced at the clock, worrying about the time, and wished she'd come earlier.

She was shaping baguettes when there was a knock at the front door. Wiping her hands on her apron, she hurried to the front and peeked out the bay window. Beneath the spill of the porch lights, David and Bart stood in cold morning darkness, rubbing their hands and stamping their feet in the frosty air. Tank was on a leash and sniffing the doormat.

She felt a rush of pleasure as she flung open the door and motioned them inside. "What are you guys doing here? Come in before you freeze to death."

"We figured you could use some help." David unzipped his parka and hung it on the rack next to Millie's. He was wearing glasses instead of his normal contact lenses, and the dark frames emphasized the sheen of compassion in his eyes. She felt her stomach twist. She really didn't deserve a guy like him.

"You really didn't have to do this," Millie said. "Get up so early and come here."

"Yes we did," Bart informed her. "Dad said that. . ." He stopped as his father shot him a sideways look of warning. "I mean, we wanted to help."

"We can stay until eight o'clock," David said. "Then I have to get Bart to school. By then Aris will be here."

"Aris?"

"She wants to help," David explained.

"She's bringing like a hundred cans of tuna fish," Bart said. "So she can make tuna casserole."

"Not a hundred, Bart."

"Well, that's really sweet of her." Millie remembered the night she'd eaten tuna casserole at David's house. The noodles had been soft and plentiful, and the sauce, although bland, had been creamy and dotted with peas. "It can be our special today."

"Great." David looked relieved. "She'll be thrilled."

"It'll be a big help," Millie said. She was suddenly conscious of her messy bun, her face bare of makeup, and the dusting of flour that coated her apron.

"So what can we do?" David prompted.

She thought quickly. "Well, could you build a fire? There's a pile of kindling stacked just outside the back door. And Bart, it'd be great if you would take down the chairs off the tables and top off the salt and pepper shakers."

It wasn't long before the fire roared cheerfully in the hearth and the chairs sat neatly beneath the wooden tables. Millie was pulling loaves of hot honey whole wheat bread out of the oven when David and Bart wandered into the kitchen.

"That smells awesome," Bart declared, coming over to inhale appreciatively as Millie set the pans on the cooling racks.

"Give it a few minutes, and then you can have some."

"Bart, we're here to work, not eat," David pointed out. He was standing in front of the grill, staring in fascination, as if he were studying the controls in the cockpit of a spaceship. "I could fry some bacon."

It was too early, but Millie knew he was itching to take the grill for a test spin. Plus he and Bart could eat it before they left. She pulled a slab of bacon out of the refrigerator. "But before you get started," she said, "you have to wear the official Dosie Dough's apron."

Bart snickered as David tied it over his scrubs.

"You, too, Bart," Millie said, handing him one. It reached his knees. "You both look pretty cute," she said and was rewarded with both Denvers males making faces at her.

As the bacon began to sizzle, Millie carried another sack of whole wheat flour out of the pantry. "Ever make bread before, Bart?"

"No, but I made a volcano erupt in science class with Diet Coke and Mentos."

"If you can do that," Millie agreed, "you can make bread." She smiled at the intense interest that formed in his eyes. David sometimes looked like that when he was thinking hard about something. "We're going to start from scratch and make a starter sponge."

Pulling out a small mixing bowl and measuring cup, she set both on the counter. Next she retrieved some honey and a container of yeast and turned on the hot water faucet. Testing it with her finger, she explained that the temperature should be warm but not scalding in order to activate the yeast, which was a live organism.

"It's going to eat the honey," she explained, "and come to life. It'll look like foam on the surface."

"Cool," Bart exclaimed and bent until he was eye level with the liquid in the measuring cup. "It's doing it!"

Millie laughed, and over the top of Bart's head, she caught David's gaze. He was grinning, and there were grease spots all over his apron and too much smoke coming off the grill. "You might want to turn that down a little," she said. "We don't want to start a grease fire."

"Dad likes to cook on high," Bart offered. "He blew up our grill."

"It was an old grill," David said, poking the bacon. "A very old grill."

"You should have seen it, Miss Hogan. It made a big whooshing noise and then *boom!*" He threw his arms open wide demonstrating.

"We'd had it in storage for a while," David said. "I probably had the propane turned up a little too high when I hit the starter."

"The neighbors called the fire department."

David's eyes crinkled at the corners. "I admit it wasn't my proudest moment."

"Well," Millie said, "usually the fire chief comes in for donuts and coffee. I think we'll be safe."

"He'd better bring the truck," Bart said, eye level with the foaming mixture.

When Millie turned, David was still looking at her. Her heart jumped in her chest. The expression in his eyes sent a wave of heat through her, and she laughed a little self-consciously. "Oh, we'll be fine. We've got plenty of fire extinguishers and good insurance." She slanted David a look. "Not that I think we'll need it."

He shrugged. "Just wait until you taste my bacon. You'll be whistling a different tune."

Millie glanced at the smoke starting to billow up from the grill and smiled. David looked manly and cute in the red apron. She couldn't remember—ever—a man being back in the kitchen working. Now she had two of them. That they were completely clueless about cooking only added to their appeal. She didn't care if David burned the bacon so badly it turned to charcoal. She'd eat it anyway.

Lottie arrived a little before six. She hugged Millie, asked about Eva, and then quietly set about the final prep work for breakfast. By seven o'clock when the first customers came through the doors, the coffee was hot; the cooling racks were full of warm, fresh bread; and a pound of bacon—only slightly singed at the edges—stayed hot beneath the heat lamps.

The aunts were among the first to come inside. Aunt Lillian glided into the café in her electric wheelchair. She was followed by Keeker, who wore an odd green cap that resembled a bathing cap with sequins, and Mimi, who marched inside with Earl Gray securely strapped to her chest in a baby carrier.

They swarmed Millie with hugs. "How's Eva?" "How are you holding up, dear?" "We're here to help you." "Don't you worry about a thing, honey."

"Quiet," Aunt Mimi ordered in the same tone of voice she'd used as a crossing guard. "Millie, honey, we've discussed this thoroughly, and there's going to be no argument. We're going to help you run the café until Eva is back on her feet."

"Before you all get too involved," Lou Pinella said from his seat at the counter, "could Millie please take my order?"

"Later," Mimi snapped at the portly owner of the movie theater. "We have more important things to discuss than bacon and eggs." She turned back to Millie. "Lillian can sit on the stool and work the cash register. Keeker and I will wait tables. You can fill in for Eva in the back."

"Thanks, but I can manage," Millie said, softening her words with a smile. The aunts, while good-hearted, had no idea what they might be getting into. Waitressing was very physical. "Why don't you all have a seat? I'll bring you some tea."

"Don't patronize us." Mimi's mouth puckered, and she drew herself up as tall as her four-foot-eleven frame would allow. "Eva is our dear friend. We're not going to sit back and sip tea when she needs us."

"We've got this, honey," Keeker said more gently. "I'm wearing my luckiest hat today. I was wearing it the night Roland called to tell me that he'd survived Pork Chop Hill—one of the bloodiest battles in the Korean War."

"We want to do this," Lillian insisted. "Please let us."

Millie looked around the room. Most of the tables were full, but she recognized almost everyone. She could almost predict what they would order. She glanced at the hopeful expressions on the aunts' wrinkled faces and sighed. "Okay," she said. "But if things get crazy, come get me." She paused. "And thank you."

"You're welcome, honey," Mimi stated firmly. "Don't worry about anything."

For the next hour, she put her head down and worked. She had taken her mother's place several times before but not in recent years. It felt strange to step into the bustle of the backroom, to see Lottie with her heavy legs braced in front of the sizzling grill, hands flying as she flipped pancakes and scrambled eggs. David was in constant motion, moving between the sink and the warming trays as he both washed dishes and monitored the ready food orders in order to block either Mimi or Keeker from carrying out any heavy trays. Bart bussed tables and was thrilled when someone left him a ten-dollar tip.

With working the ovens and helping prep the final orders, Millie barely had time to do more than thank David and Bart when it was time for them to leave. Aris arrived a short time later with two shopping bags of canned tuna. "There's more in the car," she murmured and set the bags on the counter.

Millie wondered just how much tuna casserole she was planning on making, but she had too many other things on her mind. Lottie wasn't quite as fast on the grill as Eva, and without David and Bart, Millie needed to help Mimi and Keeker serve. She thanked Aris, set her up in the kitchen, and then focused all her energy on running her mother's restaurant. When Eva came back, she would see that Millie had taken good care of everything. She would understand that this was Millie's apology to her, a way of showing her in a way that words couldn't how much she loved her.

All day Millie stored up things to tell Eva—the overwhelming smell of Aris's tuna casserole, the argument Mimi had had with Chief Glugan over the amount of mustard in his sandwich, and how Tank, the plump bulldog, had used a stool to jump onto the counter and eat two pounds of chicken salad before anyone noticed.

She was later than she'd planned, however, and the heels of her boots clicked on the tile floor as she hurried to the bank of elevators in the hospital lobby. The halls were quiet, and the nurses' station was empty as she slipped into her mother's room. The television was playing, but Eva's eyes were closed when Millie reached the bedside. The remains of Eva's dinner sat on an adjustable tray. The meat looked tough, and the potatoes lumpy. Millie resolved to smuggle her in food from the café.

Millie settled herself in the chair beside the bed. She watched her mother's chest rise and fall, the indent her head made in the pillow, and the double strands of plastic bracelets looped around her wrists. One strip identified her by name, and the other said she was diabetic.

The bands didn't say that Eva was a mother or a loyal friend or that she'd once won a box sled race. It didn't say that she celebrated the first snowfall of the year with coconut-iced cupcakes or that she got sad when it rained or that she feared big dogs and hated being helpless.

Millie stared at her, guilt-filled and sad. Despite what the doctor said, Millie feared her mother wouldn't fully heal, wouldn't be the same, and there was nothing Millie could do about it.

Nothing?

She almost dismissed the answer that came into her mind, but she felt a little desperate. She remembered how David's face had softened and recalled the sound of his deep voice praying. His faith had moved her. She knew she wouldn't be able to speak as if God were standing right next to her like David did, but something in her was urging her to try. She glanced uneasily at the doorway. When she was sure she was alone, she leaned her elbows on the hospital bed. Closing her eyes, she folded her hands and whispered the prayer her father had spoken every night. *The Lord is my shepherd. . . .*

Chapter 27

A few days later, Millie left Lottie in charge of the café and drove to the hospital. Her mother had been discharged from the hospital—or "kicked out" as she put it. Eva was in good spirits, high-fiving the nurses as she wheeled past them and inviting everyone within hearing range for free food at Dosie's. The smile on her lips died, however, when she eyed the distance between the wheelchair and the bucket seat in Millie's Subaru. Millie saw the fear in her eyes and stepped forward to help.

It took both of them straining and hauling to get Eva into the car. Afterward, they sat panting, both of them silently contemplating just how much everything had changed.

Millie drove straight to Lillian's apartment. Golden Sage was an assisted-living community. Lillian rented a two-bedroom apartment designed to accommodate a person in a wheelchair. Since there was no first-floor bathroom in Millie's house, Lillian had invited Eva to stay with her.

A nursing aide came every morning to help Lillian bathe and dress. When Millie had explained her mother's situation, the nurse had been happy to help out with Eva.

It had started flurrying earlier that morning, and as Millie stepped out of the car at Aunt Lillian's apartment, a thin layer of snow tinted the back window. Millie had the sudden urge to take her finger and write her name in the flakes, although she knew it would be covered up again within minutes.

"Be careful," Millie warned as she opened the car door. "The ground's getting slippery."

Eva stared at the two-story building ahead of them. Her face was stony. The silence disturbed Millie more than any complaint could have.

"It's not like this is forever," Millie said as she rolled the wheelchair to the passenger's side of the car.

Eva nodded. "I know."

"You'll be back to work before you know it."

"Yes," Eva agreed in a monotone.

Millie frowned. She hated seeing this look of defeat on her mother's face. "If you feel like it, tomorrow afternoon I'll take you over to David's and you can help us work on the sled."

Eva would not meet Millie's gaze. "Let's just go inside now, honey. It's cold out here."

"It's like she's an alien," Millie tried to explain to David a few days later. They were in the kitchen at the café, and as usual he and Bart had come early to help. "She's stopped complaining about everything. She says please and thank you."

"Maybe she's just trying to be a good patient," David suggested, turning a sausage on the grill.

Millie shook her head. She was mixing batter for apple cinnamon pancakes. "I know her," she said. "This isn't her."

"She's just been through a serious trauma. You need to give her time."

"Maybe." Millie put her spoon down and leaned against the counter. "It's just weird. You try to talk to her about anything and she just says she's tired and wants to watch television. She didn't even want to hear about the flowers you sent me for Valentine's Day."

"It could be the pain medication."

"She's watching the Game Show Network," Millie said dryly. "It means she's giving up."

"She might be a little depressed. Is she sleeping?"

"Not well."

"I'd give her a few more days, and if she doesn't improve, I'd call her doctor."

Millie heard herself agree, although part of her felt that David didn't fully understand the problem. Yes, Eva was upset about her hip, but it went deeper than that. Eva had never held back when it came to expressing her opinions to Millie. She spoke her mind, even when Millie wished she wouldn't. They bantered, argued, and talked about everything and anything.

It was all different now. It was as if not only had Eva's hip been broken, but the invisible bridge that had connected them, as well. Her mother didn't ask about Millie's day or anything else. All Eva wanted was her medication and to semidoze on Lillian's couch. Millie feared Eva's apathy was proof of her anger and disappointment in her. Her mother knew that once David found out about Karl Kauffman, he'd break up with her. Eva was effectively putting as much distance between herself and Millie as she could so that when the breakup happened, it wouldn't hurt so much.

"Lillian's also in a wheelchair," David pointed out. "Your mother probably relates to her pretty strongly right now. I wouldn't take it personally."

"It's more than that," Millie said, turning as the oven timer went off and pulling a tray of bread pans out of the oven. *Tell him,* a small voice said.

Immediately another voice in her head piped up. *Does he really have to know? It's not like anything big happened.*

She looked over at David. He had his back to her and was flipping the sizzling sausages. The Dosie's red apron was tied around his waist in a lopsided bow. His blue and gray finely checkered shirt outlined a strong set of shoulders that narrowed to a tapered waist. And beyond his good looks, he was the nicest person she'd ever met. He was the kind of man who understood right from wrong and never wavered, never let himself cross the line. She knew he wasn't perfect but also knew that he never would have done what she had.

How could she admit that she'd been so stupid and thoughtless? How could she make him understand what it felt like to be her?

She slipped another pan out of the oven and put it on the cooling rack. Maybe it was better that he never found out about her and Karl. Maybe she could pretend that it never happened. That would be a lot easier, but then if he ever found out from someone else—like his mother—it would make it much worse. She hesitated. Even if David's mother said something about seeing them together, she could always tell him that they'd gone out for coffee. She could leave out that little part about flirting with Karl— and kissing him. David would believe what she told him.

He never had to know, but what would it do to their relationship? Wouldn't she always have this small lie between them? Would it grow like cancer? She worried her lip, trying to quiet the voice that insisted she simply blurt out the truth.

She wiped her hands on her apron and watched him work. With her history, how could she ever make him believe that she truly regretted what had happened? That it would never happen again?

He turned around and caught her watching. "They're not burning."

Millie shook her head and managed a faint smile. "I know. They smell great." She paused, testing out words. *I'm an idiot. I made a mistake. I'm sorry.* Her throat felt squeezed. She swallowed hard.

"Then what?" He pressed gently.

Millie heard a voice in her head say very clearly that she should tell him the truth. Another voice argued that this wouldn't change anything. It would only hurt him. Confessing would be selfish. The voice said she deserved to carry her own guilt.

"I was just thinking about the meat order. I couldn't remember if I added enough ground beef." She forced a slightly brighter smile and felt the weight of her omission settle a little more heavily on her shoulders. She didn't like herself for lying, but she couldn't tell him either. Her choice had been made, and now she was going to have to live with it.

Later that morning, when Millie returned to the kitchen, she found Aris standing by the menu board. The older woman had her hands on her hips. "Why isn't my tuna casserole on the menu?"

The café had been serving tuna casserole for a week straight. Millie didn't have the heart to tell her that fewer and fewer customers had been ordering it or that an increasing number of feral cats had been attempting to breach the dumpster in the back. "Well," she said, "it is your recipe, only slightly modified."

"I don't think chicken tetrazzini sounds like tuna casserole." Aris's lips pressed together into a coral-colored line.

"We're just substituting chicken for the tuna and spaghetti for egg noodles."

Aris's eyes narrowed suspiciously. "That's it?"

"We'll brown a few onions when we make the sauce, but yeah, that's it."

"What about the peas?"

"We'll add them."

Some of the tension seemed to leave Aris's face. "I suppose we could try it."

Soon both of them were at the worktable chopping onions. Millie's hands flew over the cutting board. Tank lay at her feet. She found the dog's presence comforting.

"You know what the best thing about your mother breaking her hip is?" Aris commented.

"What?"

"Getting to know you," Aris said. "I'm impressed with how you're handling everything."

"Thank you. I couldn't have done it without your help."

A little pink color bloomed in Aris's thin cheeks. She looked up, and her eyes were bright with what looked like approval. "You're a very resourceful person. I like the way you've stepped up and taken over running the café. Your mom would be proud."

Millie warmed under the compliment. "I couldn't have done it without everyone's help. Yours especially," she added. "David's lucky to have you."

"I'm the lucky one," Aris stated firmly. "So. . .when's your birthday?"

"What?"

"I want to get to know you better. I thought your birthday was a good place to start. Were you born in Deer Park?"

Millie scraped the chopped onion to the side and picked up another. The question seemed strange, but she felt a little flattered at the older woman's interest. "Yes, at Saint Vincent's—the same place where my mother had her surgery."

"Date of birth?"

"Oh, not until July."

"July what?"

"The eighteenth."

"What year?"

Millie glanced up. Aris was watching her intently. "I'll save you the math," she said. "I'm thirty-one."

"Were your parents from around here, too?"

"No. They're both from Ohio." Millie sliced the onion in half. She didn't like the questions, but then it occurred to her that she had a few of her own. "How long have you worked for David?"

"Since before Bart was born," Aris stated, and her knife banged the cutting board as she diced the onion. "Tell me a little about your father. What'd you say his name was?"

Millie's hands stilled. "Max Hogan."

"Maxwell?"

"Maximillian, actually." She felt the small splinter of pain press into her heart at the mention of her father's name. She ordered herself not to overreact and calmly pulled out another onion. "What was David's wife like?"

"Lovely," Aris said without hesitation. "Classy and smart. Never heard her say one bad thing about anyone and was always helping others. She organized a mission trip to Africa to give children dental care. Imagine that!"

Millie didn't want to imagine that. How could she compete with someone who practically was a saint? She banged the knife down a little harder than necessary and sent a row of diced onion sailing across the cutting board.

"I want to know more about your father," Aris said. "What year did you say he was born?"

"I didn't," Millie snapped before she could help herself.

Aris retreated into silence, and Millie immediately regretted her sharpness. Aris, after all, was there to help. It was natural she'd be curious about Millie's past. She set down the knife. "Sorry," she said. "I don't like talking about him. The long and short of it is that my father abandoned me and my mother about twenty years ago."

"Did you ever try to find him?"

"No." She wouldn't admit how for years she'd clung to the idea that he would come back. How she'd loved him and hated him until she wasn't sure just what she felt at all. She thought about the night of her senior prom, how she'd pretended that it was her father's face watching her from the mirror in her vanity as she'd sat putting on her makeup. She imagined him looking at her with pride and approval. *"You'll be the prettiest girl there,"* he'd whispered in her mind.

She finished chopping the last onion and pushed it and the memories firmly aside. She no longer cared about or yearned for her father's approval. "As far as I'm concerned, Aris, he's dead."

Aris thankfully let the subject drop. But Millie pushed her sleeves up higher on her arm and poked at the onions with a little more force than was necessary. She was thankful the heat coming off the range could account for the flush in her cheeks.

Wherever her father was, Millie decided he could stay right there. He'd blown his chance to get to know her. Even if he begged her for forgiveness, she'd turn away from him. He would understand then what it felt like to be rejected by the one person who was supposed to love you. One day, she vowed, he'd regret what he'd done. She wasn't that old—it was still possible that she'd do something amazing with her life. One of these audition tapes could still hit, and she could be cast in a commercial or appear on a reality television show or land a role on a soap opera.

Her father could turn on his television, and there'd she be, filling the screen. It might take him a few seconds to recognize her, but he would. The shock would be overwhelming—he'd have to sit down. He'd realize that he made the biggest mistake of his life. He'd try to touch her face on the screen and give himself an electric shock. For once, he'd feel the pain of the years they'd lost together. He'd finally understand that he'd misjudged her, underestimated her potential. He'd be crippled with regret, and she'd be the one who felt nothing at all for him.

Chapter 28

On the way to David's house, Millie was thinking about chicken potpie. She had been running the café for almost two weeks now and was starting to play with the menu a little. As the Subaru purred through the early winter darkness, she went over the recipe in her mind. It was an old one—she'd come across it by accident in an old recipe book bound together with rubber bands. A heart and several stars had been doodled in the margins. Although the ink was faded and nearly illegible, she recognized her mother's writing. Obviously her mother loved this recipe. Millie pictured making it for her: Eva biting into the flaky crust and understanding everything Millie wanted to say but couldn't.

Lost in her thoughts, she almost passed the dark shapes half hidden in the shadows between the streetlights, but slight movement caught her eye. She slowed. Her first thought was that someone had fallen on the icy sidewalk and another person was trying to help. Pulling the car to the side of the road, the car headlights illuminated the situation more clearly, and she realized that one kid was facedown on the sidewalk and another was sitting on top of him. She pressed the car horn and held it there.

The kid sitting on top of the other kid got up and bolted. She glimpsed a shock of yellowish hair and a navy-blue jacket, but mostly her attention was on the kid who'd been tackled. He was just starting to get up, and her heart began to race as she recognized the familiar blue parka with the red trim.

"Bart," she shouted. "Are you okay?"

He didn't answer. She ran over to him, taking in the scrape on his cheek and the slightly dazed look in his eyes. Throwing her arms around him, she pulled him tightly against her. "Are you okay?"

For a moment, he stood still as a statue. His arms stayed at his sides, and the only movement at all was the uneven pull of his breathing. He was trembling a little, and she made soft, soothing sounds and stroked the short, silken hair on the back of his head. She felt him stiffen and remembered a little too late that he didn't like her to hug or touch him, and here she was fussing over him like he was a little boy. She just couldn't seem to stop herself. She was as shaken up by what had happened as he probably was.

His arms lifted. Something inside her sighed and prepared to let go of him. His hands, however, settled lightly, kind of tentatively, around her waist, and then he was hugging her hard. Something in Millie started to break. She held him tighter, silently promising him that everything would be okay. She wouldn't let anyone harm him ever again. She understood for the first time how parents could willingly throw themselves in front of a train if it meant saving their child. She bent her head so that the tip of her chin gently rested on the top of his head and breathed him in. "Oh Bart," she whispered.

It broke the moment. He pulled away and stared at her through eyes that shined a mix of embarrassment, pain, and a slight defiance. "I'm fine."

She looked him over again. There was a scrape on his cheek and a scuff mark on his jacket, but she understood his manhood was on the line. "Yeah," she said. "I can see that." She stepped back from him and assumed a brisk manner, as if she hadn't just found him helpless and flattened by a much bigger kid.

"He caught me by surprise," Bart added, straightening his glasses and then tentatively touching his cheek.

"Cowards do that," Millie said, longing to soothe away the red mark on his face but knowing better than to try. "They sneak attack you from behind. Not much anyone can do about that." She watched relief form in Bart's eyes. "He was a lot bigger than you, too, Bart."

The relief faded, and Bart scowled. "I would have been fine if my scarf hadn't gotten tangled under me."

His blue-striped scarf was hanging untied around his shoulders, but Millie nodded soberly and decided to change the subject. "What were you doing out here anyway?"

He shrugged. It could have been her imagination, but it looked like a little color came into his cheeks. "I missed the bus."

"You could have called me. I would have given you a ride." So would have David, or Aris, or Bart's grandparents. Something didn't make sense.

"I didn't have your number," Bart said and looked away. Both of them knew he'd walked right past the café on his way home.

Millie sighed and fished out her keys. "I want you to put my number in your phone," she said. "And I want you to feel free to use it anytime. No questions asked. You need me, I'm there."

Bart's eyes blinked behind his glasses several times. "Okay," he said and pulled out his cell.

She gave him the numbers and watched him program the phone. "You got it?" What she meant was, did he understand that she'd be there for him in any kind of situation? Even if he did something wrong?

He gave an offhanded shrug, but the way he held her gaze gave him away. "Yeah," he said. "I got it."

"I don't like this." David studied the small red scrape on Bart's face. Someone had hurt Bart, pushed him down and sat on him—his son, who wouldn't hurt a flea. Action had to be taken, but Bart was refusing to give him enough information to do anything. "Who did this?" he demanded for the third time.

Beneath the kitchen lights, his son's face was pale but determined. The stain on his cheek stood out like the map of Africa. "I don't know."

David's jaw tightened. If Millie hadn't been on her way to their house and stopped it, there was no telling what might have happened. "Come on, Bart. I know you know."

Something in Bart's eyes told David he was right. "Bart," he pressed. "Why are you protecting this kid?"

Bart's gaze slid away from him. "Because you'll just make it worse."

"I don't think that's possible," David snapped. He turned to Millie. "Tell me again. What did you see?"

She shook her head. "It was dark, David. All I saw was a tall, muscular kid with a blond crew cut and a navy parka." Her brow furrowed in concentration. "The hood of the jacket was partially unzipped, so it hung unevenly in the back. He ran away when I honked. I never saw his face."

"Dad"—a pleading note entered his son's voice—"you have to leave this alone. Nothing really happened."

"Nothing? You've got a scratch on your cheek and the front of your jacket is scraped up." He paused as a fresh swell of anger rushed up in him. "The next time this kid could seriously hurt you."

"He doesn't want to hurt me," Bart said, avoiding David's eyes and resting his gaze instead on Millie. "He just wants. . . Oh, just forget it."

"Wants what?" David demanded.

"Nothing." Bart's mouth turned down.

"I'm trying to help you," David said, but even he could hear the edge in his voice and tried to stamp down his anger and frustration. "We're going to stand right here until you tell me—even if it takes all night."

Bart widened his stance. "Fine."

David clamped down hard on his molars. He hadn't expected Bart to agree to his challenge, and now that he had, there was no backing down. He narrowed his gaze and settled in for the long haul. A touch on his arm made him jump.

"Listen," Millie said. "Let's all calm down."

"I'll calm down when he tells me the name of the bully."

"Maybe we need to ask why Bart won't tell us."

David didn't like being told how to handle his son. He moved his arm free of her touch and felt his already precarious grip on his temper slip another notch. He'd never argued with Lisa about Bart in front of the boy. That was the first rule of good parenting. A united front. "You should stay out of this."

"Maybe I should," Millie said, studying his eyes and frowning. "But I won't."

"This is my son. I'll handle this."

"I don't think a staring contest is going to end well for either of you."

"You don't have kids," David said tightly, keeping his gaze

pinned to his son. "You don't know what you're talking about."

"All I'm asking, David, is that you talk to him."

"I am talking to him."

"No, you're not. You're saying the same thing over and over. Only louder."

He turned to her. Part of him recognized the truth in her words, another part really didn't care. "Just stay out of this!"

"Don't yell at her, Dad," Bart said hotly. His round cheeks flushed a deeper red, and behind his glasses his blue eyes were dark and stormy.

"I'm not yelling," David snapped and watched Bart take a protective step toward Millie. He made an effort to tone it down. "I'm just trying to get to the bottom of this. You're not helping."

He directed this last remark at Millie, who drew herself to her full height and glared back at him. "Because you're not letting me."

"We'll talk about this later." When they were alone, he'd tell her that her place was to support him, be his second in command, not to question his parenting techniques.

"If you won't ask him, I will." There were twin spots of color in her cheeks. The pinched look of her mouth softened as she turned to his son. "Bart, please tell us why you won't reveal the name of the kid who's bullying you."

At Bart's silence, David shot Millie a triumphant look. "I told you he wouldn't answer."

Millie kept her big gray eyes firmly fixed on Bart. They were as soft and warm as gray flannel. David gave Bart credit for being able to hold out against that look.

"I know you're not afraid of this kid," Millie said.

"Of course I'm not afraid," Bart said with a snort. "I just don't want my dad calling this kid's parents." He pushed his glasses higher on his face in a gesture David recognized as one of his own. "I'm not a little baby."

"You're eleven," David stated.

"Almost twelve."

"You're birthday isn't until August."

"But I'm still older than eleven."

"The point is," Millie interrupted, "that you both want the same thing—to deal with the bully." Her voice softened. "Bart, what if we promise not to do anything? Will you at least tell us what happened today?"

"I'm not going to make that promise." David shot Millie a warning look.

Millie folded her arms and regarded him unapologetically. A lock of her dark hair had fallen onto her cheek, and as mad as he was at her, he found himself staring at that corkscrew curl, stubbornly defying the rest of her pinned-up hair. "The more we know, the more we can help Bart."

"We are not negotiating. We are parenting," David said firmly, pleased with how he'd put that, and then his smug feeling faded as he realized he'd used the plural instead of the singular about the whole parenting thing. Suddenly the theme to *Star Wars* jingled in the quiet room. It was Bart's cell. The boy took one look at the caller and bolted from the room.

"We're not finished," David called, stunned that Bart had disobeyed him and run away in the middle of their argument. He raked his fingers through his hair. When had his son become so defiant? Just that morning Bart had been eating Cap'n Crunch and they'd been debating if Superman or Spiderman was a better superhero. He started after his son, but Millie's hand pulled him back.

"Let him go," she hissed.

He pulled free. "I'm not letting him off the hook just because his cell rang."

"David, he had to take that call."

Scowling, he looked in the direction of the stairs. "What are you talking about?"

"It was a girl on the phone."

This stopped him in his tracks. "What?"

"A girl."

"How do you know?"

"His face, David. It was like he got hit by lightning. Guys do not look like that when another guy calls them."

David glanced at the open hallway for a second time. Bart was talking to a girl? A girl had actually called him? Possibly Lauren Mays?

"If you make him hang up," Millie continued gently, as if he were a patient lying rigidly in the dental chair as he explained a particularly extensive procedure, "you'll embarrass him. Let it be. Bart will be back when he hangs up."

David started to tell Millie that she wasn't Bart's mother and that he, David, knew his son better than anyone, but then he closed his mouth. At this very moment, Bart and a girl were exchanging sentences, sharing information, maybe even making plans to get together. His son was only eleven. Was this normal? How old had he been when he'd started looking at girls? Not much older, he realized. He looked at Millie and scowled.

"I know," she said. "I should stop telling you what to do. Sorry."

"That's right," he said, then added, "So what do we do?"

"Nothing. We wait."

It seemed forever before Bart walked back into the room. "Sorry,

Dad," he said in a voice a little deeper than it had been five minutes ago. "I had to take that call."

"Who was it?"

"Lauren Mays." Bart blushed to the tips of his ears but held David's gaze. "She had a question about the math assignment."

David suspected there had been more to the call than that, and when he glanced at Millie, he read the slight lift at the corner of her mouth and knew she thought the same. "We still need to talk more about what happened today."

Bart folded his arms and sighed loudly.

David sighed. "Asking for help isn't a sign of weakness; it's a sign of intelligence."

"Not at my school," Bart stated firmly. "Nerds are not cool."

"Your intelligence is a gift," Millie said.

"So far all it's done is get my hat stolen."

"Which we'll get back as soon as you tell us who jumped you," David said, but gentler than before. He glanced at Millie to see if she'd noticed.

"I really didn't like that hat anyway," Bart said. "It was itchy."

David sighed. "All right Bart, I haven't wanted to do this, but you're giving me no choice. Until you tell me the name of this kid, there will be no video games, no computer, and no television."

"What about homework? Sometimes I have to go on the Internet for assignments."

David exchanged looks with Millie. At this rate his son was going to be a trial lawyer. "You can use the computer for homework, but I will be checking your online history. If you delete that, I'll personally be supervising your computer time."

"Fine," Bart said, scowling.

"If you miss the bus," David continued, "you will call me. Understood?"

"Agreed."

"Secondly, I'm meeting with your teacher, the school counselor, and the principal. Obviously I can't tell them who is bothering you, but they need to know what's going on so they can keep an eye out for trouble."

"They won't do anything," Bart stated, scowling fiercely. "And if they ask me about anything, I'll just deny that it happened."

"They'll keep it confidential," David said.

"Can't you just wait until after the sled race?" A pleading note entered Bart's voice. "It's next Saturday."

"No," David said firmly. "I've put it off much too long as it is. Tomorrow I'm calling and making an appointment."

It was hard to feel good about doing the right thing when David saw Bart's shoulders sag. Millie didn't look so happy either. He saw the mute appeal Bart sent her and for a moment thought she would make one last appeal to him. She didn't, and while he appreciated this, a persistent feeling of doubt settled into his mind. He needed to be Bart's parent not his friend, but he wasn't completely comfortable with the role in which he had cast himself. Everyone said the key to good parenting was establishing boundaries then consistently enforcing them.

Bart's situation still weighed heavily on his mind as David climbed into bed later that night. Closing his eyes, he knelt by the side of the bed.

Please, Lord, keep Bart safe, he prayed. *Don't let this bully hurt him, and please help me to model Your love and tolerance for our enemies, because right now I'm not feeling either of those things. Please help us handle this situation in a way that brings glory to You. And, Lord, thanks for Millie being there today. I know things could have been a lot worse if she hadn't scared off that bully kid.*

The next morning, as soon as he got to the office he called the school and made an appointment to meet with the principal, counselor, and Bart's teacher at one o'clock that afternoon. However, at eleven o'clock, the school called and told him that he'd have to reschedule his appointment. There was a virus going around the school, and all three educators had gone home sick. She suggested scheduling the appointment for a week from Monday when classes would resume after spring break.

David countered by asking to meet with the assistant vice principal and was told the man was in a training class for the next several days. David, however, was welcome to meet with Miss Gibson, the substitute teacher for Bart's class. David actually considered it, even though he knew Miss Gibson was notoriously soft on the kids and probably wouldn't take him seriously. Only too well, he pictured her deciding to talk about Bart's problem in front of the class, which he knew would only make things worse.

Frowning, he considered his options then made the appointment for the first Monday after spring break.

Chapter 29

The population of Deer Park swelled as tourists streamed into town for the Winterfest Snow Carnival. Parking on South Main was impossible, and every time Millie glanced out Dosie Dough's front window, she saw a stream of people passing down the street wearing brand-new parkas and carrying shopping bags.

For the first time all season, customers had to wait for a table. They stood almost shoulder to shoulder near the front door, their faces rosy from the cold, their eyes reading the menu board eagerly. They had big appetites, and although Millie came in early and stayed late, she was having trouble keeping up with the demand.

She was glad for the fast pace though. When she was multitasking—running the kitchen and trying to help the aunts serve, it was easier not to think about David or Bart. She couldn't help but look at every boy about eleven years old and wonder if he was the one who'd jumped Bart.

In the kitchen, she grabbed an order from under the warmers. The race was just days away. Last night she, David, and Bart had put the final coat of paint on the sled. They'd made pizza from scratch in the kitchen and toasted each other with sparkling grape juice. She'd had to force herself to go home.

Later she'd filled the emptiness in the house by talking with

David. Lying in bed, she'd pressed the receiver to her ear and listened to the soothing deepness of his voice. She thought the last thing he'd said before she fell asleep was that he loved her. But she might have imagined that. Lately her dreams had been filled with him. Vivid ones, where she walked with her hand tucked firmly into the crook of his elbow and she was happy.

Pushing the swinging doors open, she wondered if it could be true—if David could actually love her. To be loved, didn't someone have to be worthy of it? What exactly did she bring to the table besides waitressing skills and a life full of unrealized dreams?

The front door jingled. A broad-shouldered man and a rangy, tall boy stepped inside. She recognized Martin Spikes and thought the boy must be his son. It was close to closing, and although most of the tables were full, there was no line at the counter. She set her tray down in front of the Dittmore brothers then hurried over to take the Spikes's order.

"What can I get you?"

"A Double Mountain Burger—well done—large fries, extra ketchup, and a black cow shake," Martin said. He had the same blond hair he'd had throughout high school, but the muscles that had seen him to a state championship in wrestling were going soft. He had a potbelly now and a receding hairline.

Millie nodded and turned to the boy. "How about you?"

"The same."

The boy had his dad's wide shoulders and short, close-cropped blond hair. He also had a navy coat. Millie's eyes narrowed. He was the right size, and the coat looked the same as the one she'd seen the bully kid wearing.

"So, Martin," she said, carefully keeping her face neutral as she scribbled down the orders. "Haven't seen you in a while."

"Been busy."

"Don't I know it." Millie flashed a smile at the boy. "How is your spring break going?"

"Great."

"What've you been up to?"

The boy shrugged. "Nothing much. Working on my sled for the box race."

"He's got a killer sled." Martin laughed. His brown eyes gleamed. "Gonna *eat* the competition, right, Dev?"

The boy laughed. "My cousin Thad helped build it. He's an aerospace engineer, and he says the thing can go faster than a bat out of—"

"Dev," his father cut him off. "Watch your language."

"You use that word all the time," Devon said, frowning.

His father laid his hand on his son's shoulder. "We're sorry to hear about your mother, Millie. Heard she was helping the Denvers's kid with his sled." He paused. "I sure hope her accident didn't interfere with that."

Millie's jaw tightened, and her suspicions raised another notch. They were digging for information about Bart's sled. "Thanks for your concern, but Bart's sled is all finished." She studied the pair over the top of her notepad. "So what's your sled like?"

"It's a shark. A great white shark," Devon said. Something malicious seemed to gleam in his small, dark eyes. "The side fins are designed to withstand sideways impact. My cousin Thad used—"

"All his knowledge to build it," Martin finished. "What's Bart's sled like?"

She blinked rapidly, considering. "Oh, nothing much. We call it the *Flying French Fry*."

"That's what he built?" Devon's jaw dropped open slightly, and he exchanged an incredulous look with his father. "No wonder he hasn't said very much about it at school."

Millie jotted something on the pad then casually added, "You wouldn't happen to be a friend of Bart's would you?"

"He's in my science class," Devon admitted. "Is his sled really a cardboard french fry?"

Millie's heart beat a little faster. She dropped her pencil deliberately, and when the boy bent to pick it up, she noticed the hood of his parka was partially unzipped and hung crookedly down his back. "Thanks," she said as Devon handed her back the pencil. "I'll go put your order in."

She rushed to the back room then leaned against the counter. Devon Spikes was the bully kid. He had to be. Why else the interest in Bart's sled? And his parka matched the one she'd seen. She frowned. She knew she ought to call David, but she also wanted to get a look at Devon's sled. She remembered Martin Spikes had cheated frequently in high school and wouldn't put it past him to have constructed his son's sled with illegal materials.

What she needed, she decided, was more information. The Spikes didn't live too far away, and while they were having their Mountain Burgers, she could get a quick look at the sled. Pulling her purse from the desk drawer, she fished out her keys. On the way out, she pulled Aris aside and asked her to cover for her.

Aris nodded. "Of course." Her thin face creased. "Is Eva okay?"

"Yes, she's fine." Millie started to make up a vague excuse for leaving but then had a better idea. "Look," she said. "I don't have much time to explain, but I think the kid that's been bothering Bart is at table six. He's been asking a lot of questions about Bart's sled, and he looks a lot like the kid I saw beating up Bart. Before I involve David, I want to get a look at that sled. Can you stay here and delay the Spikes?"

Aris's shoulders straightened, and her eyes narrowed. "That boy is here? I'll wring his neck for what he's done to Bart."

"No," Millie snapped. "That won't help. Besides, I could be wrong. What's more important is to look at that sled."

"Then I'm coming with you," Aris stated. "Keeker and Mimi can hold the fort." She read Millie's face then added, "I'm not letting you go there alone. You'll need a lookout."

Millie started to argue then saw the stubborn set to the older woman's face. "If you come, you'll have to stay in the car." When Aris nodded, she added, "I'll let the aunts know what's happening. They can mess up the Spikes's order then offer free ice cream to delay them."

"Good thinking. Tell them to make them big scoops." Aris's hazel eyes gleamed. "That kid might spill some good information if we get enough sugar in him."

David flipped on the overhead light in the garage. "There she is," he announced proudly. "Isn't she great? We put the final coat of paint on her last night." His gaze swung back to his mother in anticipation of her reaction. She hadn't seen the sled before, and he wanted her to be proud of it. He wanted her to see the Hogans in a new and better light. "Eva and Bart designed it. We all built it."

"Miss Eva taught me a little calculus," Bart added. "We used it to calculate the slope of the sled." He touched the shiny black hood. "Miss Millie said she's going to take a picture of me at the race and hang it in the café."

His mother stopped walking around the body of the sled and looked up at him with a crease of worry between her eyes. "Is that so?" she said.

"What do you think, Grandma?" Bart pressed. "Do you like it?"

They all studied the cardboard sled. David's gaze lingered on the giant winged french fry that covered the side of the sled. It was supposed to look like a flying, crinkle-cut fry, but if it wasn't for the lettering Millie had stenciled, nobody would have known. He suspected that Millie could have drawn the design a lot better than Bart, but instead, she'd chosen to let Bart do it and had praised everything he did. David remembered the glow of pride in his son's eyes.

"It's certainly unique," his mother said and then added, "But David, is it supposed to look like a coffin?"

"It's aerodynamic, Grandma," Bart said. "Miss Eva custom-shaped it to my body."

"Are those lightning bolts with wings?"

"Those are french fries," David explained. He glanced at his watch. Millie had said she might drop by later. He hoped he could talk her into going out for coffee. The race day was rapidly approaching and something had to be said about what would happen to their relationship. He planned to ask her if she'd like to date him for real and even had a little speech planned.

He checked his watch. Aris wasn't home either. Millie and Aris were probably still at the café getting a start on the morning's baking.

"Why is there a tail?"

"That's the rudder," Bart said. "It'll help keep the sled straight."

His mother circled the sled slowly then regarded David. "Are you sure this is a good idea? Bart entering this race? I remember when you did it—your whole sled fell apart."

David smiled but wished his mom wouldn't worry so much. "Bart'll be fine. Eva Hogan still holds the record for the fastest sled on the hill."

"I suppose." His mother's mouth puckered slightly, as it always did whenever David mentioned Millie or Eva. He straightened his back. "Will you and Dad be joining us at Dosie's after the race? I know Millie has invited both of you."

"Of course." His mother smiled but turned to Bart before he could read her eyes. "We're looking forward to meeting your friends."

Bart barely looked up. He was furiously texting—probably Lauren Mays. David had asked Bart to keep a low profile with Lauren until after he'd talked to the principal, but it obviously hadn't made an impact.

"Have I mentioned, David, that I'm going to help out with the charity ball at Saint Vincent's this spring?"

Last year his mother had helped raise a couple of thousand dollars for the children's wing of the hospital. "That's great, Mom."

"We're going to need some local business support."

"I'll be glad to do what I can."

His mother's face brightened. "We could use your input on a couple of things. Are you free Wednesday night?"

David mentally cringed at the thought of sitting around a table for a couple of hours discussing menus and venues, but then he brightened as it occurred to him that this could be an excellent opportunity to get Millie connected to the church. "Can I bring Millie?"

"Of course," his mother said, but then she added, "But I know she's awfully busy with Eva being hurt and all. She probably doesn't need one more thing on her plate." She smiled. "Maybe it would be better not even to ask her. That way she wouldn't feel obligated."

It wasn't hard to translate. His mother really was saying, *"I don't want her to come."* He bristled. "I'm sure Millie would be glad to make the time. She is a very generous person."

"Then by all means ask her." She hesitated. "But maybe I should clear it with my cochair first."

It took a second, but then he understood. "By any chance is Cynthia Shively your cochair?"

"I couldn't very well refuse her help when she volunteered, David."

He thought about the look on Cynthia's face at the skating rink when he'd walked away from her. He'd seen a new coldness in her face, a hardness in her eyes that bordered on dislike. Cynthia apparently hadn't mentioned their conversation at the lake to his mother. The whole Saint Vincent's plan had probably been hatched weeks ago. He turned to Bart, who had stopped texting and was watching them with undisguised interest. "Would you please give us a few minutes alone?"

As soon as Bart left, he said, "Mom, Cynthia and I are never going to date." He watched her body go very still as if she wasn't even breathing. "I would really like Millie to get to know our friends at the church. I'd appreciate your help in making that happen."

Beneath her carefully applied makeup, the lines in his mom's face seemed to deepen. "I'll do anything you ask me, David, but I think you should be very careful. I hate to see you getting serious with that girl."

"She's not perfect, but neither am I." David was fed up with people trying to tell him how bad Millie was. "Maybe if you stopped being so quick to judge her, you'd see that she's a good person."

"A good person doesn't act the way she does." She looked long and hard into his eyes. He saw the strength of the same woman who had grabbed him by the arm and bent him over her knee when he was a child and got into trouble. He watched her reach for the small gold cross that had hung around her neck for as long as he could remember. "I saw her a couple of weeks ago. She was with Karl Kauffman."

David made a noise that was something between a laugh and a snort. "So?"

"They were in his car. It was after dark. When she saw me, she hunched down like she didn't want to be seen." Her lips twisted. "I'm sorry, David. I didn't want to have to tell you."

His face felt strangely numb. He couldn't tell if he was smiling or grimacing, and when he tried to straighten his lips, he still couldn't be quite sure. "I'm sure there was a reasonable explanation."

But was there? In high school, Karl had been a jock, and a lot of girls had trailed him around wanting dates. Unhappily, he remembered that Millie had been one of those girls.

"She's two-timing you," his mother hissed. "That's what she does."

"She isn't two-timing me," he said firmly then heard himself ask, "When was this?"

"On Tuesday, February 10th. I remember, because it was bridge night at Gloria Kirpatrick's house."

It was also the night Eva had broken her hip. His stomach churned with the realization that Millie had been out with another man—and she hadn't told him.

"There's more," his mother added gently. "Aris did a little digging around into her background. There are things you need to know."

"What have you done?"

"I haven't done anything," she said. "Stop looking at me like I'm the bad person. I love you, but you have a curious habit of hiding your head in the sand. When there's something you don't want to see, you don't. I'm your mother, and I'll protect you with every breath in my body. You don't want to hear what I have to say? Fine. But ask her, David. She obviously didn't tell you about Karl

Kauffman—and there's more."

"Whatever it is, I don't want to hear it."

Her lips trembled as she fought for control. "You don't want Cynthia, and I'm willing to accept that. But don't ruin your life by trying to prove how wrong I am about Millie Hogan—because I'm not."

She left then, closing the door hard behind her and leaving a trace of her anger hanging as heavily in the air as her perfume. David listened to the sound of her car's engine as it roared away. He gripped his hands into fists. Right now he disliked her almost as much as he loved her.

He turned off the lights in the garage with more force than necessary. His mother had to be mistaken. She must have seen someone who looked like Millie riding in Karl Kauffman's car. If it had been Millie, she would have told him.

He stepped into the living room. What if he was wrong? Millie had never told him the full story of what had happened the night Eva had fallen, had she?

He didn't like the seeds of doubt that had taken root in his mind and seemed to grow stronger with every passing second. It all made sense. Millie had gone out with Karl Kauffman, and something had happened or else she would have mentioned it to him. He thought of another man holding Millie, kissing her, and a curious numbness seemed to settle over him. He walked into the kitchen, opened the freezer, and stood there as the chilled air spilled out. His mind turned the knowledge over and over but couldn't accept it.

There had to be an explanation that did not paint Millie in a bad light. He'd believed in her; he'd believed in them. He slammed the freezer door shut. He didn't want to think about it anymore. She could date whomever she wanted. It wasn't like they were exclusive—that had never come up in their plan, at least not that he could recall. They'd never talked about a future beyond the sled race, so it really wasn't a big deal. Only it was. He looked out the window in the living room and stared at the empty driveway. The numbness was wearing off, and this time when his mind pictured Millie with another man, it hurt.

Chapter 30

Fifteen minutes later, Millie and Aris arrived in the Spikes's neighborhood. Aris sat in the passenger seat, nose nearly pressed against the glass as she read house numbers.

"Remember," Millie said, "you're staying in the car. I'm taking a quick look at the sled, and then we're out of here."

"I know," Aris retorted. "While you're at it, though, keep an eye out for Bart's hat."

Millie doubted they'd see Bart's hat in plain view but kept this to herself. She gripped the steering wheel more tightly as they passed Karl Kauffman's house. He lived in this same neighborhood, and she hadn't forgotten the angry look on his face the night she'd broken up with him for the second time.

Her uneasiness increased as they pulled over to the curb in front of a modest raised ranch that was badly in need of a paint job. A Little Tikes plastic swimming pool was filled to the slide with snow, and a rusting Flexible Flyer leaned against the two-car detached garage. She started to get out of the car and saw Aris doing the same.

"What are you doing?"

"Coming with you." Aris slammed the Subaru's door and began to march up the Spikes's driveway.

"You were supposed to stay in the car," Millie hissed, drawing even with her.

"I lied," Aris stated unapologetically. "Let's see if the side door to the garage is unlocked."

It wasn't. But Millie bit her tongue and actually was glad to have Aris's company as they circled the structure and realized the windows were too high to see anything. They mulled it over then decided the only way to take a look was if Aris climbed onto Millie's back.

Soon Aris was sitting on Millie's shoulders. For a thin woman, she was surprisingly heavy and hard to balance. Millie struggled to keep her balance as Aris strained to see through the dusty windows.

"What do you see?" Millie hissed as the seconds ticked past.

"A lot of dust. Get closer." Aris leaned forward, nearly pulling Millie into the straggly bushes lining the garage wall.

"Hurry," Millie grunted.

"Ugh."

"What?"

"Piles of stuff. Boxes. Newspapers. It's like the town dump. Can you get me a little closer?"

She inched closer and slipped in the snow, nearly unseating Aris who grabbed Millie's head for balance. "Let go," Millie ordered. "You're almost breaking my neck."

The pressure under her jaw decreased a little, but Aris's legs clamped more tightly. "Would you look at that."

"Do you see the sled?"

"No, but there's a big roll of chicken wire."

Millie remembered Eva telling her that people had once used chicken wire to strengthen the structure of their box sleds. It was illegal now to use it. She braced herself against the increasing weight on her shoulders. "Maybe that kid is lining his cardboard with chicken wire."

Aris pursed her lips. "That's what I thought. Bend down. The sled isn't in here. We need to look in the basement."

Millie sighed in relief as Aris climbed off her shoulders. "Maybe we should just go."

"Just a quick look," Aris promised. "It'll just take a second. And it might help Bart."

Although Millie knew better, she silenced her misgivings and followed Aris around the side of the house. Beneath a wooden deck, a pair of glass doors opened to a walk-out basement.

Aris rushed up and pressed her face against the glass. "Look!" she cried.

At first all Millie could see was a large-screen television and a sagging green couch. But on the left there was a worktable, and sitting on top of it was a giant cardboard shark. It was painted black and white and had its mouth gaping open.

"It has teeth," Millie gasped. "And it's big." A lot bigger than the *Flying French Fry*. Whipping out her cell phone, she snapped a shot of it. "Is it even legal to be that size?"

"Eva will know," Aris stated. "Those teeth don't look like they're made out of cardboard either. Maybe they're lined with chicken wire."

"Martin did say something about eating the competition."

"You don't suppose they left the sliding door open, do you?" Aris's gloved hands were already on the handle. Leaning back, she slid the door open.

Aris was about to squeeze inside when a very deep voice said, "Hold it."

Millie recognized that voice. Her heart sank as her gaze slowly traveled up the gold stripe on long, blue pant legs to the ski parka with the Deer Valley Police Department badge. Swallowing, she struggled to put on a good face as her eyes took in Karl Kauffman's craggy features. "Hello, Karl," she said. "I can explain."

"Turn around slowly and put your hands against the side of the house."

"Karl, this really isn't necessary," Millie protested. "We're just looking. . . ."

"You were breaking and entering."

"We just wanted to see if anyone was home," Aris said. "Nobody answered the front door. . . ."

"Because you didn't ring the bell," Karl said. "I've been watching you."

"I can explain," Millie tried again.

"And you will explain, at the station."

"Karl—you know us—we're not burglars," Millie said.

He looked down at her and slowly shook his head. "I really don't know you at all." He motioned with his arm. "Get going."

The knowledge that Millie had lied to him was eating David up from the inside out. He had to know what else she was holding back from him, and yet he dreaded discovering what she might tell him. It was like waiting for biopsy results you knew would be bad.

He paced the living room. Every few moments he drew back the curtains and looked at the empty driveway. Why hadn't Millie talked to him about Kauffman? He felt a stir of anger. She had no problem telling him how to parent. And she'd had plenty of time. Eva had fallen weeks ago.

He waited as long as he could then did something he'd never done before—decided to leave Bart alone in the house. Millie's house was only fifteen minutes away, and he needed to confront her in person. He'd be back in an hour. Just as he started up the steps to tell Bart, he heard a car pull into the driveway.

He headed for the front door. Opening it, he was surprised to see Millie's Subaru in the driveway and Aris coming up the steps. She was barely through the door when he started firing questions. "Where were you? Why are you so late?" And then the question that ate at him. "Where's Millie?"

Aris pushed back loose strands of her silver hair and twisted her reddened hands together unhappily. "It's a long story."

David studied the haggard look of her face and the slight slump of her shoulders. "What happened? Is Millie okay?"

Aris wiped her nose with a crumpled tissue. "She's fine, but David, she needs your help."

"Just tell me where she is."

Aris's eyes darted slightly to the left. Then her gaze returned to rest unhappily on his. "Karl Kauffman took her to the police station. She's been arrested."

On his way to the police station, David thought about the story Aris had told him. He knew Kauffman wasn't going to charge Millie with anything. If anything, David suspected that Kauffman had a different objective in mind—like maybe what he and Millie had done the night David's mother had seen them in the car together. Something burned hot and deep in David's stomach. Would it always be like this? Every time a man looked at Millie in a certain way, was David always going to wonder just how well that man knew her?

To be fair, would Millie look at photos of himself and Lisa and wonder who David loved more?

He gripped the wheel tighter. *How do you do it, Lord? How do You start over? Build a life over a life?*

The answer was through faith in God—only it couldn't be just his. He had been encouraged by the way Millie had clung to him in the hospital when he had prayed for Eva. But now he doubted her. Doubted them. Maybe he'd been stupid to think that believing in God would ever be more to her than a concept. He'd even been vain enough to think that God might use him to help her personally know God.

Why didn't Millie tell me about him, Lord?

He listened hard, but there was only the hum of his Lexus's engine. His mind flashed through some of his conversations with Millie, confirming that she had had plenty of opportunity to tell him about Kauffman. He was the wronged one. And then his mind came to a screeching stop when he remembered the time in the garage when she'd tried to tell him of the men she'd dated. He'd shut her down, politely of course, but firmly.

"It doesn't matter," he'd said. *"I like who you are now."*

It had been the truth, but it wasn't the whole truth. He hadn't wanted to know about the other men. He didn't want to think about her with anyone else but himself.

He felt his chest tighten in the sudden realization that congratulating himself on being so much better than Millie was laughable. His intentions had been good, but somewhere along the line he'd let tolerance slip into ignorance.

He hadn't wanted to feel Bart's pain or loneliness, so he'd

distanced himself with work and taken Bart's good grades as a report card on the rest of his life. He hadn't wanted to deal with Cynthia's emotions, so he had used Millie to solve the problem.

Now that he knew this, there was no going back. No way of closing his eyes, of saying the world was one way when he knew it was another.

He accelerated down the quiet street.

It felt like days, not hours, had passed when Millie finally stepped out of the conference room at the police station. Karl had asked a lot of tough questions. *"Why did you flirt with me at the Blue Moose if you didn't want to get back together? Why did you dance with me? Let me kiss you?"*

Millie had shaken her head. She didn't know where to start or how to explain things she didn't entirely understand herself. It hadn't been about Kyle, she knew that much. It had been about her—about feeling afraid and confused and him being there. She apologized for misleading him and for hurting him. She'd felt small, telling him that she'd made a mistake kissing him, that there had never been a chance of them getting back together.

Karl shut the door behind them. She turned to say good-bye. "I'm *really* sorry for everything," she said. "I hope someday you can forgive me."

His response was to lift her off her feet and hold her there in a bear hug that she hoped was his way of accepting her apology. It wasn't very comfortable, but she didn't struggle, and after a long moment, he set her gently on the floor. "If he doesn't treat you right, Millie, just let me know and I'll arrest him for something."

Millie laughed and almost reached up to touch his face but stopped herself in time. "Thanks, Karl," she said. "Don't be a stranger at the café, okay?"

He nodded and then started down the hallway. Her gaze followed him until he turned a corner. He was a good man and in time would find someone to love and who would love him back. Someone much nicer than Millie. As she started down the hallway, her heart stopped when she saw a man in jeans and a blue sweater sitting on a bench just down the hall. "David," she said, hurrying over to him. "Am I glad to see you."

He stood slowly. "Are you?"

It occurred to her that he might have read more into that bear hug Kyle had given her than there was, but short of coming right out and saying it, she wasn't sure how to reassure him. "Of course," Millie stated firmly. "I was about to call you and ask for you to come bail me out." When he didn't smile, she added, "I hope Aris told you what happened?"

"She did."

"We saw chicken wire in the garage, David. Did she tell you that? And the sled is huge. It's a great white shark. I seriously think this kid is going to try something sneaky in the race."

"Right now I really don't care about the sled."

"You're mad that I interfered?"

David shook his head. He had an expression on his face she'd never seen before. "Let's just go," he said and began walking down the long, quiet corridor. He didn't offer his arm or speak as they walked out of the building. The freezing air stung her cheeks as they stepped outdoors, but the real coldness was coming from David, and Millie felt panic stir inside her. He'd gotten mad at her before, but it hadn't felt like this. She didn't understand it, but she feared it.

"David—I'm sorry."

The Lexus's engine jumped to life. David put the car in REVERSE and backed out of the parking spot. His gaze was fixed on the road in front of him. She sat silently wondering what to say. She'd already apologized. Couldn't he see that what she'd done had been for Bart?

"David," she said, "this is ridiculous. It's not like I robbed a bank or something."

He shot her a sideways look. "Why didn't you tell me about Karl Kauffman?"

Her stomach knotted, but she forced herself to smile. "Well, I didn't know he was going to arrest me."

She'd hoped for a laugh, but David didn't crack a smile. Her anxiety went up another notch.

She swallowed. "Look, there's nothing going on between Karl and me. I only came down to the station with him so he'd let Aris go home. And," she amended, looking down, "we had some unfinished business. That hug you saw—it was him saying good-bye to me."

They drove past the library with its flat, snow-carpeted lawn and towering pine, and then David turned unexpectedly and pulled into the parking spot behind the building. The streetlights had yet to come on, but the light was dim, and Millie had a sick feeling as he put the car into PARK and the sound of the running engine was the only noise.

"So what unfinished business did you have with him?"

Millie thought furiously. What was safe to say? How much should she tell him? "Well, you know we used to date." She paused. "He's having a hard time moving on."

"Are you?"

She laughed. "No. I want to be friends, but that's it."

"And is that why you went out with him the night you were

supposed to come to my house?"

She felt her expression freeze. *Oh God,* she thought, *he knows.* "We didn't plan it." She realized how bad it sounded. "It was nothing, David. He needed to talk to me, and I thought I owed it to him to listen."

"So why didn't you tell me about it?"

She shuffled her feet. "Maybe I didn't think you'd understand." How did you explain that sometimes going along with something was easier than fighting it? That she'd let Karl take the lead and closed her ears to the voice that knew she was making a huge mistake?

"Why don't you try me now?"

Because she was scared. She didn't want to hurt him, and she didn't want to lose him either. Yet once he knew that she'd basically lied and cheated, it would be over between them. There was no way he could forgive her, so why bother? She looked down at her hands. Short, blunt nails and a big, fake ruby ring. She considered simply opening the car door and running away.

"Have you ever done anything wrong in your entire life?"

"Of course," he said.

But he would never have done what she'd done, and the knowledge of this lay in her heart like a stone. What was wrong with her? Why was it so easy for some people always to do the right thing and others got caught in gray areas and messed up? It was hopeless. They should just call it a night. Yet deep inside, she didn't want to just walk away. David deserved better. Even if he ended up hating her, it was better to tell him the truth and not have to carry it around inside anymore.

Taking a deep breath, Millie told him about going for a walk and running into Karl. She told him how she'd gotten in his truck thinking they were going for coffee and then ended up at the Blue

Moose. "I had a glass of wine," she admitted, "and when the band started playing, I danced with him." She paused. "A few hours later, he walked me back to his truck, and I let him kiss me. I knew right away it was a mistake, and I told him." She looked into his eyes. "I'm so sorry, David."

He rubbed the back of his neck. "You kissed him."

"Yes. I totally messed up, but it won't happen again."

He was silent for so long she began to wonder if he was going to give her another chance.

She studied the dips and curves and contours of David's mouth. His lips were tight, serious, possibly disappointed. She swallowed. She'd come this far; she might as well finish what she'd started. She sighed. "Maybe you need to know why I kissed Karl."

Half expecting him to push her away, she reached to touch his face softly. He closed his eyes as she caressed his cheek and slid her hands into his hair. Leaning across the console, she lifted her other arm and placed it on his shoulder. He didn't move as she lifted her face to his. She heard him sigh as she kissed him, and then something seemed to release in them both, and he was kissing her back. His fingers buried themselves in her hair, and he supported her head, holding on to her as if he would never let her go. It was a kiss of apology, of acceptance, of an understanding that what they had between them was more important than anything that had happened.

Finally, they broke apart and looked long and hard into each other's eyes. "Do you understand now why I kissed Karl?"

His brow furrowed, but a hint of humor came into his eyes. "Not a clue, but I'm willing for you to show me again."

She almost laughed and gave in to do exactly that. However, as nice as kissing him was, she wanted him to understand why she had been vulnerable to Karl's advances. "It's the way you kiss."

"You don't like it?" His voice was low and private, but his eyes teased her.

"I like it very much."

"Then what's the problem?"

She held his gaze. The problem was that she couldn't kiss him like that and hold back part of herself as she did in other relationships. When she was with him, she was a different person, and it was very confusing. Folding her arms, she looked up at him and let her breath out slowly. "You scare me," she said very softly. "When you kiss me, you scare me."

"That isn't the reaction I'm going for," David said dryly.

"Maybe not," Millie said. "But you do. It's going to take me time to get used to it."

"When I kiss you, you don't feel very scared. You feel kind of wonderful, Millie."

"The scared part comes after," she admitted. "The first time you kissed me—that was the scariest because I wasn't expecting it. This time was better."

The corners of David's mouth tugged. "What exactly are you scared of?"

She shifted uncomfortably. Usually guys spilled their feelings to her—not the other way around. "For a genius guy, I can't believe you can't figure it out."

"I'm not a genius or a mind reader," he said mildly.

"And I'm not a girl who settles down," Millie said. "But when I kiss you, I kind of forget that. I guess I wanted Karl to remind me who I was."

"I know who you are, Millie Hogan, and you're a lot better person than you give yourself credit for."

"Thanks—but I'm not. I'm sorry I didn't tell you about that night."

"I'm sorry I scared you," David said gravely. "I didn't know."

Millie nodded. "My mother did. She was furious. She said I was trying to sabotage us, and she was right."

"It didn't work. I'm still here."

"Well, for now." Millie closed her mouth tightly. She'd meant to think that, not say it aloud.

He frowned. "What do you mean by that?"

She twisted her fingers together. "In my family," she mumbled, "the guy always leaves."

"I won't." He laced his warm fingers into her cold ones. "I'm not your father, and I'm not going to abandon you."

"You could get hit by a car tomorrow or have a heart attack like my grandfather."

"Or I could live to be a very old man and we could sit on the front porch in our rocking chairs together." The grip on her hands increased. "There are a lot of things we still need to figure out, but I have strong feelings for you, Millie. The past couple of weeks I've felt more alive and happier than I have in years. I feel like we're meant to be together."

"Me, too," she whispered then frowned unhappily at him. "This wasn't supposed to happen. I wasn't supposed to actually fall for you."

"I know."

"We had an agreement. With clear boundaries."

He started to smile. "I wasn't looking for this either."

"So what are we going to do?"

His smile widened. "I don't know, but I think we're going to need a new plan."

Chapter 31

Deer Mountain had its humble beginnings in 1936 when a group of skiers formed a club, built a rope tow, and used their wooden skis to trample a trail. It had been growing ever since with the goal of becoming the best family ski hill in the country. In the late forties, the owners of the mountain bought its first chairlift. Now the mountain featured a quad lift, three triple chairs, two doubles, and a J-bar for the bunny slope.

During the weeklong winter carnival, hundreds of tourists flocked to the races. Skiers of every age and level of ability could be seen schussing down the long white trails cut into the thick trees on the mountain. But what set Deer Mountain apart from other ski hills, and what brought people back every March was the box sled races.

This year's race day seems more crowded than ever, Millie thought as she squeezed her way through the people clustered on the second-story sundeck. It was not even eight o'clock in the morning, but the sun reflected off the snow, creating a shade so white the hill seemed to shimmer. Around her, people talked loudly, nearly drowning themselves out. She smelled bacon-and-egg sandwiches and the deeper aroma of coffee.

Eva, Aris, and the aunts were seated at a table reserved for handicapped people. It was nearest the wood railing and had one of the best views of the slopes.

"How'd it go?" Aunt Lillian asked as Millie walked up to the table. Lillian sat in her wheelchair with a thick wool blanket pulled around her.

"Bart's pretty nervous," Millie said. "But the inspection went fine. David is helping him bring the sled to the holding area."

"Come sit," Aunt Keeker offered, sliding down on the bench to make room. She was wearing a multitailed ski hat with bells at the bottom.

Next to Keeker, Aunt Mimi sat on a couple of blankets to give herself a little more height. Earl Gray sniffed for scraps atop the picnic table. Dogs probably weren't allowed, and Millie wondered how Mimi had managed to smuggle Earl Gray inside.

"Have some hot chocolate," Mimi ordered. "You look cold. This will warm you up."

"Maybe later." She glanced at her mother, but as usual Eva avoided her gaze. Although Eva had graduated from the wheelchair to crutches, their relationship felt as broken as ever.

On the side of the mountain, people were dragging their sleds to the top of the wide trail where the box sleds would race. Millie watched a father pull a little girl in a sled that looked exactly like Cinderella's pumpkin-shaped carriage. Behind Cinderella, a little boy wearing chaps and a cowboy hat sat in a cardboard Conestoga wagon. There was a dragon sled and a race car, all equipped with their miniature riders.

Millie's stomach tightened. Children. Would she want one with David? They hadn't discussed it yet, but they would. And soon. Bart was already eleven. And there was the whole church thing. David had made it clear it was important to him. So far she'd managed to use work as an excuse not to go, but the truth was that she was uncomfortable with the thought of everyone staring at her, congratulating David with their eyes for getting her there. She didn't want to open herself up to the conclusions they would draw.

She watched her mother sip her hot chocolate. "You warm enough, Mom?"

"Oh yes," Eva said. "Beautiful day, isn't it?"

"Yes," Millie agreed. "Aren't the little kids cute?"

"Adorable."

The old Eva would have said, *Look at that cute little girl. I want grandchildren. What are you waiting for, Millie? Instructions?*

"Did you take your pain pill?"

"Yes honey."

"Do you want to put your leg up?"

"No thank you."

Their exchange left a bad taste in Millie's mouth, as if she'd dumped way too much sugar into her coffee.

Someone tapped her on her shoulder, and Millie jerked. Aris bent over her. Her long silver braid was thrown over her chest like a sash. "I need to talk to you. In private."

The announcer's voice boomed over the loudspeaker, calling for the first heat of the peewee race. There was plenty of time before Bart's race, so Millie followed Aris into the lodge then down the metal stairs to the concession area. Nearly all the tables were taken, but when a family got up, Aris quickly slid into the seat. "I want to apologize," she began.

"For what?" Millie scoffed. "You didn't force me to drive you to the Spikes's house. And besides, Devon's sled passed inspection."

The older woman shook her head. Her eyes were downturned, and her skin was deeply wrinkled, tissue thin, and dotted with age spots. "Not for that."

Millie leaned forward. "Then what?" She wondered if the older woman had broken something at the café.

"I'm an interfering old woman, and I know it. But you have to understand that the Denvers are my family. I lost my husband in the Vietnam War. We had no children, and I was never close to my brothers. When I met Lisa and David, I was a cleaning lady who watched too much television and lived off frozen dinners and cans of soup." She sighed. "Lisa befriended me. Before I knew it, I was going to church with her, and my life started changing. It got even better when Lisa got pregnant and asked me to be Bart's nanny."

Millie sensed there was a purpose to the story, but she also was impatient to get back to the sundeck and watch the races. She had to bite her lip to keep from prompting Aris to hurry.

"So when you started dating David, I was curious about you. I love him, and besides, I promised Lisa to look after him and Bart." She twisted her thin fingers in her lap. "Remember all the questions I asked you that day I helped out at the café? I was getting information so I could research you. I had heard rumors, and I was curious about your father."

Millie felt herself go very still. "What?"

Aris's face seemed to fold into itself. "There's no excuse for what I did. You have every right to hate me."

"I don't hate you."

"You will when I tell you what I know."

Millie tried to swallow but found her throat had gone dry.

"I found him on the Internet." Aris reached into her purse and pulled out several sheets of paper. Sliding them across the table, she said, "It wasn't hard."

The pages were neatly folded and looked exactly like the cheap paper that came out of Millie's printer. She touched the edges gingerly then slowly lifted the papers.

The first thing she saw was a blue and red state seal, and then she read: *Salt Lake First District Court, State of Utah v. Maximillian Hogan.*

Her chest constricted as her eyes skimmed the page. Second-degree felony. Utah County. Embezzlement of funds. Salt Lake Christian Church. Guilty. A term not to exceed fifteen years in the state prison.

Her father was an inmate at the Utah State Prison. He was serving his sixth year.

Her father. A thief. In jail. She felt herself slump but didn't have the strength to sit upright.

Criminals were people she'd been taught to fear—the villains of the scary stories teenagers told in the dark, bad people who robbed, stole, and killed. They were the ones that made you test the lock on the doors at night.

"Millie?" Aris's voice seemed far in the distance. "Millie?"

She focused on Aris with effort. "There's got to be some kind of mistake." Her brain seized gratefully onto this possibility.

"There's no mistake. I'm sorry."

"There could be another Maximillian Hogan." Millie sat up straighter. Lots of people shared names and birthdays.

"I wrote to the First District Court of Utah County and got a copy of the judgment and commitment form. Everything matches."

"Maybe someone stole his identity."

"I don't think so," Aris said grimly. "I'm sorry, Millie. I wish I'd never poked my nose in your business."

Why did you? Millie was free-falling again. She shoved the pages at Aris then immediately wanted to grab them back. "It doesn't matter. He means nothing to me."

Aris pressed her lips together so tightly they disappeared and left a gash where her mouth should have been. Millie realized there was more bad news coming. "Tell me the rest," she said.

Aris sighed heavily. "I wasn't expecting to find out anything like this. Anything at all, really. And then when I did, I didn't know what to do with the information." She hesitated. "I went to David's mother."

"You what?"

"I couldn't go to David. I didn't think he'd be objective enough." She tried to touch Millie's arm, but Millie pulled away. "It was before I got to know you. And I'm really sorry I had to tell you this, but I think she wants to talk to you about all this."

"When?"

"Soon. Maybe today. I didn't want her to blindside you. She isn't a bad person, but she feels like David should know the truth."

Millie swallowed something bitter tasting. She supposed she should thank Aris for warning her, but the words wouldn't come out of her mouth. The weight of despair settled over her. She imagined Mrs. Denvers telling her that Millie was trash. That she wasn't good enough for David.

Millie bit her lip. Maybe Mrs. Denvers was right.

"Could I see that paper again?" Her hands trembled as she reached for the sheets. All this time she'd worried about turning into her mother and now this—this horrific news about her dad.

"Millie, are you okay? You're very pale. Let me get you a hot chocolate."

"I'm fine, Aris." She folded the papers and stuck them into the pocket of her parka. She forced herself to think. "Does anyone else know?"

"No. Just Mrs. Denvers and myself." Aris searched Millie's eyes. "It's not the end of the world. Everyone has a skeleton in the family closet. Some have quite a few rattling around." She laughed, but it ended in an awkward silence.

Skeletons maybe, but not criminals. Millie climbed to her feet. She thought of the money her father had stolen and wished he were dead. All those wasted years of dreaming of gaining his approval, of proving her worth so he'd regret leaving her. She felt sick to her stomach.

He's worse than nothing. And I'm his daughter, so I guess that makes me worse than nothing, too.

"You're upset with me, aren't you?"

I look out windows and dream about other lives. I've used and hurt other people. I'm exactly like him.

Millie struggled to speak past the interior voice grinding her into nothingness. "I'm not mad. I promise."

Anger would require emotion. She had nothing inside, nothing but this growing sense of shame and an awful voice attacking her, beating her down. She gripped her fingers into fists. Was there no way of stopping it?

She almost laughed. She'd dreamed of being famous, of people knowing her name, but never for something like this. Through the wall of glass, she could see the box sleds coming down the hill. She thought of David and Bart, and for a moment something warm and sustaining flickered through her. She thought of David telling her that he was in love with her.

A warm feeling started to fill the hollowness inside. She loved David. And love was not worthless. There was a strength to it. Inside, a new voice began to speak. *"Cling to Me,"* it said. *"I'm strong enough to hold you."*

But she couldn't. Loving David didn't give her the right to grab hold of him as if she were a drowning person and he were a life preserver. That would be selfish. That wasn't love. Love was selfless.

Despair washed through her again. Aris's mouth was moving, but Millie couldn't hear a word. She wanted to run and hide, find a dark hole and disappear. Just like her father. The realization that she wanted to run made her cringe.

She wouldn't run, and she would tell David about her father. Just not today. Today belonged to Bart.

Her mind made up, she climbed to her feet. She looked out again at the great white mountain and gathered her strength. She was going to have to pretend nothing was wrong in front of the people who knew her best. Well, she'd always believed that she was meant to act, and now it seemed she'd have a chance to prove it.

Chapter 32

Remember what Miss Eva said. If you hit a patch of heavy snow and your sled stops, sit up and use your body weight to rock it free."

Bart's ski goggles were perched on top of his head, and the boy squinted up at him through the bright sunlight. "I know, Dad."

They were standing on a relatively flat area at the top of the bunny hill. The junior girls' races had just finished, and the boys were just about to get started. Looking around at the other sleds—a pirate ship that was a clear nod to the *Pirates of the Caribbean* movie, a race car so detailed he could count the spokes in the wheel, and a spaceship the shape of a fried egg—David fought the uneasy feeling in his stomach. He hadn't forgotten how humiliating it'd been when his Huckleberry Finn raft had fallen apart and he'd had to walk his sled down the hill.

"If someone cuts you off, go around them," David coached. "You can use the rudder and your body weight to turn the sled."

"Dad," Bart said, "I had this conversation with Mrs. Hogan a million times. I know what I'm doing."

David looked at his son's round face and bit his tongue. The *Flying French Fry* wasn't nearly as fancy as most of the other sleds, and maybe it wasn't as fast either. He wanted to prepare Bart for the possibility of failure without making it seem as if he expected his son to lose.

"All I care about is that you do your best." David had already said this ten times, but what he was trying to say was that winning wouldn't change the way he felt about Bart. He squeezed his son's shoulder. "I love you, Bartholomew," he said as softly as he could and still be heard. "Remember, God is good—all the time."

Their gazes met and both nodded. As Bart shuffled off, David crunched through the snow to a spot a little farther down the slope to a free spot behind the orange safety netting.

It wasn't long before all the sleds had lined up. Inching even closer to the orange safety netting, David strained for a glimpse of his son's determined face.

"Racers—on your mark, get set, go!"

The line of sleds lurched forward. A sled shaped like a dolphin took the lead, followed by the bright yellow cylinder of a rocket ship.

"Go, Bart!" David yelled.

The *Flying French Fry* slid forward, not quite as fast as some, but better than others. A few remained stuck at the starting line and were just beginning to inch crookedly forward.

Eva had stated with clear confidence that Bart would win, but David hadn't believed her, not really. However, he couldn't deny that after a slow start, the *Flying French Fry* was picking up speed quickly.

David leaned over the orange safety net and yelled encouragement. He watched Bart navigate around the pirate ship sled, which had turned sideways and come to a stop. Next Bart passed the flying saucer ship, the race car, and one shaped like a mummy's sarcophagus.

Bart sailed down the hill and, to David's disbelieving eyes, took the lead. His gaze followed the *Flying French Fry* as it continued to put more distance between itself and the other sleds. A few heart-pounding moments later, Bart Denvers crossed the finish line and became the first qualifier for the box sled finals of the boys' junior division.

Millie leaned as far over the deck railing as she could, screaming her throat raw as Bart's sled crossed the finish line. She turned exultantly to Aunt Keeker, who was standing beside her jumping up and down and cheering so wildly that her hat flew over the side of the deck.

"He did it," they said at the same time, hugging and laughing. "He did it!"

"French fries rule!" Aunt Mimi shouted. She was dancing on top of the picnic table as Earl Gray bounced up and down next to her like a canine basketball.

"Oh my goodness," Aunt Lillian said. Her wheelchair was mashed up against the deck railing. "Did you see that?"

Eva leaned against the railing, eyes sparkling, her cheeks flushed with triumph. "I told you," she exclaimed. "I told you he could do it."

Their exultant mood, however, was tempered when in the next race Devon Spikes won his heat with the morning's best time.

"This isn't good," Millie said.

Eva shrugged. "The track is getting faster, that's all. Don't worry, honey."

But Millie couldn't help thinking of how big that kid was and how fast his sled had gone. By the time the seven finalists in Bart's category lined up, she'd bitten her nails down to stubs and was thinking about having a cup of her mom's spiked hot chocolate.

She searched the crowd on the sidelines for a glimpse of David, who surely had to be a nervous wreck. She wished she were standing next to him, but a voice inside said she didn't have the right to be there.

The finalists began to line up. The announcer introduced the racers by name and sled. Millie gripped the railing more tightly. *I don't know if You can hear me or not, but if You can, God, Bart could use some help.* Her mother squeezed her great bulk into the small space between Millie and Aunt Keeker. Millie found a small solace in the familiar feel of her body pressed against Millie's.

Leaning against the railing for support, Eva put her gloved hand over Millie's. "Here we go," she said.

The crowd roared as the sleds started down the hill. Millie leaned over the railing and yelled with all her might, "Go, Bart!"

The *Flying French Fry* slid forward. It was a faster start than Bart had had before, but not as fast as the rocket-shaped sled that slid into the lead. It was closely followed by a sled in the shape of a Wii controller. *Jaws*, the biggest sled on the hill, fought with a guitar-shaped sled for third place.

All around Millie people were screaming at the top of their lungs, and the combined weight of their excitement crushed her against the wooden railing. Millie's heart was in her throat as she watched the tight clusters of sleds progress down the hill. "Go, Bart," she screamed as he picked up speed and gained ground on the guitar and *Jaws* sled.

As if he'd heard her encouragement, the *French Fry* steadily accelerated and passed the guitar-shaped sled and the shark sled. She cheered as Bart drew even with the Wii-shaped controller.

A fat white flake plopped on her nose, startling her. It was starting to snow, and with dismay she realized the track would be slower. Some answer to her prayer, she thought as big flakes dotted the sky. Almost instantly the entire hill was veiled in a curtain of white lace.

Blinking, Millie strained to see the racers. In astonishment, she watched Bart close the gap between his sled and the rocket ship. They were almost dead even halfway down the hill. However, the *Jaws* sled was bearing down on them rapidly and moments later pulled up alongside Bart's sled.

"Come on, Bart," Eva bellowed. "Take him," she yelled in a more commanding tone of voice than Millie had ever heard before. "Take him down!"

But then Devon Spikes turned his sled into the *Flying French Fry*. It looked like the *Jaws* sled was trying to put the *Flying French Fry* in its mouth—or rather, push it sideways and out of the running.

She shouted a warning and tasted the icy flakes that spiraled into her mouth. She gripped her mother's arm without thinking what she was doing. "Bart's in trouble," she screamed.

"Use the rudder," Eva shouted so loudly it hurt Millie's ears.

The floor of the deck vibrated under the intensity of the cheering crowd as the *Jaws* sled increased its pressure and managed to alter the *Flying French Fry*'s course.

However, just as it seemed Bart's sled would be pushed completely sideways, the sled shaped like a Wii controller came up hard on Bart's right. It either couldn't turn or didn't have time because it slammed into the right side of Bart's sled. The blow straightened out the *Flying French Fry* and sent it flying down the hill.

Millie leaned as far over the railing as she could and screamed, "Go, Bart!" Her muscles strained as the *Flying French Fry* and the *Jaws* sled battled it out for the lead. Precious seconds passed. Millie measured the remaining distance to the finish line with her gaze and dug her fingernails into the wooden railing.

Seconds later, both sleds passed beneath the finish line. It was impossible to tell if it had been Bart or Devon who had won. A hush fell over the crowd as everyone waited for the results.

"I think I'm going to have a heart attack," Keeker said, fanning herself rapidly.

The silence was agonizing. Millie watched Bart get out of his sled. His gaze traveled around the crowd, probably looking for his father, but then it settled on Millie. A flush of pleasure shot through her when he grinned and waved.

"Ladies and gentlemen," the announcer's voice boomed over the ski hill. "We have the results of the closest finish today." There was a long pause. "After careful consideration, and thanks to Joseph Fairbranch photography, we have determined the winner." There was another long pause. "Setting a new record in the junior boys' division is. . .Bart Denvers and the *Flying French Fry*."

Millie jumped into the air and screamed. She high-fived Eva, hugged Aris, and leaned over to kiss Lillian's cheek. Keeker thumped her on the back.

"Never a doubt in my mind," Eva declared, beaming. She met Millie's gaze and gestured with her arm. "Now go on, honey. Don't wait for us. Go give that boy a hug."

Chapter 33

David grinned as Bart lifted the silver trophy above his head. Beside him, David's father fired off shots with a camera lens roughly the size of a canon. His mother had her cell pressed to her ear and was excitedly passing along the news to her sister in Wisconsin. A small crowd of kids Bart's age had formed a semicircle around them and were cheering. He spotted Millie in the back with Eva and the aunts and motioned for her to come closer, but she shook her head and gave him a big smile.

Bart had won. It hadn't quite sunk in yet. Nevertheless, there Bart was, trophy in hand, getting congratulated by Thomas Linklin, the tall, deeply tanned owner of the ski hill.

The award ceremony was short. Afterward there was handshaking and backslapping. Eva was triumphant and invited everyone within earshot back to the café for ice cream. Judging from the enthusiastic cheer that went up, it was going to be a big group.

Leaving Bart with the sled, David hiked to the back of the lot to get the Lexus. He planned to call Devon Spikes's parents that very evening and let them know that he was meeting with the principal and that he would not tolerate any further harassment.

His heart stopped as he pulled the Lexus to the snowy curb and saw Bart talking to the very kid he had been thinking about. He got *out* of the car, started to march right over there, and then hesitated. Instinct urged him to wait, to give Bart a chance to work this out. Part of him screamed in protest as the bully kid, a full head taller, leaned over Bart, who kept pushing his glasses nervously higher on his face.

David's fists clenched. He'd give them two more minutes, and then he was marching over there and letting Devon Spikes know what it felt like when a much bigger person leaned over him.

More words were exchanged. The bully gave Bart a small push. David stepped forward. At the same time, his son's chin came up and his hands went to his hips. It wasn't a gesture David saw often, but when he did, it meant Bart was about to get very stubborn.

His son said something, and surprisingly the bully jerked as if in surprise. Bart said something else. The bully considered and then a moment later pulled off his ski hat (Bart's hat actually), threw it on the ground, and stormed off. Bart picked the hat off the ground, dusted it off, and stuffed it in his pocket.

David crunched through the snow over to his son. "Are you okay?"

Bart's eyes blinked at him from behind the thick lenses. "Yeah."

"What just happened? Did that bully threaten you?"

His son's cheeks were reddened from the cold, and his hair stood almost upright where the wind had riffled through it. Yet Bart didn't look as if he felt the cold at all. "He tried to push me around, but I handled it." He picked up the towrope to the sled. "We can go now."

"First, I want to know what he said to you—and what you said to him."

Bart seemed to think about this then nodded. "He wanted me to give him the money I just won, but I wouldn't."

David nodded grimly. "And then he threatened you?"

"Yeah, but don't worry, Dad. He won't touch me." Bart gave a small laugh. "Miss Hogan was right."

Frowning, David tried to remember what Millie might have said. "About what?"

"That I could outsmart him."

"How'd you do that?"

Bart stood a little taller. "Well, since I got the highest grade in my class on the last science test, I get to pick my lab partner for this week. It's a double grade, Dad. I told Devon that I would pick him as my partner." A smug smile appeared on Bart's face. "I told him that I had a 99 percent average and could fail the lab and still hold my A. I asked him what a zero would do to his grade." Bart paused. "At first he said it didn't matter and that he'd still beat me up. But then he figured out that if he was failing science he couldn't play on the ice hockey team." Bart grinned. "After that he was happy to let me keep the winnings and give me back my ski hat."

David grinned. "Brilliant. That was brilliant. I'm proud of you."

Bart shrugged, but his eyes gleamed. "You are?"

"Absolutely. It took courage to do what you just did."

Bart tipped his head but not before David glimpsed the pleasure in his eyes. "Dad," he said, "I've been thinking. Even though I can handle Devon, I want to go with you when you meet with the principal on Monday."

"What?"

"Devon's a bully. He might start bothering someone else, especially if we get a new student. I don't want them to go through what I did."

David rubbed his hand over Bart's spikey hair then snaked his arm around his son's shoulders, pulling him close. "That's a fine idea," he said thickly. "A very fine idea."

Chapter 34

Millie's arm ached from digging scoops of the rock-hard ice cream. "Here you go." She smiled and passed a double scoop of chocolate ice cream into the waiting hands of a skinny, dark-haired boy.

"Thanks, Miss Hogan." The boy flashed a brilliant smile, showing off a mouthful of silver braces.

"You're welcome." She pushed back her bangs with her shoulder. "Next?"

"Triple scoop of chocolate, vanilla, and strawberry," a tall red-haired boy said. He had a face full of freckles and a sunburn that marked the line of his ski hat. "And sprinkles. I love sprinkles."

"You got it," Millie said, putting some muscle into scooping.

As she handed over the cone, she spotted Bart and David talking with Mr. and Mrs. Denvers. David's mother smiled warmly at her. Of course Mrs. Denvers was happy. She had the goods on Millie.

Millie lifted her arm to wave back and felt cold drops of ice cream dribble onto her wrist. *Act happy,* she reminded herself. *Today is about Bart.*

At the table in front of the bay window, Millie's mother sat with the aunts. They were laughing even more loudly than the kids. For a moment, she soaked up the sight of seeing Eva so happy, and then her shoulders sagged. Her mother would have to be told about Max. She hadn't thought about that before.

Overwhelmed with this new worry, Millie asked Aris to take her place then excused herself to the back. Fleeing through the swinging doors, she wiped her hands on her apron. Unseeing, she passed the grill, the sinks, and the freezer. When she reached the back pantry, she jerked the door open and stepped inside. Without turning on the light, she shut the door and walked to the back of the room.

What do I do? How do I make this pain go away? I can't bear it anymore. I just can't. I just can't.

Covering her face with her hands, she made a keening noise. All these years, she'd thought she had star potential. What an idiot she'd been.

She pulled out the court papers from her apron pocket. It was too dark to read them, but holding them produced fresh agony. How could he have done this? Stolen from innocent people? Hardworking people who gave their money to the church.

Her father was the most heartless, selfish person she knew. And yet, even now, even holding the papers in her hands, she realized there was part of her that still loved him. As disappointed as she was in him, she still wanted to see what he looked like, to hear what he would say to her.

The door cracked open, and a wedge of light broke the darkness. David stood in the entranceway. She quickly swiped her eyes.

"Millie?" David stepped forward. "Are you okay?"

She grabbed a can off the shelf and plastered a smile on her face. "Oh sure." Maybe she'd never see Hollywood, but she could certainly act her way out of the pantry.

The lights flickered and then came on. He'd found the switch, and the sudden brightness was painful.

"We were running a little low on supplies, so I came back here."

"Yes," David agreed, "the kids would be very disappointed if you ran out of tomatoes." He glanced pointedly at the can in her hands.

Millie laughed. "Oh, right. I meant to grab the chocolate syrup. Guess I should have turned on the light after all." She gave another ridiculous little laugh. "So much for conserving energy."

"Millie," David said gently, "don't do this."

"Do what?" She flashed her best smile.

"Pretend. You're pretending with me. Don't." He studied her carefully. "You don't look right. You didn't at the ski hill either."

"That's not something you tell a girl." Millie pushed her hair out of her eye and batted her eyelashes. "No woman wants to hear she doesn't look good."

"I'm not saying that you don't look good. I'm saying that you don't look *right*. What's wrong?"

"Seriously, David. Nothing." She wasn't sure how much longer she could hold it together. "Let's get back to the party."

"In a minute. First talk to me."

Millie shook her head. "Nothing is wrong."

"Ever since the box sled race you've been avoiding me."

"I've been scooping ice cream," Millie said evasively. "I had no idea preteen boys could eat like that." She made sure her eyes crinkled at the corners when she smiled and wished David would stop giving her that doctor look—the one that said he saw right through her.

Her gaze dropped to her boots. Her good ones—the ones Eva said were too thin and too high-heeled. Stylish but impractical, they'd pinched her toes since the day she'd bought them. She wondered if her father wore orange sneakers to go with the orange jumpsuit.

"Are you getting goosey about us?"

She looked up. David stood about a foot in front of her. She felt the first domino in her heart trip, and she had to steel all her willpower not to step into his arms. "I don't think *goosey* is a real word."

"You know what it means."

Her shoulders sagged. He wasn't going to let her out of the pantry until she told him the truth. She opened her mouth, but no words came out, just a long breath that if visible would have been the color of shame. "Not now, David. Please. Let today be about Bart."

"I can't do that, Millie. Talk to me."

She shook her head. "Please."

"Was it my mother? If she hurt you, I want to know."

She folded her arms firmly across her chest and looked down.

"She said something, didn't she?" David's voice had an angry edge to it. "I'm going to go out there right now and tell her to apologize."

"Don't do that," she said. "She didn't say anything." At least not yet. Apparently Mrs. Denvers hadn't told David about Millie's father. But she would, especially if David confronted her.

He touched her hair. "You've been crying. Let me fix whatever is wrong."

She dug her fingers into the palms of her hands. "That's the problem. You can't." Shame was ugly. Private. Humiliating. "I'll tell you everything, but not today."

"This isn't how it works," David said. "I told you, I'm not the leaving kind of guy. I'm not leaving you alone with whatever problem you're facing. You're just making it worse because I don't know what's going on."

"Fine," Millie said then began to laugh. "You want to know?

285

Well, my father's a crook."

"So what."

She laughed again and realized just how close to tears she was. She was not a girl who cried, and the thought helped steady her. "I found out he's serving time. He's in a prison in Utah. Aris gave me these papers today." She thrust the pages at him.

His eyes skimmed over the papers. "This is it? This is what you're so upset about?"

Millie stiffened. "David, I just said my father is a criminal."

"I heard you."

"My father *embezzled* money from a church." She was having trouble keeping her voice down. "He's a *criminal.*" She waited for his expression to change. "He's probably making license plates as we speak."

"I don't care."

"You should. He's my father—I'm his daughter."

"So? He's human and made a mistake. We all do."

"When was the last time you embezzled twenty-five thousand dollars?" As expected, he was silent. "Come on, David. There are good people in this world and bad. My dad falls into the latter category."

"You're oversimplifying," David argued. "People aren't all good or all bad. You can't heap them into two piles—one to be saved, one to be tossed."

She snorted. "You don't understand. Your father stuck around and raised you. He might have some annoying habits you don't like, but essentially you know who he is. You know who you are because of him."

David shook his head. "I don't downplay his role in raising me, but ultimately he doesn't define me." He hesitated. "Just as your father doesn't define you."

"You can look at your parents and see parts of yourself in them. How would you feel, David, if your father did something terrible? Wouldn't you wonder if you were capable of doing the same thing— or worse? Wouldn't you wonder who you were inside?"

David reached out for her hands. "I might. But I hope I would also turn to God and ask Him to save me, to define who I was on the inside."

Millie remembered her own unanswered prayers from childhood. *Bring my father home. Make my mother stop eating so much. Please don't let my grandmother die. Help me get out of Deer Park. Make me famous. Shorter. Thinner. Smarter.* "What if God doesn't want to?" She felt the hopelessness rise in her.

"That wouldn't happen." David's grip on her fingers tightened. "Your father abandoned you—that was a terrible thing—and I know it hurt you deeply." He leaned a little closer. "But you have a heavenly Father, Millie. He loves you, and He's never going to abandon you. You are His beloved daughter."

She jerked her hands free. "Beloved daughter?" She made a strangled noise. "He doesn't love me." She could feel a slow anger burning inside. How could David do this? Suggest her life could be changed by turning to God and simply saying, "Save me." "That's like throwing dental floss to someone drowning."

"God loves you, Millie. He is the Father you need."

She stood taller in her anger. "How could you possibly say that? You've never had the bottom of your world fall out."

He didn't flinch. "Yes I have. And it hurt. And I questioned. But in the end, I accepted." His blue eyes seemed to bore into her. "Sometimes it feels like you're completely torn apart, and you can't even breathe without it hurting. But you give the pain to God,

Millie, and He takes it, and then somehow—I don't know how—
He finds a way of making things new."

"Just because God helped you doesn't mean He's going to help
me. I wasn't going to tell you this today, David, but we're breaking
up." She hadn't decided this until now, but she realized her mind
was made up.

David just looked at her. "Millie, I know you're upset about this,
but—"

"We're breaking up," Millie interrupted. She was hurting, and
something unkind in her wanted to hurt him, too. She stuck out her
hand. "It's been very nice, but it's over." It was her standard breakup
line. Judging from the tightness of his jaw, he'd recognized it.

He ignored her outstretched hand. "Don't do this."

"We'll tell people tomorrow. Right along with my other big
news."

"I'm not telling anyone we're breaking up—period. Because we
aren't. Breaking up with me because your father is in jail doesn't
make sense."

"Maybe not to you, but it does to me." She reached for a bag
of marshmallows just to hold something in her hands. "Besides, it
never would have worked anyway."

"How do you know that?"

"Because we're too different."

There was less than a hand's width of space between their faces.
She could see the tightness of his skin and the storm in his eyes. She
was getting to him, but the knowledge gave her no pleasure.

"What I see," David said in a very controlled voice, "is someone
who's scared of getting hurt again. Your father hurt you when he
left, and you don't trust easily. But sooner or later you're going to
see that I'm not going anywhere. I'm not going to leave you."

Millie lifted her chin. "You won't leave me," she said. "But that doesn't mean I won't leave you." She saw his eyes flicker with surprise. "You and Bart could wake up one morning and I could be halfway to California. Maybe there's more of my father in me than either of us realizes."

Suddenly the pantry door opened, and Eva said, "Oh, sorry. I didn't mean to interrupt. I was coming back here for a box of those Social Tea Biscuits Lillian likes." She started to back awkwardly away on the crutches then paused as she took in their expressions. Her face seemed to deflate as she realized she'd stepped into the middle of an argument.

"Oh no, Millie," Eva murmured. "Don't do this. Don't break up with him."

"This is not your business," Millie said tightly. "Please leave."

Eva closed her eyes and shook her head. "Well, she may be dumping you, David, but I'm not. If you were my own son, I couldn't love you more."

"Thanks, Eva. The feeling is mutual. And by the way, Millie and I aren't breaking up."

"Yes we are," Millie said. "It's been fun, but now it's time for both of us to move on."

"My foot," Eva said. "I'll try to talk some sense into her, David."

"You're on his side?"

"Absolutely," Eva agreed.

"You're my mother," Millie pointed out. "You have to take my side."

"I don't have to do anything." She looked at David as if Millie weren't there at all. "What seems to be the problem?"

David just looked at Millie.

"The problem," Millie said, "is that David won't listen to me."

"I'm listening to you. I'm just not agreeing with you."

"Well, what is it that you don't agree about?" Eva's gaze swung back and forth between them. Her voice was conciliatory, as if Millie and David had been two kids squabbling over the same toy. "My vote can be the tiebreaker, and then we can all go back outside and enjoy ourselves."

Millie and David exchanged glances. She could see in his eyes that he wanted Millie to be the one to break the news about Millie's father. She wanted to disagree, but couldn't. "Mom," she said. "I think it's something we should discuss in private."

Eva frowned. "Whatever you have to say, you can say it in front of David."

"It's okay, Eva. Millie's right." He gave Millie a final look. "I'll just be outside if you need me."

It registered that as angry as he was with her, he was reluctant to leave her, and her fingers almost clutched at him as he released his grip on her.

As soon as the pantry door clicked shut behind him, Millie tore open the bag of marshmallows. "Here," she said. "Maybe you'd better have one."

"That bad," Eva replied, but made no move to take the marshmallow.

"Yeah," Millie said. She thought about eating the marshmallow but then dropped it back in the bag and set it on the shelf. She looked at a bar of semisweet chocolate but knew that no food was going to make this any easier. "It's about Dad. I found out some things about him today."

A stillness crept over Eva's features, and the color seemed to leave her face. "Max? What about him?" Her hand flew to her mouth. "He didn't up and die, did he?"

Millie flinched at the panic in her mother's eyes. "No," she said. "Unfortunately, he is very much alive."

"He's sick then—cancer?"

"No." She hesitated. "He's in jail." She paused. "He's serving time in the Utah State Prison."

"Prison?" Eva's jaw dropped, and her eyes widened. "I'll be darned. What'd he do?"

Millie braced herself for her mother's reaction. "Embezzled twenty-five thousand dollars."

"Oh no," she sighed. The lines in her face deepened. "Couldn't keep his hand out of the till, could he?"

"Apparently not."

"Who'd he steal from this time?"

Millie froze. "What do you mean, 'Who'd he steal from this time?' He did it before?"

Eva's face sagged. "Oh yes." She sighed. "Sometimes you close your eyes and tell yourself that things are fine. You know they're not, but you need them to be, so you make yourself believe they are."

"Mom, what are you talking about? What else did Dad steal?"

Her mother's face twisted. "I didn't want you to know, Millie. Swear to God, I loved that man, and I didn't want you to think less of him."

"Mom, please." Millie wanted to demand her mother answer her question, but her words came out barely above a whisper. "Tell me what happened." She waited a few moments then couldn't help herself. "Please."

Eva sighed. "It's a long story."

Chapter 35

Deer Park, South Dakota
Twenty years earlier

The tools clanked as Eva dropped the screwdriver into the tool chest. Wiping her hands on her jeans, she turned the dial to the spin cycle then stepped back to watch. The washing machine jumped to life. She listened as the spinner whirled inside the washer. She snorted in satisfaction as it moved smoothly through the cycle without cutting out once. All it needed was for her to tighten the drive belt.

Just how many housewives could fix a washing machine? *Saved us at least a hundred bucks,* she'd proudly tell Max when he came home from work.

She thought about rewarding herself with one of those butter scones her mother had made this morning, topped with the homemade strawberry jam, canned right from their own plants in the backyard, but a quick check of her watch confirmed that if she wanted everything just right before Max came home, she didn't have time.

"Success," she called out to her mother, who was sitting in Max's leather recliner watching a soap opera.

"Come sit for a moment, honey. You won't believe the acting—
so awful. You can see them squinting at the cue cards."

Eva smiled and shook her head. "Gotta get dinner started and
Max's shirts ironed before I pick up Millie from school."

Plus she needed to shower. Max liked it when she met him at the
door with her hair freshly washed and styled, her makeup carefully
applied, and the folds of her dress neatly pressed.

"I'll help." Her mother clicked off the television and heaved her
bulk out of the chair. "I'll peel. You can chop."

Eva hid a sigh of relief. Max didn't like it when he came home
from work and her mother was sitting in his chair. She didn't blame
him. He worked hard all day. He had a right to his own recliner.

"So Millie's late today?"

Eva pulled out the cutting board. "Yes. Someone needs to tell
that drama coach this is Deer Park, South Dakota. It's not like the
kids are performing on Broadway."

Retrieving a bag of potatoes from the pantry, she pulled two
peelers out of the drawer. She wished Millie would concentrate
more on her academics and less on the fifth-grade play. She had a
low B average, but Eva felt this reflected a lack of interest more than
a lack of ability.

Soon the sausages were browning and the dumplings simmering
in a creamy bacon sauce. She asked her mom to keep an eye on
things and headed outside to grab Max's shirts off the laundry line.
Pressing them to her face, she inhaled the aroma of sunshine and
soap—and the barest traces of Max, traces that still had the power
to make her heart race and her insides turn to jelly.

She steamed the shirts smooth, using just a whisper of starch and
letting the iron linger longest at the cuffs and collars. Max took great
pride in his appearance, and this small vanity had always appealed

to her. With his thick, dark hair and smoky gray eyes, he attracted the gazes of other women. She and Max always laughed about it, and something inside bloomed each time he told her there was no one else but her.

There was no one else for her either. She'd been living in Centerville, Ohio, working at the Marriott as an assistant pastry chef in Dayton when Sandy had raced into the kitchen with the news that a hot guy at table nine wanted to meet the person who'd baked the German chocolate cake.

She was thirty years old and lived with her widowed mother. She'd been realistic about the future—she had the broad frame of her father and the plain, unmemorable features of her mother. She hadn't expected to look into the charcoal eyes of a tall, wavy-haired man with an easy smile and fall in love, but it'd happened. Even more miraculous, he'd fallen for her.

They'd been married six weeks later. He moved into their small two-story Cape Cod in Centerville, and Eva felt as if he'd swept back the curtains of her life and let the sunlight flood inside. He did silly romantic things like write in the margins of her recipe books—*add 100 kisses gradually; hug thoroughly before baking; dust with 50 grams of powdered love.* He wrote I Love You on the steam in the bathroom mirror and slipped rose petals between their sheets.

When he was fired from his job as a salesperson at Sears because the cash register hadn't balanced, she knew it was some kind of computer error. *"Let's see this as an opportunity to start fresh somewhere else. Deer Park, South Dakota,"* he'd said. *"A small town in the Black Hills. We could raise a family there. And who knows, I might find gold in the mountains, and then we'd live like kings. What do you say? Why be ordinary when together we're extraordinary?"*

He hadn't found gold though—just a job as a conductor on

the Black Hills Central Railroad line. The family they'd imagined hadn't exactly happened either. She'd had trouble getting pregnant. Increasingly she'd see him looking out the window. She tried her best to hold on to him by cooking his favorite meals, keeping the house spotless, and greeting him at the door with a smile and a funny story. Despite her efforts, he was restless. *"What are you thinking?"* she'd ask him. *"Nothing,"* he'd say. It was only a matter of time before he left, and she knew it.

And then Eva woke up one morning, looked into the mirror, and saw something different in her eyes. Something as fragile as the wings of a butterfly. Millie had been born nine months later.

"We're naming her after you," Eva had said, holding the precious bundle out to him.

"I don't think Max is a good name for a girl."

"You're a Maximillian," she said. "Millie's close enough."

It hadn't been the girl names they'd discussed. Hannah, Trudy, Emma—these names had flowed through Eva's mind like clear, fresh water. She'd spent hours dipping her hands into this beautiful pool of possibility, picturing the moment when she'd look into her baby's face and hand her the right name like a bouquet of flowers. But then, looking at the light in Max's eyes, she'd realized that she had finally found the one gossamer thread that would tie him to her forever.

Eva hung the last shirt on the hanger then trudged upstairs to their bedroom. The closet was crowded—mostly his stuff. She smiled at the line of blue and gray suits, the hangers all facing the same direction. Clothing for *someday.*

Until then, he wore them to church on Sunday. He was an usher, and she was proud of the way the minister knew them both by name. She liked watching Max move about the church, as at ease in the chapel as he was in his own home. People's eyes lit up when they saw him. She watched his lips move, the easy smile, the way he'd squeeze a man's shoulder in affection, hold out his arm to an elderly woman.

She made space on the wooden rod for the last shirt. Stepping back, she checked to see that they hung evenly and were sorted by color and style. Frowning, she noticed the flap on one of his suit coats sticking up. She started to smooth it flat and felt a bulge. Reaching into the pocket, her fingers touched something small and square. Without thinking, she pulled it out.

The envelope was small and blue and bore the name of the Deer Park United Methodist Church. There was twenty-five dollars in cash inside, and Eva's first thought was that Max had forgotten to put their offering in the plate the past Sunday. But then she remembered that she herself had dropped their envelope into the gold plate. So what was this one doing in Max's coat pocket?

She turned the edges slowly. There was spidery handwriting on the back—*Mr. & Mrs. Edward Hobbson*. She tapped the paper and wondered if Max had found the envelope on the ground and forgotten to turn it in. It made sense, but then she looked down the long row of Max's wool suits. He'd bought a new one just last week, and she'd worried about them being able to afford it. She didn't like the direction of her thoughts but couldn't seem to stop them. The one time she'd teased Max about his suit collection, he'd about taken her head off. *"Are you starving?"* he'd almost shouted.

Eva remembered feeling every one of the twenty-five pounds she'd gained since Millie's birth.

She bit her lower lip hard. What was she thinking—that Max funded his buying habits with church money? Max was no thief. She'd been watching too many episodes of *Matlock* with her mother. Replacing the envelope, she berated herself for doubting her husband. Max was a good man. He'd never said one word about supporting her mother.

The next day, however, she kept thinking about that envelope. When she checked Max's jacket pocket, it was gone. Something nagged at her, and she began searching Max's suit pockets every Monday morning as soon as he left for the railroad. She disliked herself for doing it but couldn't seem to stop. Weeks went by, and when she found nothing, she began to relax.

But then one Thursday night in April, the trash bag burst open as she carried it to the garage. Holding back an oath, she bent to clean up the mess. Her hands had faltered at the sight of little pieces of robin's egg–blue paper. Squatting on the cold concrete, she'd begun painstakingly sorting through the trash until she'd found every scrap. Slowly she began piecing them together.

When she was finished, she sat looking at the small puzzles around her. Together they formed the answer to a larger puzzle—the one that had nagged at her ever since she'd pulled the offering envelope out of Max's pocket a month ago. He was stealing—why else were there offering envelopes with other people's names on them in their trash?

Her hands flew to her face. What was she going to do about it? She had no college education and hadn't held a paying job in ten years. She had her mother to think about and Millie. How would she support them if Max went to jail? But if she said nothing, how could she live with him? With herself?

Looking at the piecemeal envelopes, she drew a shaky breath. *My God, what am I going to do?*

The air was very still as she ripped the paper into even smaller pieces then gathered them in her hands. Throwing them into the air, Eva watched her life fall down around her like scraps of confetti.

Chapter 36

Deer Park, South Dakota
The present

Dad was stealing from the church?" It wasn't so much a question as a statement, a way of getting the facts to sink into the dry earth of her brain. Millie looked into her mother's haunted brown eyes. She wondered what else her mother had kept from her.

"For five years. Maybe longer."

"How'd you find that out?"

"I couldn't sleep. I kept thinking about the people who were giving the church their hard-earned money and how Max was using it to buy himself nice things. So one night I confronted him about the envelopes. He denied it of course. But then I began reciting names off the envelopes. I told him I would call the church if he didn't do it himself. I was bluffing, but it was the only way I could get him to stop."

Where had Millie been when all this was going on? How could she not have known? She racked her brain for any arguments or signs of tension between her parents but came out blank. "But he wouldn't?"

Her mother shook her head and frowned deeply. "He argued

that he deserved to be paid for his work at the church. He said what he took came out to less than minimum wage."

Millie tried to reconcile this image with the soft-spoken man who had encouraged her to learn Bible passages. "That's crazy."

"Of course it was crazy, and I threatened to go to the church board. We went back and forth until finally I got him to agree to stop stealing and to repay the church. We sat up late with a yellow pad and figured out how much he'd taken. We were both a little shocked at how it'd all added up." Eva sighed. "The next morning, though, when I woke up, he was gone."

Millie remembered that morning all too well. She'd thought her father had died. "How could you have known he was a thief and not tell me?"

"You were ten years old. What good would it have done?"

Millie's response ballooned inside, and it took her a moment to get the words out. "Maybe I wouldn't have spent all that time wondering why he left. Maybe I wouldn't have missed him so much."

Eva shook her head. "You adored him—as I did. I wouldn't take that away from you."

"You should have told me. I had a right to know."

"You were a child, and I was trying to protect you. Bad enough that everyone in town knew he'd abandoned us—but it'd be worse if they knew he stole. He'd have gone to jail."

Millie's eyebrows shot up. "Maybe he should have. Covering up for him was wrong. You should have gone to the police."

Eva's eyes narrowed. "Don't be so quick to tell me what I should have done. You don't know what you would have done if you were me. Sometimes it's not a matter of right or wrong but simply survival. I did what I thought was best." She shifted a little on the crutches. "Besides, as much as I hated what he did, I didn't hate him." She gave Millie a long look. "He gave me you, Millie. And he tried to stick around. He just couldn't."

"What do you mean he couldn't? Were we that bad?"

"Ah, Millie, it wasn't about us. It never was." She sighed. "His father drank. And when he was drunk, he told Max that it was a good thing God made him attractive because he was stupid. He blamed Max and Max's mom for everything that'd gone wrong in his life. When people tell you something long enough, you start to believe it. So when Max's life didn't work out the way he hoped it might, he blamed us—just like his dad blamed his wife and child. He loved both of us, Millie, but he hurt inside. I guess he thought he would hurt less somewhere else."

"Yeah—the thought of paying back the church had to be unbearably painful."

"He wasn't all bad," Eva said sharply. "That's all I'm trying to say."

"Did he. . ." Millie hesitated then took a breath. "Did he ever write you. . .or try to contact you. . .or ask about me?"

Her mother shook her head. "No." The crutches clicked as Eva took a step forward and placed her hand on Millie's arm. "He loved you. I know he wouldn't have stuck around so long otherwise."

Millie made a scoffing noise. "If this is the way you treat someone you love, I'd hate to see how he treated someone he didn't."

Eva squeezed her shoulder. "Let it go, honey. For your own sake, let it go. Look at what you have, not at what you don't."

"What I have is a father in jail and a mother who hid the truth from me." Millie wiped her cheeks, furious with herself for showing this weakness.

"What you have," Eva corrected, "is a man who loves you and an opportunity to build a life together here. Let the rest go."

Millie didn't think she could let it go—even if she wanted to. "What about the people he stole from—should they let it go, too?"

Her mother's shoulders straightened. "I repaid every cent he took from the church. Took me ten years, but I did it."

Millie's jaw dropped. "You what?"

"I went to Sarah Stockman and told her everything. I mailed the church a check once a month."

Millie's hand went to her mouth. This was the Sarah her mother had been rambling about that night in the hospital. "How did you do this without me knowing about it?"

"I wrote the check out of my personal account, not Dosie's."

Millie thought about the way her mother held on to things— the furniture that was old and faded, the ugly green shag rug. Even her clothing was dated. As a child, Millie remembered cringing when Eva came to pick her up. She remembered wishing she was fashionable like her friends' mothers. It had never occurred to her that her mother simply hadn't had the money to put into the house or her appearance.

"I wish you'd told me," Millie whispered. "I would have helped."

"It wasn't your burden. And anyway, it's all paid off. Every last dime of it. With interest."

Millie's shoulders sagged. "All these years I never knew any of this. I always thought we gave up going to church because we felt judged. That you didn't like people looking at us and wondering what happened to Dad."

"Oh no, honey. It wasn't that at all. I couldn't go to church knowing what your father had done. I was too ashamed. I should have seen it sooner." She patted Millie's shoulder awkwardly. "I'm sorry, Millie. I've leaned on you harder than a parent should. And I've thought I've known what was best for you.

"But I want you to know that breaking my hip was a good thing. It's given me a lot of time to think about things. Lillian and I have talked about this, and we've decided that we make pretty good roommates. She's invited me to move in with her. So what I'm saying, Millie, is that we can sell the house. It's all paid off, and there should be enough profit to send you to Hollywood."

"What? Are you serious?" Millie shook her head. "I'm not leaving you—not with a broken hip and all this stuff about Dad. Who'd run the café? Who'd make sure you took your medicine?"

"You're not my keeper," Eva said firmly. "I am not your responsibility, and neither is this café. I guess there was part of me that always thought you wanted to be here, but I see now that you don't, and it's time for me to stop telling myself lies. I want you to be happy, Millie. I've always wanted that."

"I'm not abandoning you," Millie said firmly.

"We don't have to decide this today, but it's something to think about."

"I don't have to think about it. I'm not leaving you."

"Of course you aren't." Her mother's eyes filled with tears, and her whole face seemed to strain with the effort to hold them back. "No matter where you go or how far you go, you're still my daughter. And I love you."

Millie's heart tightened in her chest. Stepping forward, she bent her head and carefully pressed it into the curve of her mother's neck. "I love you, too." Hugging her carefully, she added, "We're the M&M's."

"Only you're not so plain, and maybe I'm not so nutty." Eva chuckled and began to stroke Millie's hair. "Now go on back there, and if anyone asks about your father, you hold your head high and tell them that he'd probably love a visitor. That ought to shut them up. Come on, honey, wipe your eyes and put a smile on your face. We've got a party going on out there."

Chapter 37

The house on Cherry Lane felt quiet and empty without Eva. In the kitchen, Millie made tea just to hear the kettle whistle then sat at the table with her hands wrapped around the warm mug.

She glanced at the telephone, hoping David would call and knowing that if he did, she wouldn't talk to him. She didn't understand this paradox in herself—wanting something she had decided to reject. As if she needed pain more than love.

It was an odd thought, and yet she had spent years responding to online audition calls and had never gotten anything except rejection. She had played out an endless cycle of hope and despair. Over and over she had confirmed in her mind that she wasn't good enough.

Standing, Millie dumped her cold tea into the sink. She strained to see out the window, but the glass was black and reflected only her own pale image. She touched the window, and the deep cold instantly penetrated her skin. *This is what aloneness feels like,* she thought. *A cold so deep it chills to the bone.*

It would be warmer in California, she assured herself. The air would smell of the ocean, and she would take acting lessons. She would go on casting calls and walk every day on the beach. She would stay too busy to be lonely.

The rooster clock clicked off the seconds. *Are you sure?* the sweep of its tail seemed to ask. *Are you sure? Are you sure?*

Millie took her palm off the glass windowpane. The smudge remained like a ghostly handprint. No, she wasn't sure of anything, and that was the problem.

A few hours later, Millie gave up trying to sleep. She pulled on jeans and a sweater and headed for her car. The Subaru cranked wearily in the cold night. With no destination in mind, she drove through the silent streets. She thought about simply driving until she ran out of gas or money or the will to keep going.

She stopped at a red light and rested her head on the steering wheel. She'd reached the intersection of Mill Road and Route 41. One direction would take her to the highway, the other into town. *If you don't go now, you never will,* a voice said inside her. *Stop using your mother's health as an excuse to stay here. The truth is that you've let her, maybe even encouraged her to depend on you, because as long as she needs you, she won't leave you.*

The light turned green. She wanted to deny that she'd had any role in enabling Eva to neglect her health, but she knew it was possible.

The light changed again, but she couldn't lift her foot from the brake. She thought of David and the things he had said to her. Did she really want him to remember her as someone who had snuck out in the middle of the night without even saying good-bye?

When the light changed again, she turned left toward town.

Inside the café, she flipped on the lights and walked into the kitchen. Her boots clicked on the tile floor as she trudged to the pantry. Lugging the twenty-five pound bag of wheat flour to the mixing bowls, she set to work.

For once she welcomed the physical work of lifting, kneading, pounding the dough into shape. Under her hands, the dough changed form and shape. She imagined her father's face, smashed it flat, and then formed it again.

The tears fell for all the years she'd spent thinking she wasn't pretty, smart, or good enough. She thought of all the men she'd gone out with—men who had given her attention and affection but hadn't been able to fill the empty space in her heart or make the pain go away for very long.

Her hands shook as she cut the dough into smaller parts and put them in bowls to rise. Placing them in the warming trays in the oven, she started the next batch. Emptying flour into the huge bowls, she wondered if customers would taste her grief in the loaves of bread.

By the time Lottie arrived, the morning's baking was finished and she had no more tears, only the sense of one more thing that needed to be done. Leaving Lottie in charge, she headed for her car.

As she climbed the stone steps, the steeple of the church seemed to tower over her. Two people in heavy winter coats stood in front of the thick wooden doors. Her smile felt numb as she took the program and stepped into the church.

Inside, it took a few seconds for her eyes to adjust to the dim, candlelit interior. The church was long and deep, the ceiling dark and high above her. There were rows and rows of polished wood benches, most of them filled. The organ was playing something slow and ponderous. Her gaze lifted to the stained-glass image of Jesus on the cross, and she swallowed with difficulty. She didn't belong here. And yet she couldn't bring herself to leave either.

She slid into the pew at the far back of the church. Bowing her head, she avoided making eye contact with anyone. As a pianist played softly, she ran her finger along the polished curve of the pew in front of her. As a child, she used to trace her name on the wood, as if she were writing in invisible ink and God alone could see it.

The light coming through the stained-glass windows was just the same, too. If she tried, she could almost picture her father ushering people down the aisle. Moving slowly until he'd seated someone and then striding back up the aisle as if he couldn't get to the next person fast enough. Eva used to poke her, and they'd laugh about this.

The piano music changed, and people jumped to their feet singing. Millie didn't know the words and stood silently, listening.

> *Rock of Ages, cleft for me,*
> *Let me hide myself in Thee;*
> *Let the water and the blood,*
> *From Thy wounded side which flowed,*
> *Be of sin the double cure,*
> *Save from wrath and make me pure.*

The old hymn moved along slowly, gracefully. The music filled the church. But the words, what did they mean? Why did they make her chest so tight?

> *While I draw this fleeting breath,*
> *When my eyes shall close in death,*
> *When I rise to worlds unknown,*
> *And behold Thee on Thy throne,*

Rock of Ages, cleft for me,
Let me hide myself in Thee.

Millie clenched her hands so tightly that her fingernails bit into the palms of her hands. Hadn't some part of her been looking for a safe place to hide? Wasn't that part of the whole Hollywood dream—to surround herself with thick walls of success? Earn her father's love by accomplishing fame?

Maybe it didn't have to be that way. She lifted her gaze to the stained-glass image of Jesus. The pull to Him was strong, and yet she felt herself resist. Her palms were damp, and she felt so tired inside.

Millie closed her eyes. David had suggested that God was the only Father she needed. But what if he was wrong?

The next hymn started. The words stirred more memories. She wanted to believe God still loved her, but she wasn't a child anymore. She wasn't sure she could simply will her heart to open. And yet wasn't there hope inside her? Hope that He existed—and that He could feel her reaching out to Him? Wasn't that why she'd come?

She pressed her fingernails a fraction deeper into her palms and warned herself that the higher her hopes took her, the longer and harder her fall would be. She tried to be angry at David. If it weren't for him, she wouldn't be sitting here right now. She wouldn't be feeling that her life could change if only she would let it.

Reverend Stockman began the closing prayer. A sudden panic washed over her. The moments were slipping away, and she realized with excruciating clarity that she didn't want to walk out of the church as the same person who'd walked inside.

Squeezing her eyes shut, Millie gripped her hands together. *Heavenly Father, I have doubts. I am the child of the man who stole from You. There's no reason for You to help me, but I pray You will. I don't want to live like I'm living anymore.* She drew a shaky breath. *Please, Father, be my Father and save me.*

She wasn't sure if the prayer worked. She was, after all, the same person when she opened her eyes. On her way out of the church, she paused to shake hands with Reverend Stockman, who stood in a long receiving line. Clad in his black robe and collar, he looked much more imposing than when she'd last seen him. But he returned her smile, and there was joy in his eyes when he shook her hand. "Welcome home," he said.

"Thank you," she murmured.

She stepped past him into the bright morning sun. *Welcome home,* the reverend had said. As if she belonged. Here. In this church where her father had been a thief and she and her mother had avoided for twenty years. She felt a small flutter of hope in her chest. He said she belonged here.

Millie was halfway to her car when someone shouted her name. She turned slowly. Squinting in the bright sunlight, she saw David hurrying toward her. His black wool coat flapped open, revealing his navy suit and the flash of a bright yellow tie.

She pushed her hands into her coat pockets and wondered what to say to him. It wasn't like one visit to a church could change her. And it certainly didn't change the circumstances. She squared her shoulders as he came to a stop in front of her. "Surprised to see me?"

"A little. You could have sat with us." The tug at the corner of his mouth told her it was an invitation, not an accusation.

"I didn't know I was coming," she admitted. "It seemed best just to sit in the back."

"I'm really glad you came."

She shifted her weight and looked around him to see if any other of his family members were there. The prospect of facing his mother still filled her with chills. "I'm glad I came, too," she said. A sliver of wind pushed a finger's width of hair across her cheek. "Yesterday— the things you said. You were right about a lot of them." She pushed the lock of hair away. "Part of the reason I wanted to be on television was because I wanted my father to see me and realize that I was somebody."

"You are somebody," David said. "You think I don't know how special you are?"

"It's hard for me to think like that," Millie admitted. "Part of me still thinks that I have to prove it." She let him see in her eyes how deep this belief ran.

"You don't have to prove anything to anyone—and especially not to me." It was his turn to push the hair from her eyes.

"Yesterday I said some things I didn't mean. I'm sorry."

"It's okay."

"How can you see the best of me when you know the worst about me?"

"Because I love you."

"David, Eva told me more bad stuff about my father. The crime in Utah—it wasn't the first time. He stole from our church a long time ago."

He nodded and looked very sad. "What he took from you was a lot worse."

She didn't know what to say and looked down at the ground. "I've made my own share of mistakes, but I'm trying to move forward." She smiled a little. "I'm not going to let him define me. I guess that's why I'm here."

"A very good decision," David confirmed. "Why don't we go somewhere and talk?"

Millie hesitated. She wanted to go with him, but she still felt a little raw inside. It wasn't as if it no longer hurt to think of the legacy her father had left for her. The last thing she wanted was to be the woman everybody thought wasn't good enough for David. At the same time, she knew she loved him. She might not think she deserved him, but here they were. She'd take it one step at a time.

"Coffee would be great," she said.

He grinned. "We have a lot to talk about."

He was right. The last time she'd seen him, she'd been trying to break up with him. She wanted to talk about the box sled race and about the after party at the café, where she'd seen Bart talking with a very cute dark-haired girl. She also wanted to know how Devon Spikes had handled losing to Bart.

"I know a great little café where we can sit for as long as we like and talk things through," she said. "The coffee is hot, and the pancakes are the best in town." She studied his face then added, "The aunts will stare and giggle, but they'll leave us alone. I promise."

"In that case," he said and offered his arm, "we should get going."

Millie slipped her hand into the crook of his elbow and leaned into him as they walked to his car.

Chapter 38

M y mom had a nice lunch with you today," David said from across the table at Ben's where he and Millie had come to celebrate their sixth months of dating. "She raves about the tuna melt and mango-honey ice tea."

Millie laughed. "The tuna melt is really Aris's idea." Even after Eva returned to the café, Aris had remained on a part-time basis. This had allowed Millie more time to do other things—like take some night courses at the local community college and volunteer at Bart's school. Bart's sixth-grade class had produced their version of *The Mikado*, and both Lauren and Bart had had leading roles.

"To be honest, I think my mom enjoys your company even more than the food. She tells me word for word everything you talk about."

"I'm enjoying getting to know your mom as well."

Ever since Millie had started going to church, Mrs. Denvers had been coming to the café about once a week for lunch. At first Millie had found her presence uncomfortable. She feared any moment Mrs. Denvers would confront her about Millie's father. When she hadn't, Millie had finally mustered her courage. She'd set down the tuna melt in front of her and said, *"I know you know about my father."*

Mrs. Denvers had calmly cut off a piece of her sandwich. *"Let me tell you about your father."* She chewed slowly then wiped her mouth. *"A few days after my father passed away and everyone had gone on with their lives—the way people do—your father drove to my mother's house with a trunk full of rosebushes. He planted them in the backyard then sat with my mother. He laughed with her, and he cried with her. He knew that grief didn't end at a funeral and wasn't afraid to be around it."* She'd paused. *"It wasn't just my mother he helped either. He planted a lot of rosebushes for folks. Now, could you be a love and bring some vinegar for the fries?"*

That was the end of the conversation. Millie thought the story was a gift. It not only gave her another snapshot of her father, but also a new way of looking at Mrs. Denvers.

David lifted his water glass. "Happy anniversary, Millie."

She smiled as they clinked water glasses. "Happy anniversary, David."

As usual, nearly every table was filled. Across from them, a middle-aged woman wearing a hot pink dress and an expensive diamond necklace laughed at something the man sitting across from her said. An older couple—probably in their late eighties—was leaning toward each other as they ate.

How did they do it? Stay together all those years? More importantly, would it be David and her sitting there someday? She stopped herself. The old Millie worried about things she couldn't control. The new Millie trusted that things would work out as they were meant to be. Sometimes it was easy being the new Millie, and other times it was harder to put herself in God's hands. David said this was normal and that as her faith grew, she would trust God more completely.

She turned back to him. David was fiddling with the menu. She thought he looked a little nervous but couldn't understand why. "Everything okay with Bart?"

"Yeah, fine." He peered intently into the menu.

Millie stifled a little disappointment. She wanted him to be looking at her and thinking romantic thoughts, not wondering if he wanted the shrimp cocktail or a lettuce wedge. "See anything you like?"

"A couple of things." He handed her his menu. "Take a look."

This was odd—she had her own menu. She opened the cover. Instead of seeing the daily specials, she pulled out a piece of paper. "What's this?"

"An application."

"I can see that. But David, *The Newlywed Game?*"

"They're casting. I was thinking that we could include a videotape in our application. Something that would give people a flavor of our lives here in Deer Park. You know, interviews with your aunts, people at the café, Aris. . ."

"People would think we're crazy. David, this is really sweet, but you don't have to do this. I don't need to go on a reality television show anymore to be happy."

"But you'd like to, wouldn't you?"

"Of course." She still sent out applications, but she'd come to accept that if it never happened, it didn't mean God didn't love her. It just meant He had something else in mind for her. David and Bart were proof of that. And then it slowly registered. "Besides, David, aren't you forgetting something? We aren't married. You have to be married to be a newlywed."

"We can take care of that." He reached into his coat pocket and pulled out a small black jewelry box. Millie's heart started to pound with anticipation as he stepped around the side of the table and got down on one knee. "I love you, Millie. I want to be with you for the rest of my life. I want our lives together to be full of love and adventure. Will you marry me?"

Millie looked down at the top of his soft brown hair. "Are you asking me to marry you so you can go on a reality television show?"

David smiled. "I'm proposing because I love you, and if being on a reality television show is important to you, it's important to me." He smiled. "Millie, will you marry me?"

"Yes, I'll marry you. I love you, David."

Her hand shook a little as he slipped the diamond onto her finger. But then he looked at her and they both laughed, and somehow everything was all right. "I'm in shock," she admitted.

"Happy shock?"

"Extremely happy shock." Millie leaned forward to kiss him. "*The Newlywed Game*?"

His lips sealed the promise between them and sent a shiver of joy through her. "Yeah," he said. "I think we've got a great story to tell."

Epilogue

It would be a simple wedding. Neither Millie nor Eva had much money, and although David had offered to pay for everything, Millie hadn't wanted to start their married life that way. She and Eva insisted on paying for the wedding and reception. Millie did agree, however, to let David finance the honeymoon trip to Paris.

She and David wanted to be married as close to Christmas as they could, and Reverend Stockman said he'd be pleased to marry them on December 23rd. A reception would be held in the church's basement.

On their wedding day, at three o'clock in the afternoon, Fred Huey, who had a gift for all things mechanical and a passion for antique cars, picked Millie and Eva up in his Model T. Millie settled herself on the butter-soft leather and arranged the folds of her wedding gown around her. The full princess skirt filled most of the backseat, and she tucked it around her to make room for Eva. The dress was not the original one she'd ordered from the bridal shop in New York City. The store had sent her the wrong dress, but she'd fallen in love with it from the moment she pulled it from the box. When she'd called the store to straighten everything out, she'd been stunned to hear that the custom-made gown had been ordered for a woman who no longer wanted it. The sales associate offered her the dress at a highly discounted rate. Millie had been overjoyed to buy it.

As Fred backed the car out of the Hogan's driveway, Millie and Eva exchanged smiles. They were charmed by the antique engine's rapid *tick-tick-tick* sound.

"Did you ever think I'd be doing this?" Millie asked as the snow-lined streets moved past them at the rate of twenty miles per hour.

Eva laughed. "Oh yes," she said. "I just wish your grandma were here to see you. She'd be so thrilled to see you wearing her pearl earrings. You look beautiful."

Millie fingered the warm beads and felt the love of her grandmother fill her. "She's here."

It wasn't long before they reached the church. Fred opened the door, and Millie stepped into the frigid air. She shivered a little then pulled the veil over her face. It would be warm inside the church, she told herself, and David would be waiting.

As she stepped forward, several flashes exploded in her eyes. Blinking, she saw photographers lining both sides of the steps. She was a little surprised to see so many but also flattered.

It was only the sound of a helicopter circling that brought her feet to a stop. It was flying low and in a circular pattern around the church. She glanced at Eva. "What in the world is going on?"

Eva shook her head as another flash popped in her face. "Let's just get inside."

Sheila Abbott pushed a lock of her Tahitian-black, chin-length bob behind her ear. An ear-to-ear grin stretched across her face as she studied the footage coming in from South Dakota. She'd been the editor of the online celebrity magazine *Star Struck* for about two years now and was about to cement her reputation as the most influential editor in the industry. A year ago she'd broken the Matthew Langston and Katherine Heffner affair. And people were still talking about the way she'd had her cameras ready when four months ago Cleo Leonard had checked herself into rehab. Now she was about to make news once again.

For months people had been speculating when Monica Rayford and Derek Dunn—two of the hottest actors in recent years—would get married. She alone had figured it out and arranged media coverage. Her smile widened as she watched the bride—stunning, really, in the Carolina Herrera dress—make her way up the stone steps to the lovely little church.

The veil hid Monica's trademark ivory skin and huge blue eyes, but it was clearly the starlet. Who else had that elegant neck? That famous curvy figure? That slight tilt of her head?

Sheila clicked the keys that sent the video streaming live to the three networks who had already paid for the story. She'd let them edit what they wanted. She watched the train of Monica's dress disappear into that cute country church.

The dress had been the first tip-off. Sheila had been keeping her eye on Traditions, which was where the in-crowd shopped for wedding gowns in Manhattan. When Sheila learned Monica had bought a dress, she'd gone on high alert. With a little more digging, she learned that wedding invitations had been purchased from a high-end stationery store on the East Side. Although the clerk had been reluctant to give out the specifics, Sheila had gotten the clerk to admit a location and date. From there it'd been easy. There'd only been two churches in Deer Park, South Dakota, and only one wedding booked on December 23rd. Although the names had been changed, Sheila hadn't been fooled. Hogan was Monica's maiden name, and Derek Dunn had the same initials as David Denvers.

The first feed already had left her computer when her cell lit up with a text message. It was from Craig Watts, whom she'd assigned to cover the story. With a swipe of her finger, she opened the message.

IT'S NOT HER. PLEASE ADVISE.

Sheila's heart stopped. She typed, WHAT DO YOU MEAN IT ISN'T HER?

In response, a photo appeared on her screen. A bride and groom stood at the front of the church. The bride had lifted her veil, and while she was stunning, she wasn't Monica Rayford. The man, although handsome, had brown hair not streaky blond.

Sheila stifled a gasp of horror. Her brain whirled as she frantically tried to figure out what had gone wrong. In the next instant, she realized what mattered more was damage control. She tapped her fingers on the desk impatiently. A mistake like this could kill a career. She'd look like an idiot unless she came up with a new spin— and quickly. *A new spin. . .* Her mind whirled. *A new spin. . .* She thought hard, and then it came to her.

She'd turn this small-town wedding into a feel-good Christmas piece—a home-for-the-holidays wedding.

GET THEIR STORY, she typed. DIG FOR DIRT, BUT GIVE ME REDEMPTION.

Everyone loved a Christmas wedding story, she assured herself, especially when the bride was as beautiful as this one and was so obviously in love with the groom. It might be a little hick, but what was the alternative? Look like an idiot in front of her colleagues?

I can pull this off, she assured herself, then reached into her desk for her stash of M&M's. "Millie Hogan," she whispered as she popped one into her mouth, "you may not know it, but I'm about to make you a star."

Kim O'Brien grew up in Bronxville, New York. She holds a bachelor's degree in psychology from Emory University in Atlanta, Georgia, and a master's degree in fine arts from Sarah Lawrence College in Bronxville, New York. She worked for many years as a writer, editor, and speechwriter for IBM. She is the author of eight romance novels and seven nonfiction children's books. She's happily married to Michael, has two fabulous daughters, Beth and Maggie. She is active in the Loft Church in The Woodlands, Texas. Kim loves to hear from readers and can be reached through her Facebook author's page.